BOOK THREE IN THE RECKLESS SERIES

Reckless FALL

NYSSA KATHRYN

An NW Partners Book
Cover by Deranged Doctor Design
Developmentally and Copy Edited by Kelli Collins
Line Edited by Jessica Snyder
Proofread by Amanda Cuff and Jen Katemi
Cover Photography by Regina Wamba

❀ Created with Vellum

She's back in town. He needs a nanny. It should be simple. But in the small town of Misty Peak, simple is never easy.

Sadie Sandler wouldn't consider herself a quitter. But then, she did walk out on her own wedding twenty-three minutes before she was supposed to walk down the aisle. Now she's back in the small town of Misty Peak, working at her grandmother's bakery and nannying the child she basically raised. There's just one problem…the child's father. He's tall, sexy and has the kind of ocean-blue eyes she could drown in. There are so many reasons why she should stay away from Eastern. So why doesn't she want to heed a single one?

Eastern Walker has one focus—his eight-year-old daughter, Avery. She's suffered too much for someone so young. She needs stability, and he's determined to be the best father possible—so why can't he get his mind off the new nanny? The young woman with the beautiful black eyes, who treats his daughter as if she were her own? He's the town sheriff, and before that, a Navy SEAL; if there's anything he's good at, it's staying focused. But Sadie's proving to be his greatest distraction.

Soon, resisting each other turns out to be the least of Eastern and Sadie's concerns. People from both their pasts reappear, and they'll go to great lengths to keep the couple apart. And they're not even the biggest threats in Misty Peak…or to Sadie and Eastern's happy ending.

ACKNOWLEDGMENTS

Thank you so much to everyone who helped me make this story what it is. Kelli, Jessica, Amanda and Jen—you're all amazing and I could never release a book baby without you.

Thank you to my ARC team and readers. Your support and willingness to step into every world I write about is everything.

And to my family—you're my world. My reason. And you inspire me every day to work hard and keep writing.

CHAPTER 1

Scott: Come on, Sadie. Answer my calls or at least text back. It's been days.

Sadie Sandler scanned the text before shoving the cell back into her pocket.

Argh. She did not have the energy for Scott today. What she *did* have the energy for was cupcakes. Lots and lots of cupcakes.

She lifted the tray of pumpkin pie goodness from the kitchen counter. They'd just cooled, and yep, they smelled amazing. Usually, pumpkin pie cupcakes were seasonal and only sold between September and November, but they were so popular at Sugar and Spice that her grandmother sold them all year round.

On her way to the front of the store, she moved past her grandmother, who was serving a customer at the register, then crouched to fill a display shelf.

Pumpkin pie was definitely a favorite of hers, but then, she had many favorites. Golden vanilla. Red velvet. Cookies and cream. It really depended on her mood.

People often assumed that growing up spending her summers around cake, and now working in Sugar and Spice, she'd be sick of the stuff. Nope. Could a person get sick of pumpkin pie cupcakes? Or triple chocolate cookies? That was impossible, right? Especially when they were the best in Tennessee. But then, she might be biased.

God, she'd missed them during the year she'd lived in Atlanta. She'd missed a lot of things about the small town of Misty Peak, but her grandmother and the shop were right at the top of the list. They were what made Misty Peak home.

Once the shelf was filled, she rose and set the tray back in the kitchen before grabbing an overflowing bag from the trash.

A week. She'd been back in Misty Peak for one entire week after a year away, and every day that passed just reaffirmed that coming home was the right decision. The people, the familiarity...even the smells of the town made her feel something that Atlanta had never made her feel.

When she stepped outside into the alley and moved to the dumpster, a truck to the right caught her attention. It was parked behind the Misty Peak Liquor Store, which sat beside her grandmother's shop.

She frowned at the sight of Mr. Anderson, the liquor store owner, arguing with a guy, who she assumed was the truck driver. Mr. Anderson was shorter than the driver, with graying hair, but there was something in his eyes, an anger, that almost had Sadie slowing her steps. The men spoke in hushed voices, but Mr. Anderson seemed to be cutting the man off whenever he tried to get a word in.

Had something gone wrong with a liquor delivery?

Suddenly, Mr. Anderson's gaze rose, colliding with Sadie's.

Crap. She was staring.

Forcing a smile to her lips, she walked to the dumpster and dropped the bag inside. She was just turning around when her phone vibrated again.

Scott: Come on, Sadie. You left me at the altar. The least you owe me is a conversation.

That was the thing though—she didn't owe him anything. She

had a very good reason for walking out on him. A reason he conveniently wasn't mentioning in these little text exchanges.

And yeah, maybe she should have stuck around the morning of her wedding to tell him why she wasn't going through with it, but it had been a fight-or-flight moment, and she'd chosen flight.

Even so, Scott wasn't *that* stupid. He had to know that she knew what he'd done.

Sadie: I don't owe you anything. Leave me alone.

Shoving the cell into her pocket, she gave one final glance over to Mr. Anderson—who'd now moved out of sight behind the truck—before stepping back inside the bakery. Her grandmother was still in the front, filling a box with half a dozen cupcakes.

"Let me guess," Sadie said with a grin. "These are for Jenny?"

Her grandmother smiled up at her. "It's like you never left. Yes, these are for Jenny. The same order every Monday for the last ten years."

Yep, because that was Misty Peak—things rarely changed.

"People here are nothing if not creatures of habit." Why she found those habits and the predictability that came with them so comforting, she wasn't sure. Maybe because living in Atlanta for the last year had been so much harder than it should have been. But that had more to do with the feeling in her belly the entire year that she wasn't where she was supposed to be.

Her grandmother straightened and looked at her. Like *really* looked at her.

Oh, Jesus. No one knew her better than this woman, and right now, it felt like she saw everything Sadie was trying to hide.

"How are you doing, Sadie?" her grandmother finally asked. "And don't give me some wishy-washy 'I'm fine' answer that you think I want to hear. A week ago, you walked away from both your home and your wedding. That wouldn't have been easy."

She'd only told her grandmother why she'd left that day. "I *am* doing well, actually. I'm angry. But I'm also relieved because I feel like I'm exactly where I'm supposed to be."

Her grandmother cupped her cheek. "You are, darling. You're home."

Sadie's heart rippled, and without a second thought, she pulled her grandmother into her arms. God, she loved this woman. She'd come to live with her when her parents had died in a car crash when she was sixteen, and this had been home ever since. Hell, even before that, her grandmother had made Misty Peak feel like home every summer break she'd spent here.

"Thanks, Nan." When they separated, Sadie lifted the box of cupcakes. "I'll deliver these for you."

"Are you sure?"

"Definitely. A walk in the sun will do me good."

She stepped outside, only to feel the vibration of her phone in her back pocket again.

Good God. Would the man leave her alone? It was over. *They* were over. Heck, she felt like she was giving him a gift by walking away. Didn't he want that? After what she'd seen on the morning of her wedding, she'd assume so.

The scumbag.

And that was it, wasn't it? While she should feel heartbroken that after six years together, not only were they not married, they were no longer together…she wasn't. Not even a little bit.

What did that say? That she'd remained in a relationship that wasn't meant for her for far too long? That she'd held on because it had been familiar?

She shook off the thoughts and started down the sidewalk. Her gaze fell on two men walking toward her on the other side of the street, and immediately, her skin tingled in a way it *never* had for Scott. They were both tall and wide shouldered, the muscles in their arms so thick that they stretched the fabric of their shirts.

Eastern and Cody. Brothers. Both former military. Cody had

been in Delta Force and Eastern was a Navy SEAL, but now Cody ran a bar and Eastern was the town sheriff.

And good God, were they sexy.

She nibbled her lip as she forced her gaze away. She'd always had a bit of a crush on Eastern. The man was a good ten years older than her, and she'd had a thing for him since the first day she'd set eyes on him as a shy teenager who'd looked after his daughter. Maybe it was the deep blue of his eyes, or the way the gravelly undertone of his voice rolled into her belly like a fine wine.

She could still remember the first time she'd met him. It had been at his daughter's mother's house, looking after Avery. He'd come to pick her up, and she'd literally not been able to look away. It was like her eyes had been glued to him, and her jaw had dropped to the floor.

But while she'd had a massive crush on him, he'd probably never even seen *her*. Not that it mattered. She didn't see him much after that, even though she saw his daughter a lot...basically every day.

Her heart gave a small tug at the thought of Avery. She'd nannied the little girl since she was a baby. That's how she'd fallen in love with the kid. God, she missed her.

The two men crossed the road, and her heart thumped. They were going to walk right past her. She *could not* stare, especially at Eastern. Not only was he older than her, but it would be completely inappropriate, since he was potentially her future boss. Well, hopefully. He'd said he might need her help caring for Avery, and she was crossing her fingers and toes for that to be true.

Be cool, Sadie. Do not stare. And do not fall on your face.

When the two men passed, Eastern's gaze caught on hers. Only for a brief second, but it was enough for her belly to do that strange flip thing.

Then the corners of his lips lifted with a slight tilt. "Hey."

She smiled back. "Hey, Eastern. Cody."

Cody dipped his chin.

The second she passed them, the air whooshed from her chest, and she almost wanted to give herself a pat on the back.

Good. She'd been cool, calm and collected, exactly how she should be. No falling over her feet or turning beet red.

But wasn't her reaction to Eastern another sign that *not* marrying Scott last week had been the best decision of her life? Women who were supposed to be "just married" didn't crush on other men. Well, not at the start, at least. That was the head-over-heels-in-love part, right?

She was still giving herself mental congratulations when someone up ahead caught her attention. An older woman who stepped out of the bookstore—the same bookstore she was supposed to be entering.

Mrs. Chase…Scott's mother.

Shit.

She spun around. She couldn't let the woman see her. She did not have the energy for that conversation right now.

Speed-walking in the opposite direction, Sadie spotted Eastern and Cody up ahead. They'd stopped beside a truck.

Split-second decision time. It was probably crazy, but who the hell cared. It was survival right now.

She stepped in front of their big bodies, knowing the mountainous men would block her from Mrs. Chase's view.

Eastern frowned. "Sadie? Are you okay?"

"This is going to sound crazy, and I've probably lost my mind, but I just need you guys to hide me for two seconds."

The muscles in Eastern's forearms visibly flexed. "Is something wrong?"

"What happened?" Cody asked, turning his head.

"No!" She grabbed Cody's arm to tug his attention back to her —then she began talking in a rush like word vomit she couldn't stop or slow.

"Don't look. Everything's fine, I'm not in danger. If anything, that *woman* is in danger—from me. I probably shouldn't be saying this to the town sheriff and his brother, but if she sees me, she'll come over and speak to me, and then I don't think I'll be able to keep my cool, because I have a feeling she knew what her son did, and she didn't tell me. They're close. Like, *really* close. I'm not saying I'd kill her or anything crazy like that..."

The men frowned, but she barely noticed. She was too far gone.

"But hurt her? Yeah, I'm definitely capable right now. I've never hurt anyone before, but give a girl a reason and these things can just happen. Please, just let me hide for a minute while she gets into her car, then everything will be okay."

CHAPTER 2

The corners of Eastern's mouth twitched. The woman in front of him was actually admitting to wanting to hurt another person.

He studied the brown specks in her black eyes, which, in this moment, looked a bit crazed. She wore a T-shirt with a picture of a cupcake that read, "A cupcake without icing on it is good for muffin." She also sported jeans that pulled tightly around her ample curves, but fuck, he was trying not to look at those curves. Sadie Sandler was too young for him, and he'd known her since she was a teenager.

The last time he'd seen her was only a few days ago when he and his daughter had bumped into her at the grocery store. She'd looked sad. Hell, he'd almost drowned in the sadness of her eyes, it had run so deep. Today, though? Today she looked angry and a little wild.

When she finally stopped speaking, her chest heaved up and down in fast succession.

There was a short beat of silence before he asked, "Are you okay?"

"I'm not sure." She peeked around his shoulder and the air

rushed out of her. "She's gone. It's okay. I won't hurt anyone today."

His brows slashed together. *Today?* Was this something he should be watching out for?

He shot a look over his shoulder, seeing no car and no woman.

"What did she do?" Cody asked.

"Maybe nothing." A scowl cut across Sadie's face. "But if she knew what I *think* she knew, then it's bad."

Okay, Eastern wasn't following at all, and by the look on his brother's face, he wasn't either.

"Maybe you can ask her on a different day…a day when you feel less violent," Cody said, humor in his voice.

"Yeah, maybe then."

The sudden smile that lit her face was in complete contrast to the scowl a few seconds earlier, and Eastern felt it like a kick in the gut. *Fuck*, she was gorgeous. Was that even appropriate to think about his daughter's former nanny?

"Don't worry," she added quickly, "you won't be arresting me anytime soon. I promise I'm not usually a violent person."

"I know you're not. Avery's only said nice things about you." His eight-year-old barely stopped talking about her.

Sadie's eyes softened, and that familiar sadness washed over her features. "I miss her. How is she?"

"She's good. She misses you too."

If possible, that comment made the sadness darken her already black eyes. "Remember, if you need anyone to look after her, I'm here and I'm happy to help."

He dipped his head. He'd been meaning to reach out and ask, but something stopped him. Maybe because since the grocery store, he'd barely been able to get her black eyes out of his head…and that was *not* something that should even be a problem.

"Well"—she lifted the box in her hands—"I should get these to

Jenny before she passes out from low blood sugar. Thanks for letting me hide behind you."

Then as quickly as she'd appeared, she was gone.

He turned his head and watched her walk away, forcing his gaze off her ass, which looked too damn good in her tight jeans.

"Is it me, or was that…"

"Strange?" Eastern finished for his brother. "It was definitely strange."

"She's certainly grown up in the last few years."

Cody wasn't saying it in a way to infer he was attracted to her. Hell, the man was madly in love with Harper Rain, a woman who'd started working at his bar.

So why did Eastern's muscles twitch at those words?

He cleared his throat. "She has."

"She didn't end up marrying that guy, right?"

"No. When Ave and I ran into her at the grocery store, she said she wasn't married and Scott didn't move back here with her."

There was a story there, but that story was none of his damn business.

"How's the bar?" Eastern asked, trying to steer the conversation in a different direction.

"Good. Great, actually. Now that we've hired more staff, Harper and I can take some evenings off, and the more time I get with that woman, the more I fall head over heels in love."

His brother had fallen in love the second Harper had stepped into his bar. Well, less stepped and more hidden. Cody hadn't known it at the time, but she'd been running from something when she'd stumbled across Misty Peak. Her past had eventually found her. But then, pasts usually did.

"I still can't believe Kayden's settled down," Cody said with a laugh. "You ever think our brother would commit to a relationship?"

"Not in a million fucking years."

Their brother was notoriously grumpy. Not only that, he had major trust issues. But he *had* settled down, and with the last woman Eastern would ever expect—Tilly Taylor, someone most of the town had distrusted for years.

Two of their brothers were still in the military—Jace, who was a Tactical Controller in the Air Force, and Lock, who worked on a Ghost Ops team. Jace had recently let them know he was planning to come home in the next few months, which had surprised everyone.

Then there was their sister, Nylah, Cody's twin, who lived in Idaho with the guy she'd fallen in love with, Liam. Something told Eastern she wouldn't be moving back anytime soon.

"It seems we're dropping one by one," Eastern said, more to himself than his brother.

Cody grinned. "Are you next?"

"Nope. Avery's the love of my life, and that's the way it's going to stay."

His daughter was his world, so much so that he'd made an effort to align as many of his shifts as he could with her school hours so that he could be with her as much as possible. Of course, as the town sheriff, things didn't always work out that way, and he was often away from her one or two evenings a week.

Cody unlocked his truck. "You coming to the bar later?"

"Nah, I'll spend tonight with Avery."

Cody nodded. "I love that kid. Make sure you make it to Monday night dinner so I can squeeze her."

"You got it."

On the way to the station, Eastern kept his gaze on both the rearview mirror and the street in front of him. Even though he'd left his position as a SEAL almost a year ago, a part of him still expected danger to hover around every corner. Live on the edge of death long enough and it was hard to escape.

He tried to hide that part of himself. Fuck, he had to, being a single father.

His fingers tightened around the wheel at the thought of Avery's mother, Jamie. At the way she'd just left town one weekend when he'd had Avery and didn't come back. At the things Avery had started sharing after her mother left…about Jamie's drinking, and Avery being sent to school in dirty clothes and without lunch.

Jesus, he wanted to kick his own ass for not knowing. For not coming home sooner and looking after his little girl. She was his world, and if he'd known, he would have been here in a heartbeat.

The only thing that helped him sleep was the fact that, two weeks ago, he'd been granted full custody of Avery. It hadn't been hard when her mother hadn't even bothered to show at the hearing to plead her case. The woman acted like her daughter was insignificant. Like she was the easiest thing to walk away from and they weren't the luckiest two people to be her parents.

Well, because of that, she'd lost her—and one day, she might just realize exactly *what* she'd lost.

He hadn't planned to have a child with Jamie. Nine years ago, she'd been new in Misty Peak and he'd been home on leave. They'd met at the bar, Meridian, and spent the night together.

The second he'd found out she was pregnant, he'd offered to move her closer to him. Being a SEAL, he couldn't choose where he lived. His naval base had been in Virginia, so that's where he'd needed to be.

She'd said no. Hell, she hadn't even considered it. That meant he'd only seen his daughter when he'd taken leave and vacations in Misty Peak.

Fuck, he'd hated that. Exactly why she was his focus now. She needed him and he was going to give her everything he could.

He pulled into the station parking lot, trying like hell to calm down. Thoughts of Jamie always did that to him, but he couldn't take it into work with him. He needed to be solid for this town.

He climbed out of his car and walked toward the building.

Daisy looked up from behind the front desk and beamed at him. She was a middle-aged woman and easy to like. "Hey, Sheriff. Good lunch break?"

"I've told you, just Eastern, and yeah, wasn't too bad. Anything happen while I was gone?"

"Depends on what you mean by 'anything.' Denny, our favorite British local, called because he wanted us to get over to his house. Said someone was trying to break in."

Eastern shook his head. Denny had a drinking problem. He called every day, sometimes twice a day. They always sent a deputy over just to make sure he was okay, and that deputy usually found him passed out somewhere in or around his house.

"Who went down there?"

"Paxley. She said he was fine."

"Good. Hopefully, we'll have a slow day."

"Don't jinx it, boss."

"Eastern." He smiled at her before stepping away. Instead of going to his office, which was right beyond the front desk, he went down the hall to the kitchen.

"I don't care what the fuck he says. I've been here longer than him."

Eastern's muscles tensed at the sound of Jarrad's voice. He liked all the deputies in the office—except Jarrad. And right now, the asshole was on thin fucking ice. Not long ago, Eastern had suspended him for mistreatment of Tilly, Kayden's woman, when she'd been questioned at the station.

"But he's our sheriff," Charles, another deputy, said.

"Who the fuck cares?"

"A lot of people care," Eastern said, voice hard as he stepped into the kitchen.

Charles's eyes widened, while Jarrad appeared unfazed.

"You don't care what I say about what?" Eastern asked as he lifted the pot of coffee.

The stuff was instant and tasted like shit. He needed to move his ass and get Daisy to order a coffee machine already.

Jarrad cleared his throat. "Nothing. Just talking about taking some time off in the next month."

"Time off for what?"

Jarrad's jaw visibly tightened, and Eastern got the feeling the guy wanted to say it was none of his business. He didn't. "Family stuff."

Eastern lifted the mug, tempted to tell the guy he'd already gotten plenty of time off during his suspension, but just held it in.

He didn't like how Jarrad acted as if he was above the law because he was a deputy. Eastern got the feeling he'd entered law enforcement solely because he liked the power and not to serve and protect the town.

"Submit the request." He stepped out of the kitchen with his coffee and moved back toward his office.

Jarrad didn't like Eastern either. But that had more to do with Eastern being elected town sheriff over him than anything else.

In his office, he lowered behind his desk, and his gaze immediately went to the framed photo of his daughter. That's when every bit of tension in his body leached out. He'd do anything for the kid. She had his whole heart, and not a day went by when he didn't put her first.

Without his permission, his thoughts shifted to Sadie. To the way she'd hidden behind him and Cody and babbled about...hell, he still didn't even know what.

She'd given him her number at the grocery store last week. Should he use it? Call her and ask her to sit for Avery? His daughter would love it.

Why was he so damn hesitant?

CHAPTER 3

"*D*id you put olives in the pasta sauce?" Avery asked as she slid into the seat opposite Eastern at the table.

"Emptied a full jar. Can't you see them?"

His kid beamed at him. The little olive nut. Not the green Sicilian olives though. The last time he'd offered her one of those, she'd looked at him like he was trying to force poison down her throat. Actually, poison probably would have been more welcome than green olives.

"Yum!" She scooped up a big swirl of pasta onto her fork and put it into her mouth, groaning as she did. "It's good, Daddy. Really good."

Great, because he'd hidden a whole lot of vegetables in that sauce, something he'd gotten good at during his time as a dad.

He wasn't a great cook, but he wasn't bad either, just...ordinary. Did she love his cooking because she hadn't gotten enough home-cooked meals with her mother?

Fuck...his intrusive thoughts.

He needed a distraction. "How was school, princess?"

"Good. I finished three books during reading time, and Miss

Davies said I might be able to move to the next reading level soon."

Damn, this kid was something else. Despite her mother's drinking and leaving town without notice, Avery hadn't missed a beat at school. "I'm proud of you, Ave."

"Thanks, Daddy."

Her little nose scrunched. That meant she was thinking about something and a question was about to come. He didn't have to wait long.

"Daddy?"

"Yeah, princess?"

"Have you called Sadie?"

He should have been expecting that. Every day, he waited for his daughter to ask about her mother. About whether she'd called or whether she was coming home. She never did.

The only person she asked about was Sadie.

"I haven't called her, but I ran into her today."

Avery's eyes lit up, and she straightened in her seat. "Really? What did she say?"

"She reminded me that she'd love to look after you."

The kid wriggled in her seat like she couldn't control her excitement. "Did you say yes?"

"I told her I'd let her know."

"Oh, please, Daddy! The day Mom fired her was the worst day of my life."

A pulse beat at his temple. "Do you know why your mother stopped having her watch you?"

"No." She tilted her head as she spiraled some pasta onto her fork. "But the last night she watched me, I woke up to them fighting." Her brows pinched.

"Did you hear what they said?"

She shook her head, the corners of her lips tilting down. "Mom just told me the next day she wouldn't be watching me anymore, and she didn't seem to care how much I needed her."

Need…not want. "I'm sorry, princess."

She nibbled her bottom lip. "I like Mrs. Hanley, but I like Sadie more."

Their neighbor, Mrs. Hanley, often cared for her when he had a late shift at work. "I'll see what I can do."

Avery squealed and jumped off her seat to round the table. Her little arms wrapped around his waist. He held his daughter close, feeling so damn lucky to have her.

For the rest of dinner, Avery sat on his lap while they ate, and she told him every detail of her day. About her friends and her teacher and a show-and-tell she did. He could listen to her talk all night.

Afterward, they worked together to clean up and get ready for bed. It wasn't until he'd read her a few chapters of her bedtime book and she was tucked under her sheets that she yawned and turned to him.

"You promise you'll message Sadie?"

He brushed a lock of hair from her face. "I promise."

She yawned before closing her eyes. "Thank you, Daddy. I love you."

Those words…they did things to him that nothing and no one had ever done to him before. He lowered his head and kissed her temple. "I love you too, princess."

He didn't leave her room straight away, instead staying by her bed as her breaths evened out while studying every intricate detail of her little face.

Even though he and Jamie hadn't been together, the second Avery was born, he'd fallen in love with his daughter and knew she was the reason Jamie had been brought into his life for that brief moment in time.

He lowered his head and pressed a final kiss to her temple before turning off the bedside lamp and moving out of her room. The second he was in the living room, his gaze shot to his phone.

Screw it.

He lifted the cell and searched for her number.

* * *

SADIE STEPPED out of Sugar and Spice. It was late. Well, late for leaving the store. She'd stayed for a few hours after closing to do a big deep clean of the shop, something that was way overdue. The ovens, the counters, *under* the counters…even the long glass display case. Her grandmother was getting older, and Sadie knew if *she* didn't do these things, her grandmother would hurt or exhaust herself trying.

After locking the door, she glanced at the liquor store next door. She wasn't a big drinker, but apple sours were her weakness.

What the hell.

She stepped into the store and found the bourbon section. There weren't a lot of options for bourbon. Fine with her. She knew almost nothing about alcohol, and if she added enough juice, all her apple sours tasted the same.

She grabbed a random bottle and turned to the counter. The empty counter, that was. In fact, the entire store was empty.

Strange. *And* there was no buzzer or bell.

They were open, right? Their doors were unlocked, and she was pretty sure she'd seen an open sign out front.

Footsteps sounded from the other side of the half-closed door behind the counter, closely followed by hushed voices.

"I'm taking care of it, Dad."

"Good. Because I don't want any more fuck-ups. We don't have anyone to cover—" Mr. Anderson stopped abruptly when he stepped into the store, his eyes narrowing on Sadie. Another guy stepped in after him. He was tall and slim, with brown eyes just like Mr. Anderson's.

When neither of them spoke, she cleared her throat. "Hi. Just the bourbon, please."

Mr. Anderson was slow to move to the register. He scanned the bottle before putting it into a paper bag, while the other guy, presumably his son, just stood there watching her.

The air felt thick around her, and she almost wanted to squirm.

"Were you standing here long?" Mr. Anderson asked as he set the credit card machine in front of her.

For some reason, the question made her uncomfortable. It wasn't so much what he said, but more the way he said it in combination with how he looked at her. Like he was more concerned about her proximity to his conversation and whether she'd heard something.

She shook her head. "No, I just came in."

She scanned her card and grabbed the bottle before giving both men a small smile and moving out. The uncomfortable knot in her belly didn't untangle until she slid into her car. And even then, it took her blowing out a long breath before she felt okay.

God, why had the other guy just stood there and stared at her like that? And why had both of them been acting so…weird?

With a shake of her head, she drove home, forcing the exchange to the back of her mind. She didn't live far from Sugar and Spice. Her apartment was less than a five-minute drive, and even though the building was older, she loved it. It was the same building she'd lived in with Scott, just a different apartment. Thank God the super had something she could move into on almost no notice.

Unlike the last time she'd lived in the building, she'd been able to fill it with all her own things. Decorate however she wanted and use vibrant colors and items that made *her* happy, instead of Scott's favorite color—beige.

Argh. Beige was barely even a color. She liked bright shades that lifted her mood at first glance. It was all her grandmother's influence, of course. Summers spent painting the store in every color under the sun.

Man, she'd loved those summers because while her parents had barely had time for her, her grandmother had always given Sadie her full attention.

She pulled into the parking lot at her apartment and grabbed her bag and the bottle of bourbon. The cool breeze brushed over her face as she crossed to her building. Once inside, she caught the elevator to the fourth floor. When she'd lived here with Scott, she'd been on the second floor, and even those two extra floors made a huge difference. She loved opening the windows and feeling the breeze and marveling at the higher view.

The second she stepped inside, she felt that *thing*. It was a mix of comfort and peace and security. Her bright blue couch with the yellow cushions called to her. She planned to fall into it the second she'd heated up her leftover noodles.

In the kitchen, she set the bottle of bourbon down just as her phone buzzed with a text. She almost rolled her eyes when she saw who it was from.

Scott: Just tell me why you walked out on our wedding, and we can talk it out.

Uh, that was a no. He knew. He *had* to know. And if he didn't, well, he hadn't planned to tell *her* what he was doing before she walked down the aisle to marry him, so she didn't owe him any form of explanation now.

No longer feeling like drinking, she set the bourbon in her cabinet before grabbing the noodles from her fridge and popping them into the microwave. She'd just set her phone onto the coffee table and settled on the couch when her cell vibrated with another text.

God, maybe she needed to block his number and be done with it.

She lifted the phone, fully ready to tell the jackass where to go —only to freeze.

Not Scott.

Unknown: Hey. It's Eastern Walker. I was wondering if you were free this Saturday night to watch Avery? I have to work a late shift and she really misses you.

The beats of her heart stumbled over one another at the prospect of looking after Avery. Of spending an evening with the child she'd helped raise.

Her fingers moved quickly over the cell.

Sadie: Yes. I'm free and would love to.

She bit her bottom lip, excitement filling her chest as she saved his number into her phone moments before his response came through.

Eastern: Great. I'll let her know. She'll be excited.

For a few seconds, Sadie closed her eyes. Avery was both part of the reason she'd left…and the reason she'd come back.

After Jamie had let Sadie go, it was hard to live in the same town as Avery and not be allowed to see and spend time with her. No, Avery wasn't her child, but she'd loved the little girl as if she was. So when Scott had been offered the job in Atlanta, she'd encouraged him to take it, thinking the new town would help her get over what felt like a genuine loss. It hadn't.

After she'd walked away from her wedding and her grandmother had asked her to come home—while in the same sentence, mentioning that Avery's mother was gone—the decision was easy.

Sadie had never told anyone what being fired by Jamie had done to her, but her grandmother had known. Like she knew everything else.

Sadie: I can't wait.

CHAPTER 4

Sadie pulled up in front of Eastern's home. She felt nervous. Which was crazy, right? Why would she be nervous to look after a child she'd cared for almost since the day she was born? She'd never been nervous before, with Avery. But it had been an entire year since the last time it was just the two of them together.

One thing was for certain, she *could not* cry. Even if she got ridiculously emotional at the sight of her. She'd thought about Avery every day since she'd left Misty Peak, and every day, she'd felt that devastating pit in her belly over not seeing her.

With a deep breath, she climbed out of her car. She'd just straightened when the front door of the house flew open and Avery ran out. Her little face was stretched into a smile that was so achingly familiar, Sadie's pulse took off in a gallop. She barely had time to drop to her haunches before the eight-year-old ran into her arms.

And the hug…God, it was everything. *This kid* was everything.

Sadie tightened her arms around her and dug her face into Avery's hair. She smelled exactly the same. "I'm so excited to see you, Ave."

"Me too!"

From over Avery's shoulder, Sadie saw Eastern step onto his front porch, a slight crease in his brows as he watched. Why did he look worried? Before she could put any thought into the answer to the question, Avery pulled back, and there were tears in her eyes.

Sadie frowned, brushing a tear away as it fell down the girl's cheek. "Hey, you'll make me cry."

"Sorry, I just missed you so much!"

Her own eyes burned, but she held back the emotion. "I missed you too. And you were my biggest draw when it came to moving back home." She tucked a lock of hair behind Avery's ear before finally rising. "I might have brought our favorite game too." She reached into her car and pulled out the small box.

"Skip-Bo!" Sadie yelled as Avery took the worn card game from her hand and ran over to her father. "Dad, look what Sadie brought!"

Sadie turned to grab her bag out of the car. She felt Eastern's gaze on her as she walked up the path, and when she glanced at him, his blue eyes watched her intensely.

Man, oh man, why did he have to be so big and sexy and godlike?

"Hi." Jesus, her voice was so high-pitched.

He leaned forward and touched a kiss to her cheek, and holy shit, was she blushing? Because she felt like she was blushing…

"Thanks for coming, Sadie."

She almost shuddered at the way he said her name with that deep, gravelly voice of his. "Thanks for *asking* me to come."

Avery grabbed her arm and tugged her toward the kitchen. "Daddy wanted to leave money for takeout, but I asked him to buy everything we need to make my favorite spaghetti and meatballs. Is that okay?"

Memories of the countless nights they'd spent making those meatballs hit her hard. She'd barely made the dish since because it made her chest ache with memories of Avery. "Yum. I love spaghetti and meatballs. But you might have to remind me how to make it."

Avery giggled. "It hasn't been that long."

Really? Because it felt like a lifetime. "Maybe we can make cookies for dessert."

Her little eyes lit up. "Triple chocolate chip?"

A quiet growl sounded from behind before Eastern spoke. "Maybe just chocolate chip."

"Daddy—"

"You know what chocolate does to you, princess." He crouched in front of her. "I've got to get to work now. I love you, and be good for Sadie."

Avery flung her arms around her dad's shoulders. "I love you too, Daddy."

Eastern tickled her belly, causing Avery to giggle, and something in Sadie's chest clenched. She'd seen Avery with her mother countless times, and never had the woman made her laugh or smile the way Eastern did.

Which was good. Avery deserved to be loved and cared for, and Eastern was capable of that.

He rose and turned those beautiful blue eyes on her. "Thanks, Sadie. Call if you need anything." He squeezed her upper arm, and yep, there was another punch of awareness through her system.

She waited for the door to close behind him before turning to Avery. "What should we do first?"

Her little face lit up. "Bake cookies, then Skip-Bo."

"You had me at cookies."

The next couple of hours were a mix of baking, games, cooking and eating. Sadie hadn't laughed this much since the last night she'd cared for Avery. The kid was like medicine for the soul.

By Avery's bedtime, the night felt like it had gone far too quickly.

"Ten chapters," Avery said adamantly.

Sadie shook her head. "Two."

"Eight."

"Three."

"Five."

"Four."

The girl wrinkled her little nose before giving a quick nod. "Okay. Four."

Sadie lifted her brows. "Really? I remember you fighting me to your last breath that it was five or nothing."

Avery grabbed the big book before crawling into bed. "I'm a whole year older, Sadie. I'm maturing."

Even though she meant it with humor, that one sentence hit Sadie hard in the heart. She *was* a whole year older. And so much had changed in her little world. "I'm sorry."

Avery frowned. "For what?"

"For your mom leaving."

Those little brows tugged together. "I prefer being with Daddy. He doesn't drink."

She pulled back. "Your mom never drank when I was around."

"She drank a little bit, but not much. It was after you left that it got worse."

A painful knot began to form in Sadie's gut. "How much worse?"

Avery lifted a shoulder. "She slept a lot. And sometimes she forgot to buy groceries. I missed a lot of school because she was too tired to take me. My friends said I was lucky, but I didn't feel lucky."

The anger tore through Sadie like wildfire, stealing her breath. "Oh my God…I'm so sorry. I didn't know."

"No one did. You weren't the only one she stopped from

seeing me. She didn't even let Uncle Cody or Uncle Kay come over." She looked up, a hint of tears in her eyes. "I know I was supposed to be sad when she left, but I missed you more than her. I always wished you'd come back…but I kind of hope she doesn't."

The last words were spoken quietly, like Avery wasn't sure if she was supposed to admit them out loud.

Sadie pulled her straight into her chest while scrunching her eyes to fight off tears. "I'm so sorry, baby girl."

Avery sniffed. "It's not your fault. And things are different now."

Sadie waited until she knew she had her emotions under control and wouldn't cry before releasing her. "Yes, things are different now." And she would do everything in her power to ensure she stayed in Avery's life…for good.

Getting through the four chapters was hard, so much harder than it should have been. Avery's words kept rolling through her head. Her mother had been drinking to excess. Barely taking care of her. And Sadie hadn't known. Not only had she not known, she'd left town when Avery had needed her most.

She wanted to cry for the child beside her. For what she'd had to deal with alone. But she held herself together…just.

She was finishing the fourth chapter when Avery's eyes closed. She snuggled into Sadie's side, her warm little body like a heat pack. She remained perfectly still, arm around Avery's shoulders, stroking her skin.

It was a couple minutes later, when Sadie was about to creep out of the bed, that Avery whispered, "Sadie, will you promise me something?"

"Anything." If the kid asked for a kidney, Sadie would give it to her. Everything that was hers was Avery's.

"Don't leave me again."

That's when the first tear fell down Sadie's cheek. A tear she couldn't have stopped if she tried. It was accompanied by the cracking of her heart.

She lowered her mouth to Avery's head and pressed a kiss there before whispering, "Never again, baby girl."

* * *

EASTERN STEPPED into his dark house. The shift was quiet at the station, which made it seem long, and damn was he glad to be home.

The smell of pasta sauce and cookie dough tinged the air, causing a smile to tug at his lips. His daughter's two favorite foods. After tonight, he wondered if Sadie was a big part of the reason for that.

He dropped his jacket by the door before moving through the living room and into the kitchen. Both were empty. Strange. It was nine, an hour past Avery's bedtime.

He was about to search the house when the soft click of a door opening sounded, then footsteps.

When Sadie stepped into the living room, Eastern frowned. Her eyes were red rimmed and her skin pale. Had she been crying?

She lifted two empty mugs from the coffee table and started toward the kitchen.

"Hey."

She jumped, her eyes shooting up at Eastern's voice. Then she sagged, the air visibly leaving her lungs in a long exhale. "Oh my God, Eastern. You scared me. I didn't know you were home."

She headed into the kitchen and put the mugs into the dishwasher. When she turned, she didn't quite meet his gaze, instead looking everywhere but at him.

He inched closer. "Are you okay?"

"Of course." The words came far too quickly and did nothing to reassure him.

She went to move past him, but he stepped in front of her, gently touching her arm. "Hey. Talk to me. Is it Avery?"

The small flicker of emotion gave her away. It *was* Avery.

"I let her down," Sadie whispered.

Eastern frowned. "What are you talking about?"

"When Jamie told me that I wasn't needed to look after Avery anymore, I fought to stay on. I love Avery like she's my own, and hearing I wasn't going to be part of her life anymore… I felt like I was losing a part of *myself*." Tears gathered in her eyes. Eyes that were so sad he could drown in them. "I didn't think Jamie was a bad mother. Absent, perhaps. A bit cold. But never truly neglectful. I really thought I'd fought as hard as I could. But now, after what Avery told me…I should have fought harder."

Every word punched a new hole into his chest, so deep and painful he wanted to keel over. Because every word was the whisper in his head that had been repeating over and over again since he'd gotten home. Since Avery had told him the extent of her mother's drinking problem.

"If anyone should have known what was going on and fought for her, it's me. And I feel that guilt like a weight on my chest every second of every day."

There was a small flicker of her brows. "You were away. You were serving in the military, fighting for our country."

"But I'm also her father. The second she was born, she became my priority. And I failed her."

"You're here now."

"So are you."

When a tear slid down her cheek, he couldn't stop himself. He stepped forward and swiped it away with the pad of his thumb.

"Thank you." His voice sounded loud in the otherwise quiet house.

Her eyes flickered between his, and her next words were barely a whisper. "For what?"

"For loving my daughter like she's your own."

One side of Sadie's mouth lifted. "She's easy to love."

So damn true. Still, the fact that this woman loved her so much did something to him.

Suddenly, he was all too aware of the way he hadn't moved his hand from her cheek. Of the softness of her skin against his palm. For some reason, he wanted to graze her plump lips with his thumb. See if they were as soft as they looked. Hell, even the way her clothes smelled like cookie dough made him want to lean into her and do things he shouldn't even be thinking about.

When her gaze lowered to his mouth, he almost gave in. Almost lowered his mouth to hers and touched those full lips. The only thing that stopped him was his daughter. The fact that she loved this woman, and he couldn't mess that up. Because kissing her *could* mess that up. It would complicate things. Make them messy. And Avery didn't need messy right now.

He forced himself to step back. To drop his hand from her cheek and look away. "I'll just grab you some cash."

Then he left the room as if the devil himself was chasing him. Walked down the hallway and into his office to grab some money. When he returned, Sadie stood by the door with her bag over her shoulder.

He handed her the cash. "Here you go."

"Thanks. Let me know if you need my help again." She stepped out the front door, and when he followed, she glanced at him over her shoulder. "You don't need to—"

"I'm walking you out, Sadie." The man in him, the protector, had to. He scanned the street as they moved.

When she reached her car door, she was about to slip behind the wheel when he wrapped his fingers around her wrist. She looked up, and those black eyes burned right into him.

"Again, thank you. Not just for tonight, but for everything." For loving his daughter. Watching her. And coming home to her.

A small smile curved her lips. "You shouldn't be thanking me. I should be thanking you for making such a great kid. I'll see you later, Eastern."

When she just stood there, it took him a beat to realize he was still holding her wrist. Then another to force himself to release her and step back.

The entire time she drove away from him, he had to remind himself that she wasn't for him. That tonight, he'd come too close to crossing a line...a line that he could not, under any circumstances, cross.

CHAPTER 5

He'd almost kissed her, right? That hadn't been her imagination. Eastern's head had lowered, and heat had laced his ocean-blue eyes.

Sadie nibbled her bottom lip as she cleared the remaining cupcakes from the display cabinet. They'd almost sold out today. Not a surprise, her grandmother had developed a great little shop here, and its reputation was well-known amongst locals.

The thing was, if Eastern *had* kissed her last night, she would have kissed him back. And that was crazy when a couple weeks ago, she was supposed to marry another man. Had woken that very morning *thinking* she was going to marry another man.

Except, almost kissing Eastern didn't *feel* crazy. It felt right. Just like letting him touch her, stand so close, felt more right than anything else in a long time.

Nuts. She was absolutely nuts. Sure, he was only ten years older than she was, so it wasn't a huge age gap. But she was his nanny. And she'd just walked out on a wedding.

She checked the clock on the wall. Three o'clock. Time to get out of here and go home, watch some sitcom reruns and get out of her head.

She'd just finished boxing the last of the cakes when the door opened and two women stepped in. One was Matilda Taylor. She'd been born and raised in Misty Peak, but she'd left town about five years ago after her father had stolen from locals. Sadie had heard she was back but hadn't seen her yet. She'd also heard she was dating Kayden Walker, Eastern's brother.

Matilda stopped at the counter. "Hey. Sadie, right?"

"Hey, yeah. Matilda?"

"Tilly." She turned to her friend. "And this is Harper Rain. Harper works at Meridian. She's dating Cody Walker."

Harper smiled at her. "It's nice to meet you."

"You too. What can I do for you ladies today?"

Tilly leaned over the counter. "Well, we know we're here right at closing time, but we were hoping you'd take pity on us and have something left to sell, because we're both *dying* for anything with sugar."

"Actually"—Sadie lifted the box she'd just packed—"I have a mixture of cookies and cupcakes, and I can give them to you at cost."

"Oh my Lord, you've just made our day," Harper said with a sigh. "But we'll pay full price."

Sadie shook her head. "Absolutely not. They would have been given away if you hadn't stopped by, so you're saving us from a loss."

The women paid, and they were about to leave when Harper stopped and turned. "It was really nice to meet you, Sadie. Hopefully we'll see more of each other."

"I'm here a lot, so I'm sure we will."

Harper grinned. "Great."

The women stepped out, and Sadie reached behind her to grab a cloth to do a final wipe down of the shelves and counters. When the door opened again, she thought it was Tilly and Harper returning.

It wasn't.

"Mrs. Chase." The name was an angry whisper on her breath.

Scott's mother was short, with long, graying blond hair and pale green eyes.

"Sadie, I'm so glad I caught you! I came in here a few days ago, but you weren't working and your grandmother wouldn't give me your address."

Of course she wouldn't. What had the woman expected, that her grandmother would just give out her personal information?

Mrs. Chase stopped at the counter, the perfect mix of concern and confusion on her face. "Scott and I have been so worried. You just left the church that day without a word! And Scott said you haven't been answering his calls or texts?"

"I'd like you to leave." Interesting. The words were so calm, she almost sounded like she wasn't affected by this woman.

Mrs. Chase frowned, her brow creasing. "What are you talking about? Sadie, we've always had a good relationship."

Sadie rounded the counter and moved to the door to pull it open. "Now."

There was a beat of silence, during which Mrs. Chase seemed to consider what to do next. Then she shook her head. "No." The older woman stepped closer, her frown deepening. "Not until you tell me why you left my son at the altar on your wedding day."

Fine. If she wanted to play it that way, Sadie would let her. "I know what he did." What he'd probably *been* doing for a while. "And I know that *you* know what he did," she added.

The older woman pulled back like she'd been slapped. Her mouth opened and closed a few times before words came out. "What are you—"

"I saw him with his admin assistant on the morning of my wedding day. I went to find him, to tell him I couldn't go through with marrying him, and I saw them together. I turned around and walked away, but then I decided to give him a piece of my mind. Only when I turned back, I saw *you* step into the room."

This time, the woman stepped back. "Sadie, I don't—"

"Don't lie to me. I wondered if you were going to come and tell me. But then I heard that you were just sitting up there in the front row, waiting for me to walk down that aisle. So I guess not."

Mrs. Chase squirmed where she stood.

"Was that the first time you saw him with another woman or were there others?" Now that she'd started, she wanted to know everything.

Mrs. Chase cleared her throat. "I don't…"

She'd never known this woman to be lost for words before. "But that's the thing—you do."

"It was a mistake."

Was she serious? "No. The only mistake was made by me, thinking I could trust him *or* you. Now get out."

"He loves you."

That was almost laughable. She crossed her arms. "No, he doesn't, or he wouldn't have done what he did."

For a moment, Mrs. Chase just stared at her like she was assessing how serious Sadie might be. She obviously realized she was solid on her stance, because she left without another word.

Good.

For a moment she just stood there, looking out the glass door as the woman got into her car and drove away. God! She felt angry, and betrayed, and a million other things. Yes, she understood that Scott was the woman's son, but he'd screwed up, dammit, and even a mother should be reprimanding her son for what he'd done to his bride on their wedding day.

Argh.

She finished tidying up, hating that her hands shook, but it was more out of anger than anything else. Anger at herself for trusting Scott and liking his mother. Anger at the situation.

She'd thought she was at the stage of accepting it all, but after seeing Mrs. Chase and having the woman try to deny what Sadie had seen with her own eyes…the sense of betrayal was still as fresh as ever.

Grabbing the bag of trash, she headed through the kitchen and out the back door to the dumpster. She heard it the second she stepped into the alley—Mr. Anderson. He spoke in a hushed voice on the phone, standing outside the back door of his shop.

"I don't fucking care. You said you'd get it done, so get it done!"

When his gaze cut across to Sadie, she lowered her eyes and moved to the dumpster. The man did not look in the mood for small talk. But, hell, was he *ever* in the mood for small talk?

She'd just heaved the trash in and turned—only to almost walk straight into him. What the hell? How had he gotten to her so quickly and without making a sound?

"Mr. Anderson—"

"Why are you *always* listening to my conversations?"

What was he talking about? "I was taking the trash out." This was, after all, the only trash receptacle…the *shared* dumpster.

He stepped closer, glaring down at her like she was a bug he wanted to squash. "You need to mind your own business, missy."

Missy? On a better day, she might have let that slide and tried to defuse the situation, but after the altercation with Mrs. Chase, she was *not* feeling calm enough for that. "Excuse me, but I haven't done anything wrong. *You* chose to speak in a public alley. If I heard anything, that's on you."

The red in his cheeks deepened, and he inched that bit closer so there was no space between them. "I don't appreciate nosy neighbors."

"Well, lucky for you, you don't have any. Now, please move."

He didn't. And she was almost at the stage where she was ready to shove him aside—either that or stomp on his foot— when a new voice sounded.

"Everything okay out here?"

* * *

Eastern's eyes narrowed on Mr. Anderson. On the way he'd backed Sadie into the dumpster so he could tower over her, making himself appear bigger, probably so she felt small.

What the hell was going on here?

Mr. Anderson cleared his throat as he stepped back. "Eastern. What are you doing here?"

Eastern scanned Sadie from head to toe. She didn't look scared—more angry.

He turned his attention to the liquor store owner. "I came to talk to Sadie. When I stepped in, I heard voices back here." Wasn't hard, when the back door had been left open. "What's going on?"

Mr. Anderson straightened. "I've just had some trouble with this woman listening in on private conversations."

Sadie rolled her eyes. "First of all, this is a shared alley. If I'm out here, it's *not* because I'm trying to listen in on anything. It's because I actually need to use the dumpster. Secondly, when I came into your store the other day, you were *open*. If you were talking about things you didn't want anyone to hear, that's not my fault."

Mr. Anderson's hands fisted, and instinctively Eastern moved to Sadie's side. Everyone knew the man had a short fuse. Eastern didn't think he'd do anything, just based on the fact he'd never harmed anyone before, but he didn't want to take any chances.

The older man huffed. "Fine. I'm going back inside."

Eastern's hand itched to reach out and grab him. Pull him back and warn him against getting in a woman's face again. But technically, he hadn't done anything wrong.

Instead, he turned to look at Sadie. "You okay?"

"Yeah, just annoyed because he's an ass. I don't remember him being like this before I left."

"Actually, he's always been grumpy."

"Well, he can take that grumpy somewhere else." She gave one more glare toward the back door of the liquor store before turning to him, features softening. "Thanks for coming out here. You saved him from a bruised toe."

Eastern lifted a brow. "A bruised toe?"

"Only if he didn't move back after the shove I intended to send his way." Then she gave him her sweetest smile before stepping around him and moving back into the bakery.

He followed, biting back the grin at how open she was about what she'd intended to do.

She strode around the kitchen, turning the lights off. "I shouldn't be telling you about my violent thoughts for a second time, should I?"

"I would say he probably deserved it."

She tossed a smile over her shoulder as she entered the front of the store, and it damn near stopped him in his tracks. "A sheriff who bends the rules. I like it. Are you picking up Avery now?"

"I am. But I wanted to stop by and apologize."

She turned just as she reached the display counter, a crease in her brow. "Apologize for what?"

"Touching you last night." Cradling her cheek, grazing her skin…and wanting to do more. Not that she knew the last part.

Her frown deepened.

He ran a hand through his hair. "It was inappropriate. I asked you to watch my daughter, so technically I'm your employer. I shouldn't have…"

"Touched me?"

Shit, was he doing this wrong? "Yeah."

There was a flash of emotion over her face that almost looked like disappointment, but it came and went so quickly he couldn't be sure. "It's fine, Eastern. It's not like we kissed."

Why didn't she *sound* fine then?

She turned. "I've got to lock up."

"Sadie—"

"And you've got to pick up Avery."

She'd just reached the front door when he wrapped his fingers around her arm and turned her. There it was again, that hint of disappointment in her eyes…and maybe a bit of hurt.

Dammit. He inched closer. "I'm sorry."

"You said that already." Her gaze lowered to his hand on her arm. "And you're touching me again."

Yeah, it appeared he couldn't stop.

"I almost *did* kiss you last night." The words fell from his mouth.

"Would that have been so bad?"

"Yes." Another flicker of hurt. She tried to pull away, but he inched closer, tightening his fingers—not enough to hurt her, but just so she couldn't go anywhere. "You're younger than me. You just got out of an engagement. And you're important to Avery."

So many reasons to not give in to every primal urge telling him to make a move on this woman.

It was only when her breasts lifted on a deep breath that he realized just how close they stood. Close enough for her chest to graze his. For her exhale to whisper across his skin.

"Guess you shouldn't kiss me then."

Her quiet words barely registered. And even when they did, he didn't want to acknowledge them. But fuck, it was true. They shouldn't kiss or touch or do anything else that would cross a line.

Reluctantly, he stepped back, dropping his hand. "I'll see you later, Sadie."

Then he forced himself to walk away, even though it was the last thing he wanted to do.

CHAPTER 6

Sadie took a deep breath as she stepped out of her car in the Misty Peak Visitors Center parking lot. The center was right in the mountains, and God, the air up here smelled good. Of pine and dirt and just freshness…was that a smell?

She'd done plenty of hikes here over the years, but today, she was purely here for coffee. It was her first time visiting since returning to town, and if the coffee was anything like she remembered, she needed it. Plus, today was her day off from Sugar and Spice, and she needed to go somewhere different.

As she walked toward the building, her mind inadvertently drifted to that conversation with Eastern last week. The way he'd touched her while apologizing for touching her. The way he'd told her they couldn't kiss while hovering his lips so close to hers.

Dammit. It was so freaking confusing. It was like his words said one thing while his body said another. And she was hopelessly attracted to that body. Which meant his words had hurt that much more. The man she was attracted to had basically told her he couldn't and wouldn't kiss her. It felt like a cold bucket of water over her head.

She moved straight to the back deck of the center, scanning

the mountains as she walked. They surrounded her, and they were spectacular. They were the reason so many people came to Misty Peak—because it sat in a valley in the Smoky Mountains.

She only took her eyes off the scenery when she reached the café door. Elle, the woman who ran the café, stood behind the counter. Kayden, Eastern's older brother, waited on the other side.

"So he's definitely coming back?" Elle asked as she made his coffee.

"Yeah, he should be home in a couple months."

Elle's brows pinched, and for a moment she almost looked uncomfortable. Then she smiled, seeming to pull herself together. "That's great. You must be excited to have him home. Where's he going to live?"

"He actually just bought Mom and Dad's old place."

If anything, that seemed to make Elle even *more* uncomfortable.

Elle pushed a to-go cup across the counter. "I'm glad you'll have another brother home."

Kayden dipped his head. When he turned and spotted Sadie, he gave her a small smile. "Hey. Sadie, right?"

"Yeah."

"Kayden. Eastern's brother."

"I know. It's nice to see you, Kayden."

"You too."

The second he stepped away, Elle's smile widened. "Sadie! I heard you were back. I've been waiting for you to come see me." The other woman rounded the counter and pulled Sadie into a warm hug. "It's so good to see you."

"You too."

She and Elle hadn't been super close, but whenever she came in for coffee, conversation was easy between the two of them.

When they separated, Sadie studied the other woman's features. "I heard about Macy. I'm sorry."

The corners of Elle's lips turned down. "Thanks. It was a huge shock, and honestly, I'm still recovering from her loss."

Macy and Elle had run the café together until a few months ago, when her friend had been murdered right there in the mountains. Sadie's grandmother had told her the killer was identified and wasn't around anymore, but justice for her murder didn't bring Macy back.

"Are you doing okay?" Sadie asked.

Elle lifted a shoulder. "As well as I can be. I've hired another girl, but it's been…hard. I turn to her expecting to see Macy."

"I'm so sorry."

"Thanks. On a lighter note…we should catch up some time."

"I'd love that. I've still got your number. I'll text."

"Great. Now, what can I get you? Your usual almond cappuccino, no sugar?"

"You have a good memory."

Elle grinned. "It's what I do. I'll throw in one of those macarons you like."

"Oh my gosh, you're a godsend."

As Elle got started on the coffee, Sadie moved over to a table. She'd just sat when her phone vibrated with a text.

Scott: Come on, Sadie. Please talk to me. Let's work this out.

She clicked out of the text. She was sure his mother had already called and let him know exactly what had transpired between them.

Her phone rang and she rolled her eyes, immediately canceling Scott's call. A few seconds later it rang again.

Good God.

She hit the answer button. "Stop calling me!"

There was a short pause before he spoke. "You answered."

"Yeah, because you're harassing me."

"Wait, don't hang up! Please. I want to talk about us—"

"There is no us. You made sure of that."

"Sadie—"

"Stop contacting me and leave me alone."

She'd just hung up when the door to the café opened, and Eastern and Avery stepped inside.

* * *

"ONE MARSHMALLOW."

"Two," Avery said firmly.

Eastern shook his head, a smile trying to break through as they stepped onto the deck. He had a rare Saturday off work, so he'd brought Avery up to the mountains. They'd been his backyard as a kid, and he'd loved them, so he took her hiking every chance he got. Of course, it was a bonus that Uncle Kay was here. He'd joined them for the first half of their trek before being called away. While her uncle was with them, Avery had done less walking and spent more time on Kayden's shoulders.

"Fine, two," Eastern finally agreed.

Avery grinned as they stepped into the café. Yeah, she knew she'd won that one. She'd probably always win, didn't matter if they were talking about marshmallows or the last sip of water in a drought.

"Stop contacting me and leave me alone."

His head whipped around at that voice.

Sadie.

She sat by the window, phone in her hand, and damn she looked just as good as always. Her dark hair was down, falling around her shoulders in soft waves, and her skin was so silky smooth, all he wanted to do was touch it.

Avery squealed when she saw her and raced across the room to throw her arms around Sadie's shoulders. He was slower to close the distance between them.

"Hey, baby girl." Sadie's voice was muffled, her face in Avery's hair. "I didn't expect to see you here today."

Avery pulled away. "We're having a daddy-daughter day. We

hiked through the forest. And Uncle Kay joined us for a while and let me go on his shoulders."

"Oh my gosh, what a fun morning. Uncle Kay sounds like the best!"

Avery laughed. "He's always trying to be better than Uncle Cody."

Eastern ruffled Avery's hair. "And Ave takes full advantage. I'm going to order our drinks. Do you need anything, Sadie?"

"No thanks, I've already ordered." Their gazes held a beat longer than necessary before he turned toward the counter.

Elle tossed a smile at him over her shoulder. "Hey, Eastern. How are you?"

"Good. How are you doing after everything?"

That smile slipped just a fraction, but he noticed. "I'm okay. Glad you closed the case."

She didn't need to say her friend's name for him to know she was talking about Macy. The investigation had been long and frustrating, with barely any evidence to go by. Hell, her killer had almost slipped through his fingers. If Tilly hadn't caught her trying to rob the café, she might have.

"Have you hired someone?" he asked, careful not to use the word replace.

Elle turned toward the register. "I have. But it's not the same. No one will be." She blew out a breath. "Anyway, what can I get you? Medium dark roast for you and a hot chocolate for little miss?"

"Yeah, that would be great. Oh, and—"

"Two marshmallows?" Elle laughed at his nod. "You got it."

He handed over his card.

"So…" Elle said slowly. "Kayden just told me Jace will be back soon."

He nodded. Jace was the youngest of their brothers. He was also the adrenaline junkie and the guy who could never sit still for long. He was finally leaving the Air Force to come home.

"He is. You don't speak to him anymore?"

During high school, maybe some middle school too, Jace and Elle had been basically inseparable. Never dating but always best friends. Some days, she'd spent more time at their house than her own.

"No, not really." There was a tinge of something in her voice. Maybe sadness. Maybe regret. Maybe both.

His phone rang from his pocket, and he tugged it out to see it was the station. "Sorry, Elle, I've got to take this."

"Go ahead. I'll get started on the drinks."

He stepped away from the counter. "Eastern speaking."

"Eastern, it's Daisy. I know, the last person you want to hear from on your day off."

"Is everything okay?"

"Well, it's fine from a station point of view. But Jarrad called in sick for his shift this afternoon, and I haven't been able to find anyone to fill it."

"Again?" The guy had already called in sick two other times since returning from his suspension.

"Yep. Something about a stomach bug."

Yeah fucking right.

Avery sat on Sadie's lap, his eight-year-old talking at a million miles a minute while Sadie stared as if she could listen all day.

"Give me five minutes to see if I can find someone to look after Ave and I'll get back to you."

"You got it, boss."

Avery was skimming the chocolate off Sadie's drink when he stepped up to her table.

"Is everything okay?" Sadie asked, the brown specks in her eyes playing with the black.

"That was the station. We're down an officer for tonight's shift. Any chance you could watch Avery?"

Avery's eyes widened and she grabbed Sadie's arms. "Oh, please say yes!"

Sadie smiled affectionately at his daughter. "I'd love to."

Eastern dipped his head. "Thanks." Now he just had to control himself when he got home that night. Not touch her. Definitely not think about kissing her.

Easier said than done.

CHAPTER 7

*E*astern pulled into his drive and turned off the car before leaning his head back. It had been a long-ass night of house calls and drunken idiots…so the usual for a Saturday night. There'd even been one guy who'd decided to get drunk, leave Cody's bar, then try to break into the grocery store a few doors down. Of course, he'd claimed he wasn't trying to break in, just *get in,* only he hadn't realized they were closed.

You'd think the blaring alarm once he'd started shaking the door would have been a dead giveaway.

Eastern massaged his temple as he climbed out. It was late. A hell of a lot later than he'd intended to come home. He'd texted Sadie an hour and a half ago, but she hadn't replied. And that in itself had made the night feel longer, because he'd been looking at his phone for the last ninety minutes, *waiting* for a reply.

Once the front door was unlocked, he stepped inside—only to stop at the sight in front of him. All the lights were off and the TV was on, but that wasn't what had him pausing. It was the sight of Sadie and Avery cuddled on the couch. They both lay on their sides, Sadie's arm wrapped around Avery's middle, his daughter in her pajamas.

Had she already gone to bed but come back out to lie with Sadie? Or had they just fallen asleep like that?

Something deep in his chest gave an odd twist. They looked like what a mother and daughter should look like. Sadie looked like the mother Avery deserved.

After dropping his bag by the door, he crossed the room and lowered in front of the couch. They looked so peaceful that he didn't want to wake them, but he had to. Gently, he slipped his arms around his daughter's back and legs and lifted her from the couch. Neither of them stirred.

When he reached Avery's room, he realized his earlier suspicions were right. Her bed was unmade, a dead giveaway she'd started her night there but had escaped. Wasn't a huge surprise, it had happened before.

Carefully, he laid her on the bed and pulled the covers up.

A small sigh left her lips before she rolled to the side and whispered, "I love you, Sadie."

He stilled. She hadn't woken when she'd said the words, but that didn't matter.

He grazed some hair from her face before whispering, "She loves you too, princess. We both do." He pressed a light kiss to her cheek before rising and moving out of the room.

Then that twist in his chest turned into a gallop of his heart. Sadie's eyes were still closed, but it was the peace on her face that had him pausing. The vulnerability.

Damn, she was beautiful. The gentle rise and fall of her chest. The way soft wisps of hair fell onto the delicate skin of her cheeks. She wasn't the teenager he'd met almost a decade ago anymore...not even close.

As he crossed the room, her phone, which sat on the coffee table, lit up. He frowned at the message. A *lot* of messages. All from Scott.

What was going on with them? Were they on a break or was it actually over? And why hadn't they married?

He gritted his teeth, reminding himself it was none of his business, no matter how much he wanted to *make* it his business.

He crouched in front of her and touched her arm. "Sadie."

Nothing. Not even a flicker of her eyelids.

He lifted his hand to her face, gently cupping her cheek. "Sadie, wake up."

This time there was a small scrunching of her eyes, then another, before they slowly opened. She frowned. "Eastern?"

"Yeah, honey, it's me. Sorry I'm home so late."

Her gaze moved between his eyes before her own widened. "Avery—"

"She's in bed."

Sadie nodded slowly before pushing up to a seated position. "Sorry I fell asleep."

"Don't apologize. I'm the one who got home so much later than expected. Next time, you're welcome to take my bed." Even if the thought of her sleeping between his sheets knotted his gut. Would the bedding smell of her after? Sweet like honey.

She shook her head. "Oh, no, that's okay. The couch is comfortable."

Hell no. Having a woman sleep on his couch went against every gentlemanly instinct inside him, and his father *had* raised him to be a gentleman.

He reached behind him and grabbed her phone, handing it to her. "This was lighting up."

Her brows flickered. She only looked at it for a moment before turning it face down on the couch. "Thanks."

He should keep his mouth shut, but the question was out before he could stop it. "Everything okay there?"

She lifted a shoulder. "It would be...if he'd just leave me alone."

Something hard lodged in his throat. "He's harassing you?"

"It's partly my fault. I walked out on our wedding day and never told him why. Although, by now, I'm sure his mother has."

He sat beside her on the couch. "Want to talk about it?"

Her gaze returned to the phone. "Have you ever been confused about something, then at the last hour, finally gotten clarity?"

"Everyone's probably experienced that at some point."

She laughed, but the sound didn't have much humor behind it. "Not like this. I sat there on the morning of my wedding day, in my ivory wedding dress. My hair and makeup were done, and I was holding the most expensive flowers I'd ever held in my life…flowers that I chose so carefully six months prior. It was twenty-six minutes until I was supposed to walk down the aisle. I remember because that number seemed almost ominous, staring back at me from the clock on the wall. I was waiting for the next minute to tick by, and it felt like I was waiting for my death sentence. Dramatic, I know. But that's when I realized…I couldn't walk down that aisle."

He watched every flicker of emotion that moved across her face, and each seemed darker than the last. "Because you were scared that you were making the wrong decision?"

"Because I was *terrified* that I was making the worst decision of my life. All I could think was…my heart had never beat fast for Scott. My palms had never felt clammy in his presence. And everything I could see in front of me just felt so…ordinary."

"And you didn't want ordinary?"

"No." This time when she looked up, the darkness was gone, and a hopeful bliss crossed her face. "I want delirious happiness. I don't need easy, but I want a love that makes me excited and breathless. I want to feel wildly happy when I see his name pop up on my phone. I want my belly to clench when he's near me."

Some deep part of him wanted her to have that too. All of it. "So, you walked away from the wedding twenty-six minutes before you were supposed to walk down the aisle because you knew it wasn't right?"

"Actually, I went to find him, to tell him that I couldn't do it. I knew the room he was using to get ready, and I just hoped he was still there. He wasn't answering my calls."

When she stopped, he almost leaned into her, needing to know how this ended. "Did you find him?"

"I did. I saw him…but he didn't see me."

"What do you mean?"

She took a breath as she glanced up. "He was making out with his admin assistant, and they were kissing like they'd kissed a thousand times before."

* * *

SADIE SUCKED IN A DEEP BREATH, not sure why she was telling Eastern all this but unable to stop. The only other person she'd told the whole story to was her grandmother, but it had been fresh and raw then and she'd been so angry. This time, saying it out loud again, she almost felt relieved that the morning of her wedding had played out the way it had. That she'd realized he wasn't for her, then seen with her own eyes how much of a mistake marrying him would have been.

Anger darkened Eastern's expression. "That son of a bitch. I'm sorry."

"I'm not. I wasn't sad when I saw them together. I was mad. But also relieved, because imagine if I *hadn't* seen that and had walked down the aisle?"

What would her life have been like? Would she have woken up the next morning with the pit in her belly, knowing she'd made the worst mistake? Or would she have steadily become more and more unhappy?

"But you did, because you were meant to find out the truth." Eastern looked at her phone.

She followed his gaze. "He's been calling and texting, asking to talk, and I probably should talk to him about it but honestly, I don't want to. I want to stay far away from him. I want nothing

50

to do with him. Because even though we didn't love each other like we should have, we'd made a commitment to each other, and I would *never* have done to him what he did to me."

"I don't understand how he didn't realize what he had."

Her breath caught. Had Eastern meant to say that? Or had the words just slipped out?

"I'm no prize, Eastern."

He gave her a skeptical look. "Do you really believe that?"

Yes. The word was on the tip of her tongue, but she couldn't quite release it into the room.

"What about you?" she asked, trying to get off the topic of herself. "You were never married to Avery's mother, were you?"

"No. I met her at Meridian when I was home on leave. We spent the night together and a month later she got in contact and told me she was pregnant."

"Wow. That would have been a shock."

"It was, but as soon as it sunk in, the idea of being a father… fuck, I liked it. I offered to move her to Virginia where I was stationed so we could be a family and I could take care of them both. Jamie didn't want that."

Sadie frowned. "Why not?"

"At the time, I thought it was because we weren't dating. We weren't anything. She didn't want to uproot her life for a man she barely knew. Now I wonder…"

When he stopped and pain flickered across his face, she frowned. "You wonder what?"

"I wonder if she didn't want me too close so she could do what she wanted. SEAL teams are away a lot for training and deployments, but if she lived in Virginia, I would have seen anything that was out of place."

She shifted closer. "Eastern, I spent a lot of time at Jamie's house, caring for Avery. There were no red flags. Sure, she had a few drinks on the weekend. But I never would have suspected she'd developed a drinking problem and was neglecting Avery."

He nodded, but when he still looked unconvinced, she inched forward, eliminating that last bit of space between them, and cupped the side of his neck. "Eastern…stop blaming yourself. You're here now. And you are Avery's world."

Something hot flashed in his gaze as it collided with hers. "We both are."

For a moment, their eyes held, neither of them wanting to look away. She should remove her hand. She should shift back and put some space between them. But before she could do either of those things, he wrapped his fingers around her wrist.

His touch was so soft it was almost a graze. Then he trailed his hand down her arm. "You should get up and walk away from me."

His words confused her. Was he telling her to do it because he couldn't? "You first."

His hand trailed to her shoulder, down her side, slipping so dangerously close to her breast that the fine hairs on her arms stood on end.

"If you don't walk away," he said quietly, "I might do something neither of us can take back."

Her breathing became choppy, those full lips of his taking up all of her attention. "Just because you can't take something back, doesn't make it a mistake."

Fire. It lit his eyes, darkening the blue.

Then his mouth crashed to hers.

The kiss was instant heat, and even though it was firm, his lips were surprisingly gentle. They grazed across hers, exploring, and when she opened her mouth, his tongue slipped inside, dueling with her own.

She groaned, a deep, primal sound that slipped into the air, cutting through the quiet of the room.

Then his hands were on her hips, sliding beneath the material of her shirt and touching bare skin. Instinctively, she leaned back, tugging him down with her. His weight settled over her, heavy and hard, causing a dull throb to beat into her lower belly.

He made her feel small and vulnerable and safe...yes, so safe under his large frame.

She curled a leg around his waist and tugged him closer as one of his hands inched higher, teasingly close to her breast.

His tongue swiped across hers one more time before his hand closed over her breast. Even though there was material between his hand and her flesh, it felt like he was touching bare skin, the roughness of his skin in complete contrast to her softness.

She arched as he palmed her, the throbbing in her core intensifying. Consuming and blacking out the world around her until it was just them.

Desperately, she slipped her fingers into his hair, tugging at the roots as she arched into his touch. He found her hard nipple and rolled it between his thumb and forefinger, drawing a guttural groan from her throat.

She was right on the verge of asking—no, begging—for more, when he suddenly released her, his mouth lifting, his hand disappearing from her breast. He stood quickly. Then his hands were in his hair, pulling, and the expression on his face...it was almost agonized.

"Shit, Sadie. I shouldn't have done that."

The words, combined with the separation, were like ice in her veins.

Her heart still beat at a million miles an hour as she tugged down her shirt and rose from the couch on shaky legs. "You don't have to keep apologizing for touching me," she said quietly, voice not nearly as steady as she would have liked. "We both wanted to do that."

The shake of his head felt like a kick to her stomach. "No. It's not appropriate. You're my nanny, and I'm older than you."

"I'm twenty-five. I'm hardly a child, Eastern. We're both consenting adults."

When he continued to stand there looking tortured, as if he'd just made the biggest mistake of his life, she forced her spine to straighten, refusing to let the hurt show on her face.

"I'm going to go."

She grabbed her phone and bag, then headed to the door, suddenly wanting to be anywhere but here. She was outside and almost at her car when strong fingers wrapped around her wrist.

"Sadie, I'm—"

"Don't." Her whispered word barely reached air. *"Don't* say you're sorry for kissing me. Having you say you shouldn't have done it already hurt enough. Having you say you feel *sorry* about it… No. I don't want that."

"What *do* you want?"

Wasn't that obvious? Hadn't she *made* it obvious by the way her body responded to him?

Instead of answering his question, she gave him a small smile that she knew went nowhere near reaching her eyes. "I'll see you later, Eastern."

CHAPTER 8

"Get off me, ya big plonker!"

Eastern didn't ease his hold on Denny's elbow as he marched him from the car to the station doors. "Plonker? Haven't heard that one before. You make it up?"

"No, it's British, ya wanker."

"See, now wanker's been used quite a few times." He stepped into the station and pulled Denny down the hall.

"I didn't do nothin'."

Eastern stopped in front of a holding cell. "That's where you're wrong. You started a fight in my brother's bar. Then you went out to your car and tried to drive down the street while drunk." Very fucking drunk.

"Try? There was no tryin' about it. I *did* drive that car down the street and if you hadn't pulled me over and arrested me, I would've been fine."

"You crashed the car, Denny." He opened the holding cell door and pushed the guy inside. "You hit a pole. A pole that could've been a person. You can sleep off the alcohol in here, and when you wake up, you'll find you've been charged with reckless driving while under the influence." He spun Denny around to uncuff him.

"You takin' these cuffs off to have it one-on-one?"

"Denny, you try anything, and I'll have you on the ground in a second."

"You couldn't knock the skin off a rice puddin', ya plank."

Despite everything, Eastern's lips twitched.

Once the cuffs were off, Denny spun, but he moved so quickly he fell on his ass.

"Sleep it off," Eastern said, not taking his eyes off the guy on the floor. "And you drink and drive in my town again, you'll be spending a hell of a lot more than one night in a cell."

Denny had just managed to get to his feet when Eastern tugged the door closed and locked it. He blew out a breath as he moved down the hall, ignoring the curses being shouted at him from the cell. This wasn't the first time Denny had been brought in for drunk and disorderly behavior, but it was the first time he'd decided to get into a car.

When he reached his office, he collapsed into his chair and leaned back. It was only seven o'clock, but the night had already been busy. And the second he had that moment of peace, his mind went to Sadie. To what had happened in his home a few nights ago.

He'd kissed her. Pressed her into the couch. Touched her.

His dick twitched just thinking about it.

Fuck. He had to stop. He kept telling himself they were a bad idea, that nothing could happen, but the second he was within arm's reach of the woman, all he wanted to do was close the remaining distance between them.

What the hell was wrong with him? He was a grown-ass man, but he was acting like a fucking teenager who had no restraint.

Sadie hadn't been able to sit for Avery tonight. She'd said her grandmother was sick and she needed to close the shop and get some stuff done, but a part of him wondered if what had happened between them contributed to her not being available. And that was exactly the reason it shouldn't have happened. He didn't want anything *he* did to affect her relationship with Avery. His daughter had already lost enough.

A knock sounded at the door, and he looked up to see one of his deputies, Lenard, standing there. "Hey. Heard about the call out for Denny. Everything okay?"

"Nope. The drunken idiot's in a holding cell. He's gonna spend the night and be charged. I'll do the paperwork before I go."

Lenard's eyes shot down the hall, a small smile on his face. "Did I hear him call you a plank?"

"Oh, he called me more than that. And I'm sure I'd be offended if I knew what any of the insults meant."

The deputy chuckled. "Okay. Well, don't stay too long."

"I'll be out of here once I'm done with the paperwork."

He tapped the door. "Great."

Eastern turned to his computer and started writing up the report. He was just finishing when his cell rang, Sadie's name flashing on the screen.

* * *

ANOTHER LATE EVENING. Well, late for her. Working at a bakery, she started at six in the morning, so seven o'clock felt very late.

Time to go home and die on her couch.

She stepped outside and was just locking the door when a car pulled up in front of the liquor store next door. The guy who climbed out had a phone pressed to his ear. She recognized him instantly—he was the man who'd been speaking to Mr. Anderson the other week in the back room. Presumably his son, because he'd referred to the liquor store owner as "Dad."

When their gazes met, she offered a small smile. He stopped

talking to whoever was on the other end of the call and gave her a pointed glare.

A pointed. Freaking. Glare. For smiling at him.

Well, looked like rudeness was genetic. Which was absolutely fine. She wasn't in the market for more friends anyway. Not him at least.

She climbed into her car and pulled onto the road. She hated that she hadn't been able to watch Avery tonight. Usually she'd leap at any opportunity to spend time with the kid, but with her grandmother and a couple of their part-time workers not feeling well, she'd had no choice. And the decreased staff numbers today meant that most of the prep for tomorrow needed to be done tonight, hence her late evening.

Of course, there'd been the smallest, teeny-tiniest part of her that was also relieved that she wouldn't be seeing Eastern. It sounded awful, but anytime she thought about what he'd said, something inside her experienced a sharp jab.

"I shouldn't have done that."

She pulled onto the road. Each time he touched her, he went out of his way to make sure she knew it was a mistake. But the thing was…it didn't feel like a mistake. Not to her. To her it felt good and real and right.

She clamped her teeth on her bottom lip, the flicker of pain forcing the heat out of her body. And dammit…she wanted him. A lot. But she wanted him to want her too, without the regret that immediately seemed to follow.

She'd only been driving for a couple of minutes when her gaze went to the car behind her. The driver wasn't overly close, but they'd been trailing her since she left the shop. They'd actually pulled out at almost the same time she had, from a spot at the curb a few doors down.

They couldn't actually be following her…could they?

Instead of driving straight, like she normally would have to get to her apartment, she took the next left, her pulse picking up speed when the car also turned.

It's fine. Maybe they live in this direction.

On the next left turn, she sped up and quickly followed it with a right. For a second, she thought she was okay. The air even started to flow with a bit more ease into her chest.

Then the car showed up behind her.

What the hell?

Maybe it was the thudding of her heart, or maybe she'd just watched too many true crime documentaries, but she instinctively reached for her phone. Instead of calling the sheriff's station, she called Eastern's direct number.

He picked up on the first ring. "Sadie? Is everything okay?"

"I'm not sure."

She paused, and when Eastern spoke again, his voice was on alert. "Tell me what's going on."

"I think someone's following me. I keep taking random turns and they're always behind me. I don't want to go home in case they follow me there."

A curse sounded over the line. "Where are you?"

"Adams Street."

"That's not far from me. Drive toward the station. I'll wait for you outside."

She worried her bottom lip as the car behind her started to put some distance between them.

She sped up and took the next right, her gaze barely on the road in front of her as she looked in the rearview mirror.

"Sadie? Are you coming to the station?"

The headlights of the car kept going straight instead of turning right. The air whooshed from her chest. "They went straight."

"What?"

"I'm sorry. I must be on edge or something. I turned, and they went straight. No one's following me."

"I still want you to come to the station so I can follow you home."

She opened her mouth to tell him that wasn't necessary when her car suddenly shook, almost like it was going over a series of small bumps. What the hell was that?

Then it hit her.

"Crap." The word was muttered under her breath, but Eastern must have heard it.

"What's wrong? Is the person back?"

"No, I got a flat tire." She pulled over to the side of the road. The businesses around her were all closed for the night, but at least the streetlights were on.

Eastern cursed again. "Send me your location. I'll come to you."

"It's fine, Eastern. I know how to change a tire. I—"

"Send me your location, Sadie."

He wasn't going to let this go. "I'll text you."

"Good. I'll see you soon. Stay in your car with the doors locked until I get there."

She opened her mouth to tell him that wasn't necessary, but he'd already hung up.

She frowned, sending him a pin of her location before looking out the window. For a moment, she considered listening to Eastern and staying in her car, but there was no reason. It wasn't even seven thirty, and she lived in the small town of Misty Peak, where barely anything bad happened. Plus, she didn't need a man to change her tire.

Knowing Eastern wouldn't be happy but too tired to care, she climbed out and moved to the trunk. She'd just popped it open when a car pulled onto the street. She assumed it would drive straight past her...but it didn't. Instead, the car pulled over and stopped behind her.

It couldn't be Eastern. She'd just sent him her location two minutes ago.

She waited for their blinding lights to turn off. It wasn't until the person climbed from the car that she saw who it was.

Every muscle in her body tightened as Scott walked toward her. She hadn't seen him since the morning of their wedding—and suddenly, everything she'd felt when she watched him with his admin assistant came screaming back to her.

"Sadie." He crossed the space between them, looking far too much like a concerned fiancé. "I'm so glad I finally caught you. I've been so worried—"

She slapped him.

She'd never slapped another person before in her life. Hell, she'd never *hurt* anyone, but it was like her hand had a mind of its own, and she slapped him right across the cheek.

He gasped, red-hot anger slashing across his features. "Sadie —what the hell?"

"*You're* saying what the hell to *me*?"

"Damn straight I am! You leave me standing at the altar looking like a damn fool. You don't write me so much as a note. You refuse to take my calls." With every word, he moved closer, his overpowering cologne, which she actually used to like, causing nausea to sweep through her belly.

"Come any closer and I won't just slap you, I'll nail you in the balls."

His brows slashed together. "What the hell is wrong with you? You've never been this—"

"Angry before? Well, I guess no fiancé has ever cheated on me on my *wedding day* before."

There was no flash of surprise in his eyes. No reddening of his cheeks. He knew what she'd seen. No doubt because his mother had told him.

"Look," he started, as if he was going into a negotiation at work. "I know what you saw must have been distressing—"

She laughed, and he stopped. "Oh, please go on, Scott. I'm

actually really interested in hearing how you plan to talk your way out of being the bad guy in all this."

A muscle ticked in his jaw. "It was a mistake. A one-time—"

"Don't lie to me. That was *not* a first kiss. If you're going to tell me anything, tell me the truth. How long?"

"It's not like that, Sadie. She was—"

"How. Long?"

The beat of silence that passed between them stretched, until finally he sighed. "A few months. Maybe a year."

Her fiancé and his admin assistant had been hooking up behind her back for a freaking *year*? "Was it just her?"

There was a small flicker of emotion that crossed his face, and she knew—it wasn't just her.

God, she wanted to slap him a second time.

"She was a mistake. I don't love her like I love you," he said quietly, inching toward her again.

Sadie pressed a hand to his chest. "Don't. I am barely holding on to my anger right now. I don't even know why you came here. It's over."

"Don't say that. You love me."

"Actually, that's the thing…I don't think I did. I don't think either of us ever truly loved the other."

"Sadie—"

"When I saw you with her on the morning of our wedding, my heart didn't break. I didn't crumble. I felt hurt and angry because I thought you were loyal and that we at least respected each other. But I also felt relieved."

"You don't mean that."

"I do. When I found you, I was on my way to tell you that I couldn't marry you, Scott. That I didn't love you the way I was supposed to love you."

Another wave of anger washed over his face. Maybe because he was a proud man who was used to getting what he wanted. "You're just trying to hurt me for hurting *you*."

God, he was delusional. And in this moment, she couldn't do anything but wonder how she'd ever thought she could spend the rest of her life with him. Was it because he was the easy option? Because she was afraid of being alone?

"You need to go."

"No." He gripped her arm, and she was a second from following through on that threat to nail him in the balls when a car screeched to a stop in front of hers. And a very large, very angry looking Eastern stepped out.

CHAPTER 9

Rage ripped through Eastern so fast that his breath heated. An asshole had Sadie pressed against the back of her car. Had his fingers wrapped around her upper arm.

"Everything okay here?" he asked through clenched teeth. What he really wanted to do was shove the asshole aside.

"No," Sadie answered.

At the same time the guy said, "Yes."

Eastern glared at him. "Release your hold on her. *Now.*"

"Look, I'm just trying to have a private conversation with my fiancée—"

"*Ex*-fiancée," Sadie cut in.

"I don't care if you're her damn husband," Eastern ground out, moving another step forward so that he was so close he could feel the heat radiating off the guy. "Release. Her."

Another second passed—a second too long.

Eastern grabbed his wrist and squeezed, instantly forcing him to release Sadie, then twisted his arm until it was bent behind him. The guy cried out in pain, and Eastern shoved him against the trunk of Sadie's car.

"Eastern!" Sadie cried.

"Were you following her tonight?" Eastern growled. When the guy didn't answer, Eastern pulled his arm higher. "Answer me."

"I followed her from the shop, yes! But only because I need to talk to her and she's refusing to see me."

Sadie gasped. "That was you? What the hell, Scott! You could have just spoken to me at the bakery."

When Scott was silent, Eastern shook his head. "No. Because he wanted to know where you lived. But he almost lost you, so when you pulled over, he couldn't wait any longer."

Another trickle of quiet passed before Sadie finally asked, "Is that true?"

The silence from Scott told them it was.

"You want to file a report for harassment?" Eastern asked, hoping like hell she said yes.

When Sadie didn't answer, the guy cocked his head to look at her, shock on his face. "Sadie!"

"No." She sighed. "Let him go."

That was the last thing Eastern wanted to do. But if she didn't want to report him, he had no other choice, dammit.

He released the asshole but didn't move, effectively blocking him from Sadie. "Go home."

Scott's brown eyes darkened as he straightened to his full height. He was tall at about six feet, but he couldn't compete with Eastern's six-three and sheer muscle mass. "I'd like to talk to Sadie. *Alone.*"

Like hell that was happening. He opened his mouth to tell the guy exactly that, but Sadie spoke first.

"We're done, Scott. Go back to Atlanta. Stop calling and texting. It's over."

"You can't just—"

"She can," Eastern cut him off. "*Go.*"

Red bloomed across his cheekbones before he turned and stormed toward the driver's side of his car.

Eastern waited for him to get in and drive away before turning to Sadie. "You okay?"

She rubbed a hand over her temple, looking more tired now than anything else. "I almost married that jerk."

Every muscle in Eastern's body locked. That asshole didn't deserve her. Five minutes in his company and Eastern knew that. "But you didn't."

Her hand dropped, and she looked up at him. "There has to be something wrong with me, right?"

"With my shitty dating track record, I'm probably not the right person to ask."

The corners of her mouth lifted. Only slightly, but it was enough.

He inched closer and lifted her arm, swiping his thumb over the spot the guy had touched. "Did he hurt you?" Because if he had, Eastern wasn't opposed to going after the fucker and teaching him a goddamn lesson.

She shook her head, and when the silence between them stretched and thickened, feeling far too intimate, he released her wrist and stepped back. "I'll change your tire and follow you home."

She frowned. "I don't need you to do either of those things."

Ignoring her, he reached into her trunk, lifted the base and pulled out the spare tire.

"Eastern, did you hear me?"

"Heard you, but it wasn't the answer I wanted." Once the tire was beside the flat, he went back for the tools before squatting beside the car.

Sadie huffed. "I told you, I can change it."

"Ah, but you see, my parents raised me to be a gentleman, and a gentleman would never let a woman change a tire if she doesn't have to." He placed the jack under the car and got to work.

"Will you at least let me help?" she asked.

"Nope."

Another huff. "You're a stubborn ass, you know that?"

He bit the side of his cheek to stop the smile. "I've been called worse tonight."

"Really?"

"Yes, ma'am. I didn't even understand half the insults that were thrown my way, but I'm sure if I had, I would have been deeply offended."

At the silence, he looked up to see her bottom lip between her teeth and a ghost of a grin on her face. "Well…at least you've been put in your place."

Maybe. But now, looking up at her beautiful midnight eyes, all he could think was that he'd been completely knocked off center.

* * *

SADIE'S BELLY did a little flutter. He was following her home. Back to her apartment building. Of course, she'd told him he didn't need to follow. She'd told him a whole bunch of times, but he didn't seem to be listening to a word she said tonight.

Once she'd pulled into the parking lot in front of the building, she climbed out of her car to see Eastern already out of his, his gaze skirting the streets around them.

Why? Because he was expecting danger? Or because he was always on guard? Something told her it was the latter.

He crossed his arms, and her throat dried when his thick biceps stretched his shirt.

God, he was just so much…man. Big and protective and strong. Yeah, he definitely radiated strength. And that did things to her belly that she should *not* be acknowledging.

She straightened her spine and forced her features to blank as she crossed the space between them, not wanting him to see the effect he had on her. "Thank you for following me home. I'll see you soon?"

In a few days, or a month, or longer, depending on how long it took her to get over this little crush.

"I'll walk you up."

Her brows shot up. Eastern in her space? No. No, no, no. Absolutely not.

She opened her mouth to tell him exactly that, but then his hand went to the small of her back, the heat from his touch zipping into her skin, piercing her belly, and the words just died on her lips.

She'd always thought she was strong and able to put up a good fight to get what she wanted, but when it came to this guy, she was powerless.

As they walked, she worried her keys in her fingers. "I'm sorry I couldn't look after Avery tonight."

"It's okay. My neighbor, Mrs. Hanley, was free. Avery might not like her as much as she likes you, but I have a feeling there aren't *many* people she likes as much as you."

Her heart gave a little twist. "There aren't many people I like as much as Avery either."

An odd expression crossed his face before Sadie slotted the key into the foyer door and let them in.

Eastern frowned at the door. "It's a pretty old-school lock."

"Yeah. Unfortunately, this building doesn't get much TLC. We have a working elevator though." She hit the call button.

Eastern was still looking back at the door like it was on the verge of letting in an ax murderer. "This is a new apartment for you, right? Not the same place you lived before moving to Atlanta?"

The elevator doors opened and they stepped inside. "New apartment in the same building."

His gaze swung back to Sadie. "So Scott could have a key to the building."

What was he getting at? Did he think Scott was going to come here and harass her some more? "No, Scott and I both turned in our keys before we left town. And besides, Scott wouldn't do that. I know what he did tonight was…"

"Inappropriate?" Eastern finished for her when she couldn't. "Dangerous? Bordering on stalker behavior?"

"Eastern. I don't think he'd hurt me. I think he just wanted to talk."

The look Eastern gave her said he didn't believe her.

"He plays it tough, but he's really not," she added softly as the doors opened and they stepped out onto the fourth floor. "Trust me, if my slap didn't make him want to run, then your arm-twist move did."

Eastern frowned as she stopped at her door. "You slapped him?"

"Yep. Right across the face." The door opened, and she cringed. "Wait, I probably shouldn't have said that to you, right? Is that assault? Damn, I just keep coming off as this crazy, violent person."

Humor sparked his eyes. "It's not assault if it's self-defense."

Ha. It was less self-defense and more unresolved anger, but sure, she'd let him think it was self-defense.

She stepped into her apartment and dropped her stuff onto the side table before grinning at Eastern. "Yeah, it was definitely that then."

He chuckled as he stepped inside after her. "I wish I'd been there to see it."

"Maybe next time you will." Crap, she needed to stop admitting to her combatant tendencies.

She opened her mouth to take it back, but the way he was looking at her stopped her cold. It was a look filled with heat and pride and…something else. Something much more primal.

Swallowing, she slipped past him into the kitchen. "Do you drink tea? It's a bit late for coffee, and not everyone's a tea person, but I love a chamomile before bed."

Not only was she rambling, but with the pantry door open,

she was hiding. Hiding because she didn't trust herself around this man. He was in her apartment, taking up all the space, smelling far too good and looking way too kissable.

When she had the tea box in her hand and had no other reason to stand behind the pantry door, she finally closed it to see Eastern in her kitchen. God, he really did make her place look tiny.

"Tea would be nice," he said, voice like silk.

Shit. Hold it together, Sadie. Do not give him another reason to kiss you—it'll just be followed by a painful apology.

Turning, she filled her kettle with water. "So," she started, desperate to fill the silence with anything. "You were a Navy SEAL?"

"I was."

She turned to look at him over her shoulder as she set the water on the stove and pulled out two mugs. "But you left."

"Yeah, Dad got sick before he passed away, and that was a wake-up call I needed. I'd missed his last few years, and I knew if I didn't get out, I'd miss too much of Avery growing up."

Something inside kicked at his words. She set the mugs onto the island and put in the tea bags. "I know what you mean. I was only away from Avery for a year, and yet she seems so much older." She grabbed honey from the cupboard. "Do you miss it?"

"Every damn day. I loved my time in the military. But I don't regret leaving, and I'd do it again in a heartbeat to be her full-time father."

Barely thinking about what she was doing, she reached over and slipped her hand over his. "You're a good father, Eastern. Avery's lucky to have you."

"It doesn't always feel like that."

She wasn't sure if he meant to say those words out loud or if they'd just slipped out, because a frown creased his brow immediately after and he almost looked surprised.

She grazed her thumb over the back of his hand, wanting to

give him some form of comfort. "Jamie hired me to watch Avery from the time she was a baby. Six months old. And from the second she could talk, all she wanted to talk about was you. Her big strong daddy, who lifted her up into his arms and made the rest of the world disappear."

"When he was around."

Those words cut into her. So did the guilt and vulnerability in his voice. "You can't be everything to everyone all the time, Eastern. But you've come pretty close."

He dipped his head, and she had to force herself away from him to grab the boiling water from the stove and fill the mugs.

As they drank their tea, they shared stories of times Avery had made them smile or laugh. They spoke about Sugar and Spice and her grandmother, and all their favorite cupcakes and cookies. Eastern even told her the funnier details about Denny's arrest.

It felt strangely easy to talk to him. Like they'd never run out of things to say, and even if they did, she'd talk about nothing just to keep hearing his voice. To keep his eyes on her and keep him with her in this moment.

When they'd both finished their teas, it felt far too quick.

He rose from her small kitchen island. "I should go. Avery will be in bed, but sometimes I do that stalker-dad thing where I just watch her sleep."

A tinge of jealousy weaved through her chest that he got those moments with her whenever he wanted. "Give her a kiss for me."

A flicker of some emotion she couldn't name shone in his eyes.

Clearing her throat, she walked him to the door. She'd just opened it when he touched her arm.

"Hey. Will you do me a favor?"

She turned and looked up, way up, into his ice-blue eyes. If the man asked her to sign over everything she owned to him, she'd probably agree just because of the way he looked at her. "Sure."

He stepped closer. "If Scott returns…tell me."

"He's—"

"Harmless. I know you think he is. But when a man loses something, and the realization of exactly what he's lost finally hits him, he can become dangerous in the fight to get it back."

Her heart rippled in her chest. Because he was saying *she* was worth fighting for.

"Eastern…" His name was a whisper on her lips, and she wasn't sure *why* she'd said it, just knew that she needed to. "I'll be okay."

His gaze roamed over her face. "I don't know what it is about you that makes me want to risk everything to kiss you."

This time, her heart stopped, and the air in her throat became stuck. "Would it be so bad to kiss me *without* calling it a mistake or a risk?"

That familiar frown tugged his brows together. "Avery needs me to do what's best for her. She's lost so much, and I can't do anything to make her lose more."

So he was assuming that if they kissed, if they allowed themselves to give in to what they both clearly felt, it would end in devastation. And then Avery would lose her.

Why was he so sure of that?

Swallowing, she nodded and forced herself to step away when what she really wanted to do was lean closer. Touch her lips to his. Taste him one more time. "You'd better get back to her then."

A muscle worked in his jaw, and he dipped his head before stepping out.

The second the door closed, she leaned her temple against the wood, wondering how on Earth she was supposed to live in the same small town as a man who made her want him with such conviction…yet she was unable to have.

CHAPTER 10

Sadie rushed from her apartment building to her car. She wasn't technically late. In fact, she was actually early to open Sugar and Spice. But she'd barely slept last night, which meant she needed coffee—stat.

It had been damn near impossible to sleep with thoughts of Eastern rattling around in her head. Of his beautiful blue eyes. His silky-smooth voice as he spoke about wanting her...

Oh, Jesus.

The sun was only just starting to rise as she slid behind the wheel.

Why? Why did she find everything about him so goddamn attractive? Out of all the men on this planet, she was crushing on the one who under no circumstances wanted to be with her.

Obviously, she just had to accept that she and Eastern were never going to happen. It didn't matter how fast he made her heart race or how clammy he made her skin feel, he wasn't for her.

He wanted to protect what she had with Avery, and how could she argue with that? She wanted what was best for Avery too. The difference was, she wasn't afraid to see where their attraction could lead, because even if they broke up, they could be adults and remain amicable, right? Or was that naive of her to think?

She took a right turn, driving faster than she should have.

It was fine. Absolutely fine. She hadn't been single in years. It was about time she learned to live without a partner. She'd fill her nights with cupcakes and cocktails. Which reminded her, she still hadn't cracked open that bottle of bourbon. Maybe she'd text Elle and ask if she wanted to come over for a girls' night. Yeah, that would be good. They could drink and talk and laugh, and the other woman could be a big, fat distraction from Eastern.

As she pulled up out front of Sugar and Spice, she was already making mental notes of what she had to do before opening. All the cookie dough was already prepped, so it just needed to be taken out of the fridge and popped into the oven. She was also going to get started on a few of her favorite cupcake recipes, one of them being red velvet.

She grabbed her bag and climbed out of the car, dreaming about the iced coffee with caramel syrup she planned to make herself.

Her stomach rumbled, a reminder she hadn't eaten anything this morning and had barely touched her dinner last night.

She unlocked the shop doors and stepped inside, only to abruptly stop.

Not just stop—completely freeze.

The place was trashed.

The glass display case had been smashed, shards everywhere. The register was on the floor, the drawer open and empty. Even the chairs had been thrown, with legs broken and seat material torn.

This wasn't real, right? Someone hadn't actually broken into her sweet grandmother's cupcake shop and broken everything.

She blinked hard.

Still trashed.

The farther she moved into the space, the more nausea cramped her belly.

Who had done this? And why?

She neared the back room, only to stop again...this time because she heard something. A small crunch, almost like someone had stepped on glass.

Her heart hammered loudly in her chest as she forced words out. "Hello? Is someone here?"

Silence. It hummed through the shop, sliding over her skin and icing her insides.

Everything in her demanded she turn around. Get out.

The last time that happened had been the morning of her wedding, and thank God she'd listened.

She spun around—and the second her back was turned, fast footsteps sounded. She didn't have time to look behind her before pain radiated throughout her skull.

Sadie cried out as she fell forward, hitting the floor hard. Pieces of glass dug into her palms, making her whimper in pain.

The heavy crash of footsteps sounded again, this time moving away from her, toward the back door. By the time she lifted her head and looked that direction, the door was open, the room empty.

For a moment, she just lay there, shock spiraling through her limbs, making movement feel impossible. It took a long time to feel capable of pushing up to a sitting position, then another few seconds to actually rise to her feet. Her head throbbed and her hands were bleeding, bits of glass still digging into her flesh. But she needed to call for help.

When she finally managed to stumble to her fallen bag and tug out her phone, she dialed the sheriff's office. As the phone rang, she went to the back door. She already knew what she'd find though...the alley was empty. Whoever had done this was gone.

* * *

"Leaves."

Eastern shook his head. "Nope. I wouldn't make it that easy."

Avery's little brows tugged together as they walked from his parked car to her school. "Grass?"

"If it's not leaves, it's definitely not grass, kid."

They were playing their usual morning game of I Spy. Sometimes they spied on things that started with a letter. Sometimes it was a certain texture or function. This morning, he'd chosen the color green.

Her eyes suddenly lit up as she spotted the kid in front of them. "The star on Noah's shoe."

"How'd you get that in three guesses?"

She grinned up at him, the freckles across her nose sparkling in the sun. "Because I like stars."

Exactly why he'd chosen it. Some of his best memories were of the nights he let her stay up late so they could stare at the stars.

They'd just reached the front of the school when Avery gasped. "Quinn's here! Okay, see ya, Daddy."

"Hold on there, kiddo." He grabbed her wrist before crouching in front of her. "Are you too cool to give your dad a kiss now?"

Her features softened and she threw her arms around his shoulders. "I'm never too old for that. I love you, Daddy."

A piece of his heart ripped right out of his chest and went straight to her. "I love you too, princess."

Then she was gone, running over to her friend and grabbing her hand.

God, she was getting big. And he'd missed so much of it already.

Not anymore.

She was about to step through the doors when she paused and

turned her head, a grin crossing her face before she waved to him and finally disappeared.

"That kid adores you."

He turned at the female voice, internally groaning at the sight of Marie Alvaro. A local single mother who was not only a gossip but also flirted with him any chance she got.

"She's lucky to have such a good father," she continued.

The way she said *good* while checking out his chest and arms made him take a step back. "I'm the lucky one. I'll see you around, Marie."

He started to step away, but she gripped his arm. "Wait. Before you run off, I have something I need to talk to you about."

"What is it?"

"I think someone's been lurking around my apartment building." She inched closer, her gaze once again going to his upper arms. "It's made me feel a bit unsafe. Maybe you could come check it out?"

"I can have some patrol cars do a few drive-bys. But if you feel unsafe, call the station and we'll write it up. Excuse me. I've got to get going."

He started toward his car, but she followed close behind. "To see Sadie Sandler?"

He stopped. "Why do you say that?"

"I live in the same building as her. Used to live on the same floor back when she was with that fiancé of hers. I saw you two together out the window last night."

So she spied on her neighbors too?

Marie cocked her head. "Are you two—"

"I need to get to work." He cut her off before she could finish her sentence. "Remember, call the station if you feel unsafe."

He slid into his car, his muscles tense. If there was anyone he didn't want to know his business, it was Marie. She'd probably spread the news around town by lunchtime that he and Sadie were dating, even though it wasn't true.

He pushed the woman to the back of his mind as he drove to work. He'd always loved that it was so close to Avery's school, because it meant if he ever needed to get to her quickly, he could. And today, it meant he didn't have time to get caught up in his head.

At the station, he took his usual parking spot. What kind of day would it be? Quiet? Chaotic? Busy? He never knew. When he stepped into the office, Daisy was the first person he saw, as usual.

She smiled up at him. "Hey, boss."

At what point did he stop correcting her? "Just Eastern. Anything happen while I was gone?"

"Well, we gave Denny his fine and let him out. Told him he'd lost his license."

Eastern almost wished he'd been there to see that. No doubt whichever poor soul had given him the news had received an earful. "I bet he wasn't too happy."

"That he was not. Made quite the spectacle of himself, threw a few insults around. Well, things I suspect were insults. Didn't really understand what he was saying."

He chuckled and headed toward his office. "Thanks for the update."

"There was also a break-in at Sugar and Spice."

His muscles locked and he spun. "What?"

"Yeah, that poor granddaughter who just returned to Misty Peak actually walked in on the perp."

The *fuck?* "Did she get hurt?"

"I think she's at the hospital now. I'm not sure which officers went to the scene—"

"I'm going to her."

Daisy's brows shot up, but he barely paid her any attention as he stormed out of the station and raced to his car.

Someone broke into the bakery? Who? Why? And what exactly had happened when she'd walked in on them? Why was she at the fucking *hospital*?

He made it to the hospital in half the time it should have taken. He was told she was in room eight, and when he walked in, he saw two of his deputies closing notepads. They both turned, Charles lifting a brow. "Boss. What are you—"

"I'm here to check on Sadie."

He frowned. "But we—"

"Go back to the station. Write up the report."

They each frowned but nodded before stepping out. That's when he took in Sadie and the gauze on her hands.

He bit back a curse as he stepped in front of her, not even trying to stop himself as he cupped her cheek. "Are you okay?"

"Yeah. The person who broke in hit me with a cake stand when I turned my back." She laughed, but there wasn't much humor behind it. "A cake stand as a weapon, can you believe it? Your officers found it at the scene."

He couldn't believe any of this. "But you're okay?"

"No concussion. I have a small bandage on the back of my head from a cut. I also fell on some glass." She lifted her bandaged hands to prove it.

"Male or female?"

Disappointment filled her eyes. "I don't know. I don't know *anything*. They came at me after I turned to leave, and by the time I got up, they were gone."

He trailed his fingers gently through her hair, his eyes never leaving her black gaze. "You never answered my question. Are you okay?"

"Honestly, I don't know. I'm shocked that my grandmother's store was broken into. Sad that it was trashed, and we'll have to close for a while to fix everything. And I'm confused. So confused. Why would someone do this? They obviously stole some money from the register, but we don't keep much in there because most people pay with card. If it was a money thing, wouldn't it make more sense to break into the liquor store next door?"

Eastern frowned, suddenly remembering the altercation between Sadie and Morris Anderson. "Have you and Morris been getting along?"

Her brows shot up. "Me and Mr. Anderson? We don't talk. We haven't talked since you saw us in the alley."

"What about Scott?"

She shook her head. "No. He wouldn't do this. Why would he bother?"

"Maybe he wants you scared and running back to him? Or maybe he's angry you left him and wants to get back at you."

Her eyes flared before she shook her head. "I still don't think he would do this. I *know* Scott. Well, at least I *think* I do."

"I'll question him."

"Eastern—"

"It's my job, Sadie. I'll just ask him a couple of questions and cover all our bases." When she didn't respond, just nibbled her bottom lip, he closed the remaining space between them and clasped the back of her neck in his hand. "Someone hurt you today. They put you in danger."

"I'm okay."

This time. The words were a whisper in his head that never made it to air.

He tugged her against his chest, needing to hold her. Reassure himself that she was safe. Even though that same little whisper told him he shouldn't care as much as he did.

CHAPTER 11

"Nan, I'm okay."

Her grandmother looked at her like she saw everything Sadie was hiding. The residual fear. The uncertainty. "You're not okay. You caught someone breaking into the store and they hurt you. You don't need to be brave with me."

Sadie cut the ham, avocado and tomato sandwiches in half. It was a favorite of her grandmother's. During the summers she'd spent in Misty Peak as a child, this was their go-to lunch. Maybe that's why it was a favorite of hers now too.

"You're right," Sadie conceded without looking up. "I did catch someone breaking into the store, and yes, they scared and hurt me, but I'm lucky that I only came out of it with a few cuts and bruises. And after speaking to the insurance company and ordering replacements for everything, I feel good."

Okay, maybe not good, but better than she had yesterday, right after the break-in had taken place.

She set the sandwiches onto plates and carried them over to the round table, then set one in front of her grandmother and the other at the empty seat beside her. Her grandmother's house looked exactly as it had when Sadie was little. Wooden floorboards with brown curtains across the windows. Photos and paintings on every inch of the wall. And trinkets and memorabilia everywhere else.

Some would describe it as cluttered. She called it comfortable. Comfortable open living room and kitchen, with cozy recliner seats in front of the TV.

Her grandmother raised a brow, and Sadie suddenly felt like she was about to be interrogated. The second she was seated, her grandmother touched her hand.

"Sadie. I'm worried about you."

"It was *your* shop that was broken into. If anyone should be worried, it's me about *you*."

Her grandmother shook her head. "No. I'm worried because you've been through a lot in the last month. Walking away from your wedding. Scott's infidelity. Moving home. Now this."

That was her grandmother, always putting others first. "You're right, there's been some crappy stuff happening in my life in the last month. But there's also been good stuff. Leaving Scott and moving home were the best changes. And being back with you? That's everything. You're my last family, Nan. I love you. And being here feels right."

Her grandmother shifted a lock of hair from her forehead to behind her ear. "I love having you home, darling." Her voice lowered, a hint of sadness in her voice. "When you came to live here after your parents got into that terrible accident, I was so worried I wouldn't be enough."

"Oh, Nan. You were everything. You *still are*. You're the reason I could get out of bed in the morning those first few months. You're the reason I didn't crumble." She tilted her head, fighting back tears. "Now, I want to be what you need after what happened to the bakery."

"The bakery is not a person. And everything in it that was broken can be fixed. Things can be replaced. People can't. Just promise me one thing."

"Anything."

"Look after yourself. I can't lose you."

There was so much concern in her grandmother's voice. She was really worried about something happening to Sadie.

"I promise," she said quietly.

Her grandmother held her gaze for one long beat before nodding and looking down at her plate. "Good. Now tell me what's going on with you and Eastern Walker."

Sadie almost choked on the water she was sipping. "What?"

"You and Eastern. You said he visited you at the hospital."

"He's the sheriff, and I was involved in a crime."

Her grandmother lifted her sandwich. "You also said you've cared for Avery on a few occasions, which of course means spending more time with him."

Jesus, this woman could have been a detective. "We've been seeing a bit of each other, sure, but nothing's happening between us." Eastern was making sure of that.

"All right. But if something *did* happen, it would be okay. You're allowed to move on quickly or slowly or at whatever pace you want."

That made her pause. "So you don't think it would be too soon after Scott?"

"There's no such thing as too soon to meet the person you're supposed to be with."

Well, she didn't want to get ahead of herself. "He's older than me."

"Pfft. Age is just a number. Your grandfather was twelve years older than me, and I always saw it as a good thing. He needed a few more years to get to the same point in maturity as me."

Sadie laughed. "Okay. Maybe that was my problem with Scott. He was the same age as me."

"Maybe. But I think you and I both know that the main problem, other than the cheating of course, was that you fell out of love with him a long time ago."

She frowned at her grandmother. How did she know that?

"I know what love is," her grandmother said softly, as if reading her mind. "And what you shared with Scott was companionship. Maybe a bit of comfort because you'd been together for so long. And familiarity."

"I don't know how you do that," Sadie said quietly. "You see everything, even what I try to hide."

Her grandmother cupped her cheek. "You may have only spent summers with me growing up, but they were the best part of my year. You were my baby as much as your father was."

Tears pricked Sadie's eyes. "I love you, Nan."

"I love you too, darling." She turned back to her sandwich. "This is the last thing I'll say on the Eastern matter, then I'm minding my own business."

Sadie's lips twitched. "Okay."

"If either of you are being hesitant because you both love Avery, and you think it might change things, remember—your love for her is so pure that you'll *both* protect her, no matter how things turn out."

She ran her finger over the crust of bread. "It's probably Eastern you should be saying that to. He's the one who has a million reasons we can't be together."

"Give him time. He's in pain because he didn't come home to Avery earlier. But soon, he'll realize that you can't run from love for long."

She almost choked. "It's hardly love. We barely know each other."

The smile her grandmother gave her said she had a secret no one else knew. "When I met your grandfather, he wasn't sure it was love either. But slowly, he saw what was right in front of him."

Her grandfather had passed away when Sadie was a baby. She'd always wished she'd met him. "You don't talk about him much."

"Oh, but I think about him every day. And every day, I'm reminded of how lucky I was to have him. I can only hope you experience that kind of love. When you were with Scott, I wasn't so sure. Now…"

She was talking about loving Eastern.

Sadie opened her mouth, not entirely sure what was about to come out, when her phone vibrated on the table—Eastern's name on the screen.

Her grandmother gave her another of those knowing smiles. "Now, something tells me you will."

* * *

THE DOORBELL RANG, and Avery squealed before jumping off the island stool and running toward the door.

"Slow down, Ave, you're gonna trip." Either that, or she'd run smack into the door, and it wouldn't be the first time.

She tugged the door open just before he got there. Sadie stood on the other side, a box in her hand and a huge smile stretching her lips as Avery threw her arms around her.

"Hey, baby girl," Sadie said.

Avery giggled. "Sadie, I'm not a baby anymore. I'm almost a teenager."

Sadie gasped and pulled back. "You are not! And even when you are, you'll always be my baby girl." She tugged Avery into another hug, kissing her cheek a dozen times before straightening and looking at Eastern. Something flashed in her eyes… heat? But it came and went so quickly he almost wondered if he'd made it up in his head.

She stepped inside and Eastern moved forward, setting a hand on her hip and pressing a light kiss to her cheek. Damn, her skin was soft. "Thank you for coming, Sadie."

"Thank you for inviting me."

He'd had to. The previous night, she was all he could think

about. How was she after the break-in? Was she hurting? Scared? Inviting her over for dinner tonight allowed him to make sure she was okay.

He moved back to the kitchen.

"When Daddy said he invited you to dinner, I was *so* excited!" Avery gushed, words coming out so quickly they ran into each other. "He asked me what your favorite food was, and I said pasta with fish in it."

Sadie laughed, and the sound floated throughout the room, punching him right in the damn chest. "Seafood marinara."

"Daddy said he could make it, but I told him I wasn't sure he could."

Eastern frowned. "Hey!" Avery glanced up at him from where she and Sadie had stopped at the kitchen island. "I'm a great cook."

"Daddy, you already burned the garlic bread, and you had to look up how to cook mussels."

"I'm sure lots of people need to look up how to cook mussels, and the burned garlic bread was supposed to be our secret."

Avery giggled. "Sadie always told me I don't need to keep secrets from her."

Sadie cringed before lifting a shoulder. "Sorry."

"It's true," Eastern admitted. "I didn't know what to do with the mussels, and I put the garlic bread in too early and it burned a bit."

"A bit? Daddy, one side is black."

"Charred," he corrected. "And I'll have that side."

Sadie lifted a shoulder. "I don't mind some charred garlic bread. It actually sounds kind of good."

Avery wrinkled her nose, looking at them like they'd both lost their minds. "I'd like the un-charred part." Her eyes lit up. "Sadie, I made you something at school today. Hang on, I'll go get it!"

She sprinted out of the room—and the second it was just him and Sadie, the air thickened.

He studied the circles shadowing her eyes. "How're you doing?"

She lifted a shoulder. "The store has been cleaned up. Replacements for everything that was broken have been ordered, and my grandmother seems okay."

He inched forward. "No. How are *you* doing?"

"I'm okay." Her words were quiet, almost not crossing the scant distance. "You and your deputies don't have any idea who it might have been?"

Frustration kicked him in the gut. "Not yet. We've questioned those in the surrounding stores and asked about surveillance footage, but no one has any." He shifted his gaze between her eyes. "Morris Anderson was home with his wife and has home security to support that."

"You still thought it might have been him?"

He lifted a shoulder. "It has to be someone, and I didn't like the way he was talking to you in that alley. Even though the register was open and the money gone, it could have been a random robbery, but everything else, the trashed display cases and furnishings, point to a deeper motive."

Her brows flickered.

Unable to stop himself, he reached up and cupped her neck. "I'll find this person."

Her eyes flared and she opened her mouth to respond, but before any words came out, the patter of Avery's steps sounded in the hall. He stepped back, dropping his hand, not missing the hint of disappointment on Sadie's face.

Over the next hour, Eastern tried like hell to concentrate on preparing dinner and not burning anything else, but every time Sadie smiled or laughed or pushed that lock of hair behind her ear, he was too fucking distracted. She offered to help half a dozen times, but he always declined, and honestly, he preferred watching her play and bond with Avery.

Their connection was like none he'd seen between his

daughter and anyone else. Sadie looked at Avery like she was the center of her world, and Avery looked just as in love with Sadie.

When they finally sat down for dinner, Avery was still speaking at a million miles an hour, telling Sadie about all the kids at school. Her teacher. Even what she'd eaten for lunch.

When Sadie finally got a word in, she looked up at Eastern. "This is delicious."

One side of his mouth lifted. "I'm not just a pretty face."

Avery's face screwed up. "Boys aren't pretty, Daddy."

"I think boys can be pretty," Sadie said.

"No. Girls are pretty. Boys are handsome. Or strong." She gave Eastern an assessing look. "You're definitely strong."

He bit back a laugh "But not handsome?"

"Ew! I can't call my dad handsome!" She turned to Sadie. "Scott was a little bit handsome."

The smile fell from Eastern's face and his muscles tensed, while Sadie's fork stopped halfway to her mouth.

Avery angled her body toward Sadie. "Why did you break up?"

"Avery—"

"No, it's okay," Sadie said quickly, cutting him off. "We broke up because we realized we didn't love each other the way we were supposed to."

"How are you supposed to love someone to marry them?" Avery asked.

Sadie gave her a soft smile. "Well...and this is just my opinion...you should love them so much that the idea of spending the rest of your life together excites you. You don't always have to like each other, but even on your hardest days, you should never question whether or not they'll always be there for you. You should just know you're in it together, good or bad."

Her brow furrowed. "And you didn't feel that with Scott?"

"No, baby girl. I didn't."

"Then why'd you move to Atlanta and almost marry him?"

That question took a bit more time for Sadie to answer, and again, he wanted to step in and tell her she didn't need to respond, but a part of him wanted to know as much as Avery.

"Because sometimes we get so used to what we know, and maybe a bit scared of what our lives would be like if they were different, that we just...ignore the warning signs."

Avery frowned, and a second passed before she nodded. "I'm glad you stopped ignoring the warning signs and came back."

The smile that spread Sadie's lips was wide and genuine. "Me too, baby girl." Her eyes met Eastern's. "Me too."

CHAPTER 12

Sadie watched as Eastern read the book to Avery. She'd read the first chapter, and now Eastern was on the second.

The story was about a ten-year-old girl who had an albino Irish wolfhound. Every time the dog in the book barked, Eastern screwed up his face and did the most realistic bark Sadie had ever heard. Everyone laughed, especially Avery.

They sat on either side of Avery on her bed, with just the bedside table night light offering a dull glow over the room. There was something about being here, listening to Eastern's voice and Avery's laughter, that made her feel so...content. Like everything that had happened over the last month had been worth it because it had led her here, exactly where she was meant to be.

This was all she'd ever wanted. Family. Love.

But this wasn't her family. Something she needed to remind herself.

She swallowed, forcing her mind to switch off and focus on the story.

It didn't take long for Avery's eyes to start closing. She fought off sleep. But then, she always had. Right from when she was a toddler, she never wanted to fall asleep, because she'd always wanted one more book or one more chapter.

Sadie brushed some hair from Avery's face and snuggled in beside her, the warmth of her little body through the sheets reassuring.

Eastern was still reading when Avery's whispered words sounded. "I wish you were my mom, Sadie."

Eastern paused, and Sadie's heart cracked. Because Avery deserved a mother who was not only there for her but *wanted* to be. And Sadie definitely wanted to be there for this little girl.

Tears pressed to her eyes, but she blinked them back. Sadie pressed a kiss to her head. "I'll always love you like you're my own, baby girl."

By the time Eastern was finished, Avery's eyes were well and truly closed, her chest moving up and down in slow succession as she slept.

Sadie didn't want to move though. That was always the case. There was something about lying beside a sleeping child, who you loved more than life itself, that just brought so much peace.

Eastern rose, and too soon Sadie knew she needed to get up too. With a small sigh, she pushed up. She wasn't expecting him to take her hand, but when he did, she didn't pull away.

He led her straight into the kitchen, where she sat on a stool at the island.

"Are you okay?"

Her gaze flew up at his question. Did she look as emotionally raw as she felt? "I just wish her mother treated her the way she deserves to be treated." *Loved her* the way she deserved to be loved.

"Me too."

"I don't understand. Jamie has this beautiful child. This *gift*. And she just walked away from her. How? How did she do that? Did she not realize what she had?"

Eastern's eyes darkened. "I've asked myself that same question a thousand times. She didn't even show up to the custody hearing to fight for her child. It's wild to me."

For the second time that evening, tears pressed at her eyes. "I almost feel sorry for her because I know *exactly* what she walked away from—and it's huge."

"Massive." He brushed a tear from her cheek. She swallowed as he lifted her hands. "How are the wounds?"

"They're fine, just small cuts that are healing already." She'd changed the bandages to Band-Aids, but that was mostly because the bandages had been so bulky and annoying.

"They shouldn't be there at all."

There was an edge to his voice that was in complete contrast to the gentleness of his touch.

"Are *you* okay?" she asked quietly.

He studied her hands, his thumbs running over the small, covered cuts. "I hate what Jamie did. I hate it so much that I actually hurt when I think about it. And I hate that even before she left, she wasn't the mother she should have been. But the one thing I'm grateful for...is that she gave Avery *you*."

Sadie met his eyes. There was so much emotion in the blue depths. Pain. Anger. Frustration. But also something else. Something deeper.

Reaching up, she cupped his cheek. "No, it's the other way around. I was given the gift of Avery. She was taken away from me for a bit. And I think, even though I didn't acknowledge it at the time, that's the main reason I left. Because her memory was everywhere, and being here was too hard. But you returned her to me. Thank you, Eastern."

He inched closer, eliminating the small space between them. "I can see why."

His breath whispered across her skin, like a warm breeze on a cool day. "Why what?"

"Why she loves you so much." Her breath hitched. "You're

kind. When you smile, you smile with your eyes. And you love her. Like, *really* love her, and if I can see and feel that, so can she."

"She's easy to love."

The fingers of one hand moved to her wrist, thumb skimming over her pulse, his other hand slipping to her waist. "I shouldn't do this. But I'm realizing I'm fighting a losing battle."

"A losing battle?"

"You, Sadie. You're my biggest battle right now."

Another hitch of her breath, then his head lowered.

He moved so slowly, giving her all the time in the world to pull away. She didn't. Couldn't. When his lips touched hers, it was like a bolt of electricity shooting through her body. She felt it in every limb. Every organ. Every beat of her heart.

His lips moved slowly, so much softer than she remembered, and the hand on her waist tugged her to the edge of the stool. She almost felt like she was floating, Eastern the only thing keeping her steady.

Her lips parted and he swooped in, his tongue tangling with hers.

She moaned deep in her throat.

Her hand eased from his cheek, slipping back into his hair, tangling with his locks, while the other grazed up his chest. God, he was hard. Layer upon layer of muscle. But then, she'd known he would be.

Suddenly, she was lifted and set onto the kitchen island. Then he was between her thighs, so close she could feel him straining against his jeans and pressing into her. Instinctively, she wrapped her legs around his waist and pulled him closer, wanting no space between them. Wanting to feel all of him.

His lips moved from her mouth to her cheek before kissing down her neck.

When his hands touched her waist under her shirt, a warmth zipped into her core. Those big calloused hands inched up her ribs, almost wrapping around her entire waist. Still, there were too many layers between them. She wanted nothing. To feel his skin against hers. His hard against her soft.

She reached for the hem of her top and tugged it over her head.

Eastern's mouth only lifted for a second, and when it did, his eyes flared. He tugged off his own shirt before his mouth crashed back to her neck, sucking and nipping as his hands once again smoothed up her sides.

The second his hand closed over her breast, she gasped, her head flinging back.

God, it was heaven. The way he palmed her. The way his thumb found the hard bud of her nipple and grazed it back and forth.

She bit her bottom lip to stifle a moan, a deep throb building in her core.

The cup on the other side of her bra was yanked down, then his mouth lowered. The second his lips closed over her nipple, she cried out. He licked and sucked, his tongue rolling her nipple back and forth, causing a riot of sensations to pulse through her.

Christ, she could barely breathe. Every attempt to inhale felt like it got stuck. He switched to her other breast, and it was the same explosion of need. The same torment.

She wasn't sure how long he sucked and played with her, but when he released her nipple, it was too soon. She groaned in protest, wanting more, needing all of him.

"Don't stop," she whispered, desperation weaving through her words. "I need you."

A deep, masculine growl rippled through the air before she was lifted and carried out of the kitchen and down the hall. He stopped in a dimly lit room. She barely took in the dark-sheeted bed that centered the space or the other masculine tones throughout the room.

Eastern's room.

Gently, he laid her on the bed. She watched, eyes heavy, as

Eastern rose, thick cords of muscle straining every inch of his chest and arms, causing her heart to flutter. When he shoved down his jeans, she noticed his thighs were the same. Thick and muscled, not an inch of fat on him.

A warrior. This man was a warrior.

Without taking his gaze from hers, he leaned over her body, his hands going to the waistband of her jeans, unbuttoning and unzipping before pulling them down her legs. When she wore just her panties and bra, Eastern braced himself over her, and oh Lord, his weight in combination with the heat of his body was like a drug. It made her heart gallop and her belly do little flips she'd never felt before.

He lowered so his mouth hovered just above hers, and there was no other space between them. Then he looked into her eyes like he saw all of her. Every fragment. Every tiny secret she hid from the world.

"You sure you want to do this, honey?" he asked quietly, his hand grazing down her side and leaving a trail of goose bumps. "Once we do, there's no going back."

"Good. I have a feeling after tonight, I won't *want* to go back."

* * *

SADIE'S WORDS were like gas on the fire of his need.

Yet again, he crashed his mouth to hers, plunging his tongue between her lips and tasting her.

Fuck, she was sweet. Like sugary candy and tart strawberry mixed together. And the softness of her body made him fucking wild.

When he reached behind her back, she arched, allowing him to unclasp her bra. The second her breasts were free, Eastern's cock hardened so quickly, it was painful. Her breasts were perfect. The pink tips of the nipples. The way they pebbled for him.

He lowered his head, took one of those peaks between his lips and sucked. Sweet, just like the rest of her. He rolled the bud with his tongue, enjoying her soft moans and hums. He couldn't get enough of her. Every sound, every graze of her skin against his, sent the blood pumping and shockwaves of awareness rippling through him.

As he continued to play with her breast, he reached down to slip a hand inside her panties. Her thighs immediately widened, giving him more access.

He stroked her clit, causing her entire body to jolt. So damn sensitive. He swiped again, receiving another of those earth-shattering moans.

Fuck, he could drown in those moans.

He switched his mouth to her other breast as he circled her clit with his thumb, working her body, wanting her right on the edge with him.

Her fingers dug into his shoulder. "Eastern…please!"

The need in her voice spurred his own. Still, he didn't stop, instead running his tongue back and forth on her nipple as he teased a finger at her entrance. Slowly, he slipped inside. Sadie gasped, her hips lifting, pushing him deeper.

So. Fucking. Wet.

His mouth trailed back up her chest, then neck, before once again claiming her lips as he worked her clit with his thumb and thrust his finger in and out.

He was vaguely aware of her reaching between them. But it wasn't until she slipped a hand into his briefs and wrapped her fingers around his cock that his entire body tensed. It was like he suddenly couldn't move. Couldn't breathe or speak or think, because the feel of her fingers around him paralyzed his brain.

Her hand moved over him from tip to base while her leg slipped around his waist and she ground into him, swiping him against her core.

Jesus, at this rate, he wasn't going to last.

He scrunched his eyes, trying to control the sawing air that moved through his chest. It didn't fucking help.

When he couldn't take it anymore, he grabbed her wrist, halting her, forcing his breaths to even out. Once he had a semblance of control again, he shifted to the side and eased her panties down her soft thighs, never taking his eyes from her wide stare.

He removed his own briefs before reaching into the side table and pulling out a foil square. He was so fucking on edge there was almost a violent shake in his fingers as he opened the condom and slipped it over himself.

When he returned between her thighs, Sadie's chest was moving quickly, her eyes so hauntingly beautiful, she gutted him.

He cupped her cheek. "Last chance. You sure you want this?"

She leaned up and nipped his bottom lip. "There's no turning back now. We're in too deep."

Blood roared through his veins, and he eased inside her. She was tight and hot, her walls wrapping around his cock so fucking perfectly.

Once he was seated deep inside, he touched his forehead to hers. "What do you do to me, Sadie?"

"Everything."

Damn straight. He kissed her before lifting his hips and pushing deep. She groaned, her leg wrapping around his waist once more, tugging him closer. He thrust again and again, getting lost in her. In her body, he lost awareness of time and space. He forgot everything that had ever come before this moment. Everything but *her*. She became his center. His whole world.

He nibbled her bottom lip and reached for her breast, then rolled the bud of her nipple between his thumb and forefinger. She whimpered, her hips lifting as she met him thrust for thrust.

He didn't want this to end. He wanted to draw this out, remain inside her for endless fucking minutes. But too soon, he knew that was a battle he wasn't going to win.

He increased the pace of his movements, sliding deeper inside her, faster.

Her breaths became choppy, her eyes closing tightly as she tossed her head back. "Eastern…"

The whisper of his name on her lips thrummed through his veins.

"Fall for me, baby," he whispered back.

Her lips parted, and an almost tortured cry released from her throat as her walls throbbed around his cock and she broke.

He watched, wanting to drown in the sight of her, so free and vulnerable. He kept pumping, kept slipping in and out of her until he had nothing left, until he was all hers. Then his body tightened, and he shattered along with her.

He growled as he found her lips and kissed her. It was so fucking perfect. *She* was so fucking perfect.

Once his thrusts slowed and their heaving chests became the only movement in the room, they both lay there, Eastern bracketing her body with his, and it almost felt like nothing could ever touch this moment.

He looked down, studying her hooded eyes, her swollen red lips. "You're so beautiful, Sadie."

The slow smile that crossed her lips was fucking glorious. "Says the man I've never been able to take my eyes off of."

Slowly, he slipped out of her, then dropped to the side and tugged her against him. He'd thought being inside her was the best it could get. But this, holding her while she pressed into him, her entire naked body sprawled across his, was pretty damn close.

CHAPTER 13

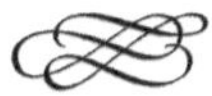

*N*oises pricked Sadie's sleep. Quiet voices that sounded like they came from somewhere far away.

Who *was* that? Even though she lived in an apartment building, it was always quiet. Her neighbors barely made a sound.

She rolled to her belly, only to frown at the scent of the sheets. Not *her* scent or the scent of her bedroom. This scent was masculine, reminding her of—

Her eyes popped open, immediately spotting Eastern's dark sheets beneath her. Her heart hammered as she rolled onto her back once again and sat up. Dark tones, closed navy-blue curtains…Eastern's room.

Suddenly, everything from the previous night came back, hitting her so hard in the chest she almost couldn't breathe.

She'd had sex with Eastern Walker. Avery's father.

A million different emotions rolled through her system. Shock. Uncertainty. And maybe a bit of breathlessness. Was that an emotion?

Last night had been… God, she couldn't even describe it.

Eastern's touch had sent her spiraling into another world. The second he'd put his hands on her, all she'd wanted was more. Even after they'd fallen asleep together, she'd been awoken a few times by the feel of his lips on her neck. The warmth of his stomach against her back.

She closed her eyes on a frown.

How had they gone from him apologizing every time he touched her to sleeping together? Would he apologize for last night?

Pain punched through her belly at that thought, right as those hushed voices sounded again. Even though they were too quiet to understand what was being said, she knew who they belonged to…Avery and Eastern.

Crap. Avery. What would she say when she saw her here? She was eight. She'd know what Sadie and her father had done, right? Or maybe not. Maybe Eastern had already fabricated a story about Sadie sleeping over. Please, Lord, say he'd made up a story, because Avery *could not* know about their night together, not while Sadie didn't know what it meant for the future.

At the clattering sound of a pot, she shoved the sheets off her legs and all but fell out of bed. Clothes. She needed clothes and to make herself look semi-presentable. Was that possible?

She scanned the floor for her panties, but they weren't there. That's when she saw her clothes from yesterday folded on the dresser, panties on top.

Heat crept into her cheeks at the thought of Eastern picking them up and folding them so neatly.

She rushed toward the pile, the twinge of tenderness between her thighs once again reminding her of the previous evening. Yeah, like she needed another reminder.

As she dressed, nerves tingled her spine at the prospect of seeing Eastern this morning.

It would be fine. They were both adults. Adults had sex all the time. Okay, *she* didn't have sex all the time, and certainly not with someone she wasn't dating, but it was common for some people, right?

Once her clothes were straightened, she moved into the bathroom, grimacing at the sight of her flushed cheeks and messy hair. Good God, even an eight-year-old could look at her and know exactly what she'd done the night before.

Quickly, she ran her fingers through her hair, trying like hell to untangle the knots and smooth it out. Ten minutes later and she looked kind of okay, which was probably as good as she was going to get.

She walked toward the bedroom door, her belly doing nervous rolls. The door creaked as she opened it.

Calm, Sadie. Just remain calm.

She found them in the kitchen, Avery sitting at the island and Eastern standing by the stove, flipping bacon. Avery's eyes lit up when they fell on Sadie, and she jumped off her stool and ran across the room. Sadie barely caught herself from falling backward as the little girl hugged her.

"Sadie! Daddy said you slept over. I'm so excited you're still here!"

As she wrapped her arms around Avery, her gaze rose to Eastern looking straight at her, his eyes so intense, they looked ten times darker than usual.

She swallowed, trying to clear the lump in her throat. "I'm excited to be here too, baby girl."

Avery grabbed her wrist and tugged her toward the island. "Daddy's making smiley face pancakes."

Sadie's brows rose. "Smiley face pancakes?"

Eastern nodded. "Yes, ma'am. Blueberries for the mouth, bananas and blueberries for the eyes, a strawberry for the nose and bacon for the hair." His deep, gravelly voice slid into her veins, turning her blood molten.

"And maple syrup as skin cream." Avery giggled.

Despite her nerves, Sadie chuckled. "I like it."

"Did you sleep well in Daddy's bed?" Avery asked. "I think his bed is too hard. He should have let you sleep on the couch, not the other way around."

Ah, so he'd told his daughter he'd slept on the couch.

"*Did* you sleep well?" he asked, voice once again all too sexy.

"I slept great." A lot better than she had in a long time, actually.

He dipped his head. "Good. Me too."

When his gaze held hers, it almost felt like something passed between them. But Avery soon cut through the silence, her words spoken so quickly they ran into each other.

Avery was in the middle of telling them about a project she was doing at school that day when a phone beside her vibrated on the island. It wasn't Sadie's phone, so it had to be Eastern's. Her gaze flicked down to the cell—and something hard and uncomfortable coiled in her belly.

Because there on the screen was a message from Jamie.

What exactly was *in* the text, Sadie didn't know, because it didn't show on the screen. It was just her name.

She grabbed the cell and passed it to Eastern, keeping the screen angled away from Avery. His brow furrowed when he looked at it, and he clicked a few things before locking the screen and dropping the phone back onto the island.

"Wait, I'll go get the project and show you," Avery said, oblivious to what had just happened as she jumped off the stool and ran out of the kitchen.

Sadie nibbled her bottom lip as she watched Eastern. "Is everything okay?"

"It's fine."

That was all he said before giving her a smile that didn't quite reach his eyes and turning back to the stove.

Hurt cut through her chest. It was probably irrational. Anything said between him and Jamie was exactly that, between them. And even if it wasn't, this wasn't the best time to talk about it.

But it was a little reminder that Eastern and Jamie were Avery's parents...Sadie wasn't. And their family dynamics were none of her business.

* * *

JAMIE: I need to talk to you.

That one fucking sentence had been toying with him all day. What exactly did she need to talk to him about? And why not just call?

His hands tightened on the steering wheel. Jarrad, his least favorite deputy, sat beside him as he drove.

Eastern hadn't called her back, because after breakfast, the morning had been a rush of saying goodbye to Sadie, getting Avery ready for school and him getting to work.

He scrubbed a hand over his face as he pulled the car to a stop in front of a house, still thinking about the hurt that had crossed Sadie's face after Jamie's text. Hurt because he'd brushed it off and hadn't explained it. And even though it hadn't been the right time to talk to her about the text, she *did* deserve to know what was happening with Jamie, because she loved Avery as much as he did.

He just needed to find out what the hell the woman wanted first.

"Going in?"

Eastern glanced at his deputy. He hadn't wanted to bring Jarrad this morning, but he'd been the only officer available. He'd witnessed the guy treat people like shit far too many times, and lately, his work ethic just wasn't there.

"Yeah, let's go."

Eastern climbed out of the car and headed toward the door of the small Cape Cod. The house was owned by Scott Chase's parents. It was a second home, usually rented out, but if the town gossip was right, it was where Scott was currently staying.

He stopped at the front door and knocked. Jarrad scanned the yard as they waited. For a few seconds, there was nothing. Then something sounded from inside, and a moment later, the door opened.

Scott's brows slashed together at the sight of Eastern. "What do *you* want?"

Eastern was careful to keep his composure even though he wanted to be a lot more direct. "Hi, Mr. Chase. We were wondering if we could ask you some questions."

"Regarding what?"

"Where were you between the hours of four and six a.m. Monday morning?" Eastern asked.

Scott's brows shot up. "Why the hell do you want to know that?"

"Answer the damn question," Jarrad said before Eastern could respond.

Scott's throat bobbed, an angry scowl etching his features. "I was here, asleep. You know, like a normal person."

"Can anyone verify that?" Eastern asked.

Scott looked like he was going to say something but changed course. "No. My parents live in their other house, so I'm here by myself."

There was something about Scott's clipped tone that Eastern disliked.

"Now tell me what this is about," Scott demanded.

"There was a break-in at one of the shops here in town," Eastern said, studying Scott's expression. You could tell a lot by a person's reactions and expressions. Whether they were genuinely surprised by a fact or they feigned shock.

The frown on his face deepened. "And you think I did it? Why the hell would I come back to town to break into a shop?"

"I think the better question is, why are you still here?" Eastern asked calmly.

For a moment, Scott was quiet, then he gave a half laugh that had no humor behind it. "Not that it's any of your business, but I have leave from work. Are you trying to get rid of me by pinning a crime on me, *Sheriff*?"

"No," Jarrad answered, inching forward. "He's trying to do his *job*. And guess what, you have a shaky-as-hell alibi *and* you have motive. Seems to me that's worth investigating further. Care to let us take your prints and see if they're a match for the ones found in the store?"

Scott pulled back. "Motive? What the hell are you—" He stopped, understanding crossing his face. "The store was Sugar and Spice."

"It was," Jarrad said, taking another small step forward. "But you already know that, don't you?"

"Jarrad, stop," Eastern said firmly.

"Why?" he asked. "Maybe this asshole just needs some *incentive* to talk."

Scott frowned at him. "Go to hell."

Jarrad attempted to grab him, but Eastern gripped his deputy's arm and tugged him back. "Hey. *Stop.*"

Scott once again frowned at them. "You want something else from me, you come back with a warrant. Otherwise, leave me the hell alone."

The door slammed in their faces, and fury exploded through Eastern's veins as he turned to Jarrad. "What the hell was that?"

Jarrad wrenched his arm from Eastern's hold. "I was doing my job, *boss*. Some people need pressure applied to admit to the shit they do. Not everyone's just going to come out and say 'Hey, I committed a crime.'"

"Even if that was the case, forcing your way into his home and grabbing him is *not* the way to do it. You ever pull a stunt like that again, you won't just be suspended. Do you understand?"

Anger reddened Jarrad's cheeks, but he remained silent.

"*Do you understand?*" Eastern demanded, voice so loud it was almost a shout.

"I understand."

The words were clipped and said through gritted teeth, but Eastern knew it was the best he was going to get. "Good. Now get in the damn car."

CHAPTER 14

Sadie ran her paintbrush carefully over the edge of the wall, near the baseboard behind the counter. The wallpaper had been damaged during the break-in, and with not enough time to order new wallpaper, painting would have to do.

A few staff members had been in throughout the day to help with getting the bakery cleaned up and back in order, but now it was just her again. Not that she minded being alone. She had her music, snacks, and a whole lot of intrusive thoughts about her and Eastern to keep her company.

Okay, maybe she could do without the intrusive thoughts. If sex with the man hadn't been so damn good, she might not be so on edge. It was annoying as hell that the guy was sexy, a good father *and* great in bed. That had to be criminal, right?

Argh.

She rose to her feet and turned, about to walk into the back room, when the door opened. She'd left it unlocked for deliveries. She frowned and stepped around the counter.

"Mr. Anderson...is there something I can do for you?" She was tempted to remind her not-so-friendly neighbor that *he* was the one who'd told *her* to leave him alone.

He scanned the inside of the shop in a slow sweep, his expression so clear of emotion she had no idea what he was thinking. "I heard there was a break-in. Thought I'd stop in and check if you need anything from me."

If she needed anything from him? Like what, a wall to erect in the alley between her store and his? "Thanks, but we've got everything under control. Just waiting on a few items to be delivered so we can get back up and running."

He shoved his hands into his pockets and nodded before casting his gaze back to her. There was something unsettling about the way he looked at her, to the point she wanted to squirm. Either that or push the guy right out of the shop.

"Glad to hear you've got everything sorted out." He paused. "I wonder why they did it. Or what message they were trying to send."

She raised a brow, but before she could say anything, he dipped his head.

"You have a good day, Ms. Sandler."

The door closed behind him, and she didn't move for a full five seconds, because the tone of his voice in combination with the way he'd looked at her…God, it made her skin crawl.

But Eastern had looked into her neighbor, and he'd had an alibi for the morning of the break-in. And more than that, he didn't have a motive…did he?

Trying to settle the suspicion in her belly, she grabbed her phone, turned up the music, and continued with her painting. She was just finishing when the ding of the door opening sounded again. This time, it wasn't Mr. Anderson. Not that the next visitor was much better.

She stepped around the counter. "What are you doing here, Mrs. Chase?"

The older woman had her hands in her pockets, an uncertain expression on her face. "I heard the shop was broken into, and after everything that's happened with Scott, I just thought I'd check on you."

Check on her? After she was going to knowingly let Sadie marry a cheater? "I'm fine. You didn't need to come."

She started to turn, but Mrs. Chase stepped forward. "Sadie, wait! Can't we talk? My son misses you."

Was she kidding? "Really? Or is he just missing stringing along multiple women?"

Hell, maybe he was still doing that.

Mrs. Chase's lips thinned. "He's not a bad guy."

Sadie crossed her arms. "Tell me, do you know what his plan was exactly? Because he still planned to marry me after making out with his admin assistant minutes before the wedding. After all, he waited for me at the end of that aisle. So was it a goodbye kiss? Or was it an, 'until our next work trip,' kiss?"

"It was a mistake."

She shook her head. "But that's the thing, it wasn't. Scott told me he was sleeping with her for months. Months is not a mistake. It's a choice that he made again and again."

The other woman's mouth opened and closed. Had she not known about how long her son had been cheating?

"Sadie—"

"No. I'm sorry, Mrs. Chase, but at some point you have to accept that your golden boy isn't so golden. He may be your son, but he did a bad thing." More than one bad thing.

Mrs. Chase straightened. "Good people can still make mistakes."

"Yes, and they pay the price for those mistakes. His price was losing me."

Mrs. Chase shook her head, huffing out a breath before storming out the door.

God, what was *wrong* with that woman? Was she so blinded by loyalty to her son that she couldn't understand the severity of what he'd done?

And who'd be the next person to step into the shop? Scott himself?

She turned toward the kitchen—only to kick her foot right into the corner of the counter. She was only wearing sandals, so pain immediately blasted up her leg, causing her to cry out, scrunch her eyes and grab her foot. "*Goddammit*, would the universe give me a freaking break?"

"Are you okay?"

She straightened and spun at the voice behind her, eyes widening at the sight of Eastern standing in the doorway. Where the heck had he come from? Although, he *was* a far better option than Scott.

"I didn't hear you come in."

His brow was furrowed, concern in his gaze as he closed the space between them. "I can be quiet when I want to be. Did you hurt yourself?"

"It's nothing. I just stubbed my toe." And now she just felt like a grade A drama queen.

His gaze lowered, and before she understood what he was doing, he gripped her hips and lifted her onto the counter behind the display cases.

She gasped, grabbing his arms. "What are you doing?"

"Checking your toe. Right or left?"

"Eastern, I'm fine."

"Right or left, Sadie?"

When he just continued to look at her with challenge in his eyes, she sighed. "Left. Big toe. But it's fine. I just have a low pain tolerance."

He lifted her ankle and removed her sandal. A part of her thought she should feel self-conscious about him touching and inspecting her foot so closely, but when his gentle fingers grazed over her skin, it was impossible to feel anything but a stream of tingles running up her leg.

He focused on her toe like it was a puzzle. "It doesn't look too bad."

When he started massaging her foot, she had to bite back a groan. Holy Christ, his hands felt good.

"How did you stub your toe?" he asked.

"I was distracted." A bit like right now, but for a completely different reason. "And I was frustrated."

His gaze lifted to hers. "Frustrated about what?"

"A lot of things."

"Would one of those things be me?"

Gosh, he just got straight to the point.

At her silence, a muscle ticked in his jaw. "I'm sorry we didn't get a chance to talk this morning."

"It's not your fault. Avery was there, and it was busy with everyone getting ready for work and school."

"Still, I wanted to talk to you about last night."

A nervous prickle ran down her spine. "You're not going to apologize again, are you?"

If he did, she wasn't sure if she'd scream or cry. Probably the former.

One side of his mouth lifted. "No. I'm not going to apologize. The opposite, actually. I wanted to tell you that I really enjoyed our time together."

She bit the inside of her cheek to stop the smile. "Really?"

"Mm-hmm…and if you're interested, I'd like to see where this takes us."

This time her heart went into a full-blown gallop. "What about the age gap, and the relationship I just got out of, and Avery?"

"Age is just a number. And you said your relationship ended long before the engagement did. And we don't have to tell Avery yet."

"It's a risk."

"But is it a risk you want to take?"

Yes. The answer was a shout in her head, but she kept it inside because she wanted to hear his answer first. "Is it a risk *you* want to take?"

He inched closer, releasing her foot as his hands glided up her thighs before bracketing her hips. "Yeah, it is."

For a moment, she had to remind herself to breathe. To suck one breath in after the next. Then, finally, she whispered, "Me too."

A slow smile curved his lips, and he lowered his head. "Good."

The second he touched his mouth to hers, she leaned into him, letting the softness of his lips send sparks of awareness straight to her core.

She wrapped her arms around his shoulders, her fingers sweeping into his hair, sliding through the thick locks. She felt him everywhere. His chest against hers, his hands sliding beneath the fabric of her shirt, his tongue as it tasted and explored.

She wanted more. She wanted to grind against him. To feel every inch of skin. But too soon, he was pulling away. She groaned, only to have him chuckle in response.

"Sadie, we can't—"

When he stopped, her eyes flicked open to see him looking out the window, brows tugged together. She followed his gaze, but there was nothing there.

"Everything okay?" she asked, turning back to him.

"Yeah. I just saw the back of someone, but they were probably just walking past." The frown cleared from his face. "How's your day going now?"

She couldn't stop the gigantic grin from curving her lips. "Better. A lot better."

CHAPTER 15

*E*astern scrubbed a hand over his face as he watched Denny be hauled into the station, an officer on either side of him.

"What the hell are you doing back here?" Eastern growled.

"I'll tell you what I'm doin' back here," Denny slurred. "I'm being dragged by these goons who took me against my will after having a simple fuckin' drink."

Charles rolled his eyes. "Denny was served by a new guy at Meridian who didn't know he wasn't welcome. Then he decided to go outside and throw rocks at cars."

Eastern was surprised Denny had slipped past his brother.

"I'm gonna sue the lot of ya," Denny growled. "For unlawful arrest. For manhandling me."

"Sleep it off in a cell." Eastern sighed, shaking his head.

Denny continued to shout and curse as the officers dragged him down the hall.

Eastern returned to his office, hating that he was doing another evening shift. But Jarrad had called in sick…again. And the only other person available was Angie, who was a mother and had already done three night shifts this week. He didn't want to ask her to skip her son's school pickup and bath time again. And even though he hated missing nights with Avery, she had Sadie now, and he was pretty sure his kid liked *her* more than she did him.

He lifted his phone to send a text.

Eastern: Hey, everything okay?

Her response was instant.

Sadie: It's great. We've painted each other's nails, baked cookies, and eaten said cookies with ice cream while watching a girl movie.

Eastern: A girl movie?

Sadie: You would have hated it. Just getting ready for bed now.

Eastern: Thank you, Sadie.

Sadie: You never have to thank me for spending time with Avery.

He leaned back in his seat. The last week with her had been… Hell, he couldn't even describe it. Sadie had stayed over almost every night, and every minute he spent with her, he wanted more.

They hadn't explicitly told Avery what was going on, but the kid was likely getting suspicious with Sadie eating dinner with them most evenings and breakfast with them in the mornings.

He shot a glance at the clock. Time to go home.

Grabbing his empty mug from the desk, he rose and headed down the hall. He'd tried calling Jamie a dozen times in the last week, but for some damn reason, she wasn't answering. So much for needing to talk to him.

He was about to step into the kitchen when a hushed voice sounded.

"I'm just saying he needs to be careful. Eastern can't be paid off like Jack."

Eastern stopped. Jack had been the sheriff before him.

There was a scoff before Charles spoke. "When's that asshole ever careful? He's not even coming in for his shifts anymore."

They were talking about Jarrad. He'd paid off the last sheriff? Why?

When the voices quieted so Eastern couldn't make out the next words, he stepped into the kitchen to see Charles and Lenard standing close to each other.

Lenard's eyes widened. "Boss! I thought you'd headed off by now."

Eastern moved to the sink and rinsed the mug. "I'm about to leave. Couldn't help but overhear something about Jarrad paying off Jack."

The two men exchanged uncertain looks before Charles gave a smile...a very forced smile. "You know what we mean. Donuts. Cupcakes. Our old sheriff had one hell of a sweet tooth."

Eastern put the mug into the dishwasher before turning to face the guys. He didn't believe them. "Why did he have to buy off Jack?"

They both lifted their shoulders, and it was Charles again who answered. "You know Jarrad. He's always screwing up in one way or another."

Yeah. He still didn't believe them. "You'd tell me if there was something more going on around here, wouldn't you? Because I'd hate to think of the consequences involved if I learned something on my own."

Lenard swallowed hard. "Of course. You'd be the first to know, boss."

The men gave him tight smiles before heading out the door.

Eastern scrubbed a hand over his face, making a mental note to ask Daisy in the morning if she knew anything about it, before heading out of the kitchen.

The drive home was quick, and when he passed the spot where Sadie had pulled over for her flat tire, his fingers tightened on the wheel.

He didn't like that asshole Scott. He didn't like that the guy had returned to Misty Peak to win back Sadie after what he'd done. He hated that the guy was still in town when Sadie had already insisted she didn't want anything to do with him. And, more than that, he didn't trust a word the cheating bastard said.

When he pulled into his driveway, the house was dark. Not a surprise. Avery should already be asleep. The kid was usually out like a light by the time he'd gotten halfway through their nightly reading.

He climbed out and moved into the house, the quiet slipping over him. When the kitchen and living room were empty, he checked Avery's bedroom, and his chest squeezed at what he found.

Avery and Sadie were asleep, both on their sides, with Sadie's hand on Avery's waist and their foreheads touching. Avery was under the sheets, while Sadie lay on top of them.

There were so many things he liked about Sadie. So many parts of her he wanted to bottle up and keep. But her love for his daughter, their connection…that was his favorite.

For a moment, he didn't move, just soaked up the scene in front of him, let it weave itself into his heart. They looked so peaceful, he didn't want to disturb them.

After a few minutes, he forced himself to step forward. First, he leaned down and kissed his daughter's temple. She didn't so much as stir.

"Love you, princess," he whispered before sliding his hands under Sadie's back and legs and lifting her. A hum slipped from her lips as he carried her down the hall toward his bedroom. He put her into bed and began slowly removing her top and pants.

"Eastern…"

Fuck, his name whispered on her lips sounded good. "Yeah, baby, I'm here."

"Did you catch the bad guys tonight?"

His lips twitched. "Just one drunk guy."

"Hmm, better one than none. Come to bed with me."

She didn't even need to ask. "I'll just check over the house and be back."

He kissed her forehead before heading out of the room. Once he was sure everything was locked up, he returned to her, crawling between the covers. All he wanted to do was hold her. Drown in her.

His phone vibrated, but before he could reach for it, she hummed again and gripped his arm. Then she whispered, "Don't let go."

He tightened his hold around her waist. "Never."

* * *

WARMTH PRESSED to Sadie's back, making her want to snuggle deeper into the bed and keep her eyes closed longer. She wasn't sure what had woken her, but sleep was just tugging her back under when something warm and soft touched her neck.

A kiss?

Then the hand on her waist grazed down her thigh.

She moaned. "Eastern…"

"Mm."

The man didn't even need to speak words, and he managed to stir desire in her belly. "We should get up before Avery wakes."

"We should."

But instead of rolling away to get out of the bed, his hand on her thigh kept running up and down, dangerously close to her core.

"I can't move when you do that," she whispered. "You need to make the first move."

"I *am* making a move. A move to touch you. And God, you feel good."

Well, his hands on her felt good too, but that wasn't the point.

When his hand shifted again, this time to stroke her over her panties, her breath caught. "Eastern!"

He sucked gently at her neck, his tongue running over her already heated flesh. "You taste too good to stop."

117

Even though she knew she should get up, her body betrayed her, her head moving of its own volition to give him better access. He continued to kiss her, to nibble her flesh and lick her, as his hand moved inside her panties and stroked her clit. She gasped, parting her thighs, wanting more, the voice in her head telling her to get up now barely a whisper.

His other hand roved between her and the mattress before reaching for her breast.

She groaned as he dipped his hand into her bra and swiped his thumb against her nipple.

"Eastern, we shouldn't." Her words were too quiet and held absolutely no conviction.

"So why does it feel like we should?"

She had no freaking idea.

As he continued to stroke and suck, she began to grind her hips against him, her blood like lava as desire throbbed through her lower abdomen.

Suddenly, he pushed a finger inside her and pinched her nipple at the same time. She bit her lip to stop the cry, her back arching, ass pressing into him. Then he began a slow, torturous thrust of his finger, his thumb working her clit, moving in circles and strokes.

She groaned and writhed under the onslaught, reaching behind her to run her fingers through his hair. When she turned her head, he kissed her, his tongue sliding between her lips and into her mouth.

A second finger joined the first inside her, and this time, her cry was suffocated by his kiss. The thrusts of his fingers became deeper, each stroke of her clit firmer.

She was so close, her body on fire, then he rolled her nipple between his thumb and forefingers, and she broke. She arched and ground against him as her entire body fell off that cliff's edge.

His tongue continued to tangle with hers, swallowing her groans and whimpers.

Her body was pulsing, the air still whooshing from her chest as he pulled his fingers out of her and she turned, tugging his mouth down to hers. She was just reaching beneath the sheets for him when the soft patter of footsteps sounded down the hall.

She gasped and tugged away, eyeing the bathroom door, itching to run toward it, but it was too late. And in addition to being flushed as hell, she only wore her freaking bra and panties.

She tugged the sheets up to cover herself.

Eastern chuckled softly moments before the door flew open and Avery burst in. "Daddy! Sadie!"

She ran over to the bed, jumped onto the mattress and threw her arms around Eastern.

"Hey, princess, you sleep okay?"

God, he sounded completely fine. Meanwhile, if she spoke, her voice would probably be croaky as hell.

"Yes!" Avery beamed. "I think the cookies and hot chocolate made me sleep extra good."

Despite everything, Sadie laughed. The kid would say anything for treats. "Well, it *is* called sleepy hot chocolate for a reason." Oh good, she sounded just about normal…somehow.

Eastern cleared his throat. "So, Avery…Sadie and I shared a bed because—"

"You're dating." There was a moment of total silence before Avery giggled. "Daddy…I've known you weren't sleeping on the couch for a week."

"How?" Sadie asked.

"He always leaves a big sweaty imprint. I can't sit on the couch forever after him."

Sadie threw her head back and laughed, while Eastern looked less than impressed. "I do not."

"You do." Avery looked at Sadie. "It's *gross*."

"That's it!" He tackled Avery to the bed and tickled her.

Sadie's heart exploded at the sound of her laughter. At the joy on her face and the smile on Eastern's as he played with her.

Avery was still laughing when he stood and picked her up before tossing her over his shoulder.

"Daddy!" She giggled as she playfully hit his back.

"Come on, Miss I-Know-Everything, it's time for clothes so Sadie can get changed, and you can tell me any other secrets I thought I was keeping from you."

Once Sadie was alone in the room, the space felt ridiculously quiet.

She climbed out of bed and took a quick shower before changing into some clothes. Over the past week, she'd stockpiled a few things here because she'd been staying over so often. Heck, she'd barely been to her apartment in days.

Dressed and ready to go, she was heading toward the kitchen when the doorbell rang. Frowning, she glanced toward Avery's room, but the door was still closed.

When a second ring sounded, Sadie hurried to the door and tugged it open. Her jaw dropped at the sight of the woman on the other side.

Jamie.

It had only been a bit over a year since she'd seen her last, but the woman looked much older, with lines around her eyes and circles shadowing them. Her blond hair, which used to look impeccable at all times, was flat and dull, as if it hadn't been washed in a few days, and her clothes were wrinkled.

Jamie's mouth gaped. "Sadie! What are you doing here?"

Before Sadie could answer, a door opened down the hall, followed by footsteps. "Sadie, who's—" Eastern stopped beside her. "Jamie." All friendliness left his voice, replaced by a low growl. "What the hell are you doing here?"

"Daddy...Sadie!" Avery slammed to a stop between Sadie and Eastern before she gasped. "*Mom?*"

Sadie's heart broke at the uncertainty in Avery's voice. And maybe something else… Fear?

Jamie swallowed before lowering in front of her daughter. "Hey, sugar. Got a cuddle for your mama?"

Instead of stepping forward, Avery inched behind Eastern—and suddenly every protective instinct Sadie possessed made her want to step in front of the young girl.

But it was Eastern who took a half step forward. "You need to leave."

Jamie frowned as she rose. "I need to talk to you."

"Fine, but not here. Not now. I'll text you."

"Eastern—"

Before the woman could get another word in, Eastern closed the door.

CHAPTER 16

Fury coursed through Eastern's veins as he stepped into the station. Jamie sat beside Daisy's desk, waiting for him. Daisy gave him a small smile and nod, probably knowing that with Jamie here, he wouldn't be in the mood for small talk. He'd texted Jamie and told her if she wanted to talk, the station was the only place that would happen.

Jamie rose from the seat and without a word, followed him into his office. He told himself to remain calm, but the second his door was closed, he spun, unleashing a world of fury with his words.

"What the hell were you thinking, showing up at my door this morning, Jamie? Avery was *right* there."

She flinched as if he'd hit her. "I was *thinking* that I wanted to see my daughter and speak to the father of my child. I have every right to see her."

Was she serious? "No. You lost that right when you walked out on her. When you skipped town and texted me that you weren't coming back, then didn't show up at the custody hearing." He stepped closer. "You lost the right when you *deserted* her."

Jamie rolled her eyes like what she'd done was no big deal. "I explained why I left. I needed a break. You left all the time when she was in my custody, so it was my turn. And I couldn't make it to the custody hearing because I was across the country."

The fuck? "I left because I was in the Navy, and that was my *job*. I didn't just fuck off to God knows where and abandon my daughter without so much as a goodbye."

"I didn't *abandon* her—I left her with her father."

She really didn't get it, did she? She truly believed she hadn't done anything wrong.

She straightened. "Look, Eastern, I didn't come here to fight. I came home because I had my time to travel and explore, and now I want my daughter back."

Jesus Christ. "You're a piece of work."

"She's mine."

"No, she's not. By law, she's *mine*."

Her eyes narrowed. "You're really going to keep my daughter away from me? I *raised* that kid."

"Actually, I don't think you did. The more time I spend with her and Sadie, the more I realize that *she* did more of the raising than you."

Jamie's back teeth visibly ground together. "That's not true. Sadie was her nanny. I was her *mother*, and I deserve access to my child."

"And you might have stood a chance if it was just the abandonment we were dealing with."

Jamie went very still. "What are you talking about?"

"You don't think Avery told me all about your drinking? About how some days you couldn't even take her to school, you were so out of it? And the days she *did* make it, she was often sent without food or clean clothes?"

There was a flash of surprise in her eyes. Surprise that Avery had outed her?

She shook her head. "She's seven. You really believe what she says?"

"She's *eight*. And it wasn't just her. The school supported every statement she made, writing up reports to support my appeal for full custody."

Her hands fisted. "So what? I have to go through you to see my daughter now?"

"Damn straight you do. I'll talk to Avery and see what she wants to do." But if her reaction to her mother this morning was anything to go by, she wouldn't want to see her anytime soon. "And if you show so much as a single sign that you've had a drink, you won't see her at all."

Red tinged Jamie's cheeks. "That's bullshit!"

"No. It's me protecting my child."

"I'll fight you on this."

"Good luck."

She spun toward the door but only took two steps before she turned back. "You really expect me to just go along with this, Eastern?"

"I don't care what you do. Avery's my priority. Her well-being and making sure she has a safe and secure upbringing from this point forward."

"And what? You and Sadie fucking Sandler are going to give that to her?"

"*Hey!* You should be thanking her for giving your daughter what *you* couldn't."

Another narrowing of her eyes, and for a moment, Eastern almost saw her mind working. "So you fuck her, and she gets the job of being my daughter's mother."

"Leave. *Now.*"

She shook her head. "I never denied you access to her or the chance to be a part of her life. Mark my words, you'll regret doing this to me." She grabbed the door handle and was about to step out, but before she did, she turned back again. "And if Sadie thinks she can take my place in my own kid's life, she's *dead* wrong—and yeah, that's a threat."

Then she stormed out without a backward glance.

$$* * *$$

SADIE'S FINGERS wrapped around Avery's hand as they walked from the car to her school. After making sure Avery was okay this morning, Eastern had rushed to get dressed and leave, no doubt to find out what was going on with Jamie.

Avery had said she was okay. She wasn't. She'd been unusually quiet all morning, not to mention she'd barely picked at her sugary cereal, her favorite breakfast treat that she rarely got.

Sadie bumped Avery's hip. "Penny for your thoughts?"

Avery was slow to glance up, and when she did, her brows were knitted together. "Why do you think Mom's back?"

Man, that was a loaded question. And even though it made this intangible fear clench at her belly, she was careful to keep her features neutral. "I'm not sure, Ave. But your dad will find out."

The memory of Eastern after Jamie had left this morning almost made her shudder. He'd been all rage. She'd never seen him like that before. Like he was ready to go to war for his daughter.

It wasn't so much anything he'd said, more the hard line of his jaw. The way he'd barely looked at anyone before leaving, both stuck in his head and trying to tamp down a fury he wanted no one else to see or hear.

"I don't want to live with her again."

At the small crack in Avery's voice, Sadie's heart fractured. They stopped in front of the school, and Sadie crouched down opposite Avery. "Hey. Look at me, baby girl."

It took a moment, but when Avery finally shifted her gaze from the pavement to Sadie, there were tears in her eyes.

Sadie grazed her cheek. "I may not know what your mother being here means, but you know what I *do* know?"

Avery shook her head, her ponytail flicking behind her.

"That you are loved by the greatest protector in this town, and that love is fierce. Your father will do everything in his power to keep you. He will *fight* for you, and if I wanted anyone fighting for me, it would be him."

Avery sniffed, blinking back the tears, but one still fell down her cheek. "He *is* pretty good at getting what he wants."

"Oh, he's better than good. He's the best." She wiped the tear from Avery's cheek. "And no matter what, he's not going anywhere. And neither am I or your uncles. You've got a whole army of people who love you and will fight for you."

Avery flung her arms around Sadie's shoulders and dug her head into her neck. "I love you, Sadie."

"I love you too, baby girl. So much."

Sadie held her for long seconds, not letting go until Avery was ready to step back.

"Are you going to be okay today?" Sadie asked gently. "If not, I could call your dad and ask if it's okay for us to have a sneaky girls' day."

Avery chuckled, and that sound was everything. "That's okay. Miss Davies is choosing groups for a project today, so I need to be here."

Always so conscientious. "Okay. But if you need me or your dad, you go to the office and ask them to call one of us, okay? We'll be here in minutes."

Avery nodded and gave her one more hug before turning and walking up the steps.

Sadie was still watching the school doors after they closed, and even then, it took her a while to head back to her car.

On her way to Sugar and Spice, her mind was still on Avery. On the sadness in her eyes. The fear that she could be put back into her mother's custody.

Pain rippled through her. It must have been really bad after Jamie had fired her, if the fear on Avery's face this morning was anything to go by. If Sadie hadn't left town with Scott, was there a chance Jamie would have let her back into Avery's life? Probably not. But that didn't stop the guilt from sinking its claws into her.

She pulled up in front of Sugar and Spice. Okay, this morning had been a mess, but Avery was at school and hopefully feeling better, and Eastern was dealing with Jamie. She had to focus on the bakery.

With a deep breath, she looked up at the building. The new display case glass would be going in sometime within the next week, then they'd be ready to open again.

A tinge of unease settled in her belly at the prospect of opening the store before the culprit of the break-in was found. But honestly, she was losing hope that the person *would* be found. How could they, when she hadn't seen them and they'd left no evidence?

With a sigh, she got out of the car and entered the shop. She'd just closed the door behind her when a rustling noise sounded from the kitchen. For a moment, fear rendered her utterly still. Her breathing shifted from a normal rhythm to short, shallow pants.

Memories of stepping inside here to find the place trashed flashed in her mind. Of hearing something in the kitchen, then being hit.

She was about to turn around and leave when her grandmother bustled past the open kitchen door.

The air whooshed from Sadie's chest. Oh, Jesus, she was a mess.

Quickly, she crossed into the kitchen to see her grandmother kneading dough. Despite everything, a smile stretched Sadie's lips because the sight of her grandmother baking in this store brought back all her favorite childhood memories.

Her grandmother glanced up. "Sadie, honey, perfect timing. Could you take the cookies out of the oven?"

"Sure." She kissed her grandmother on the cheek before turning to the oven. "Is this for orders?"

"Yes, I got quite a few thanks to your alert to the locals."

Sadie grinned as she took out the steaming-hot sheet of cookies. She'd gotten word around town that the kitchen was functional again, so they could do deliveries until the storefront reopened. "Well, people love your baking."

Her grandmother smiled, but the expression dipped a fraction when she saw Sadie's face. "What's wrong?"

Oh, man. Sometimes she forgot about her grandmother's freaky ability to know when something was wrong.

She opened her mouth to say "Nothing," but her grandmother shook her head. "Don't lie to me, Sadie Ann."

Jeez, now she was being middle-named.

She sighed. "Jamie's back."

Her grandmother stopped kneading the dough. "No."

"Yes. Eastern's meeting with her this morning. He might already be done."

"And you're worried."

She lifted a shoulder. "I'm worried about Avery. She was clearly scared when she saw her mother. She thinks she might have to go back to her. She deserves stability. To have a happy and safe childhood."

"Eastern has custody, doesn't he?"

"Yes. And if she wants Avery back, he'll fight her."

Her grandmother wiped her hands on her apron before stepping over to Sadie and cupping her cheek. "That child is so lucky to have her father *and* you. It will all be okay."

"How do you know?"

"Because I have faith."

Maybe that was it. Her fear for Avery was messing with her faith that good would prevail. "I told Avery it would all be okay, but a part of me is still scared."

"You didn't lie. Deep down, you know it will be. She didn't

show up at her custody hearing. She lost her. And now that Eastern has her, he won't be letting go." Her grandmother leaned in and kissed her cheek.

"Thanks, Nan. I needed to hear that." More than she probably knew. "I love you."

"I love you too, darling."

As her grandmother went back to her dough, Sadie pulled out her phone, unable to hold off the text any longer.

Sadie: How did it go with Jamie?

His response was instant.

Eastern: She wants Avery back.

Sadie's pulse sped up, fear trickling into her veins as Eastern's next text came through.

Eastern: She won't get her.

Sadie: Is there anything I can do?

Eastern: Actually, I was thinking...maybe we should pause what's going on between us for a few days.

Us...him and her.

A painful twist in her chest made breathing hard for a moment. She wanted to help him. To help *both* of them and be a part of this fight. But at the same time, this wasn't about her. She wasn't Avery's mother, so if he thought they should take a break, then she had to agree...didn't she?

Sadie: Okay. Whatever you think is best.

CHAPTER 17

"Are you avoiding him?"

Sadie wrinkled her nose at Elle's question. "No. He asked for a pause, so I'm giving him that pause."

Even if it was the hardest thing she'd ever done. All she wanted to do was navigate the Jamie stuff with Eastern as a team. But he clearly didn't want that.

They turned the corner and headed down the street. Elle had stopped by the shop to go for a walk and coffee with Sadie while the glaziers replaced the glass for the display cabinets. The fresh air and conversation were definitely needed after what could only be described as a hard week.

Elle frowned at her. "You said Jamie wants her daughter back."

"That's what Eastern told me." Well, not told—texted. They hadn't talked since that morning. "We've texted a little bit over the week, but not much. And the responses I get from him are really short, with not a lot of detail."

"I'm sorry, Sadie."

She shook her head. "It's fine. I don't want to make this about me. Having Jamie back is big and heavy, and it affects Avery and him so much, so I want him to be a hundred percent focused on that."

No matter how much it hurt that she was considered an outsider.

"You must miss Avery."

"I miss both of them." So much that some days her heart literally ached. And it had only been a week. "But at the same time, I feel like I shouldn't miss him as much as I do. We're not even really dating."

"Then what are you doing?"

Sex? Companionship? Exploring things between them? Who the hell knew? "I'm not sure." She shook her head. "You know what I need?"

"For a certain alcoholic, no-good mother to leave Misty Peak?"

"Well, that, and a night of drinks and girl time. I've got an unopened bottle of bourbon at home, which would make great apple sours. Are you free this Sunday night?"

"For apple sours? Hell yes, I am. Plus, now that I've hired another girl at the café, I have the next day off."

"Great. I'll text you my address." They stopped at Elle's car. "And because I've done nothing but talk about the romance troubles in *my* life, you can tell me about yours."

Elle scoffed. "That will be one short and uneventful conversation." She pulled open her door. "See you tomorrow night."

Sadie waited until Elle had pulled away before heading back to the shop. That's when she finally let the smile drop. This last week had been exhausting. Every second of every day, she'd wanted to pick up her phone and call Eastern. Ask to see him. Ask to see Avery. To go over to their house and just be with them.

But she'd forced herself not to.

She turned back toward Sugar and Spice, only to frown. The glass guys' van was gone. Had they finished already? They'd told her it would take a couple hours. Had she actually been gone that long?

Reaching the front door, she tried the handle and found it unlocked. But then, of course it was—she hadn't left a key, and that was the only way to lock it from the outside.

Why on earth would they just leave without her here, or at least without calling her? Particularly when they knew the shop had just been broken into?

She checked her phone in case she'd missed a text or call. Nope. Nothing.

As she stepped inside, her gaze ran over the glass in the display shelves. It was installed, as expected, and it looked great. But jeez, leaving a business unlocked? Were they lazy or just not thinking?

Something sounded in the back. Her eyes shot up and her heart did a little rattle.

No, don't work yourself up, Sadie. The last time you did that, it was just Nan.

Besides, she couldn't live her life forever being afraid of every small noise.

Straightening her spine, she headed toward the back kitchen. She'd just entered the room when the door to the alley drifted open a bit in the breeze. What the heck? They'd left the back door open too? She'd noticed one of them using it to go back there to smoke, but Jesus, the decent thing to do was close and lock it when you were done.

The glass company would be receiving a less than happy customer complaint.

She was reaching out to close the door when something outside caught her attention.

Mr. Anderson—or the back of him, as he stepped into the liquor store next door.

She hadn't seen him since he'd come in a couple weeks ago and made her feel uneasy. Whether he'd done that intentionally or not, she wasn't sure. Honestly, after the Jamie stuff, she hadn't given it much thought.

She pulled the door closed with a bit too much force. Time to call the glazier company and tell them exactly what she thought about them leaving the shop unlocked and open.

Her feet stumbled to a stop when she spotted a woman standing in the front of the store.

"Jamie," Sadie gasped. "What are you doing here?"

Jamie had one hand on her hip while she leaned against the counter. Her eyes were cold and narrowed. "I should be asking you that question. I thought you left for Atlanta with...what was his name? Steve?"

"Scott. And that didn't work out." She kept the counter between them as she closed the kitchen door behind her. When she'd first started working for Jamie, the woman had always been friendly. Sure, a bit cold, but she'd never looked at Sadie like she was right now.

Jamie crossed her arms. "Tell me, was it always your plan to steal my family?"

Sadie's brows rose. "Excuse me?"

"I hired you when you were a teenager. I thought you were sweet. Good for my kid. Never thought you'd try to take her—or my ex—from me."

Anger lit Sadie's spine that this woman actually had the gall to accuse her of anything after what she'd done. "I haven't stolen *anything* from you. Stealing would imply I took something that you still had."

Jamie's arms fell to her sides. "Avery is *my* daughter, and Eastern is the father of my daughter."

"I know that. Do *you*?"

"Excuse me?"

"You left, Jamie. You abandoned her. And before that, you fired me so I wouldn't see your drinking problem."

Sadie hadn't known the last part for certain, but the flash of guilt on the woman's face confirmed her suspicions were correct.

Jamie opened her mouth, but Sadie spoke first.

"You were thinking about *you*, not Avery. She needed me, and you let her struggle so you could keep drinking. Then, when her father moved back to town, you took off, once again prioritizing what *you* wanted."

"You little bitch!" she snarled, taking a threatening step forward. "How dare you judge me?"

"I judge you because I love your daughter. That child deserves the world." Tears burned at her eyes at the truth behind her words. "Are you here because you want to do better for her?"

"I'm here because I'm her mother and she's *mine*," she said firmly, appearing completely unaffected by anything Sadie had to say. "And not that it's any of your business, but I left because after eight years of being stuck in the same place, I finally had a chance to *live*. So I took it."

Sadie shook her head, not understanding how this woman's mind worked at all. "You talk about being her mother like it's a burden you can just walk away from."

"He got his time—why shouldn't I get mine?"

Was she serious? "He was serving his country in the military."

She scoffed. "I don't give a shit about anything you have to say, because it's not your damn business. I came here to tell you to back off."

Sadie frowned. "Excuse me?"

"Stay away from Avery and Eastern."

"You can't ask me to do that."

"Yet I am. Don't make me do something I don't want to do."

A chill slipped over Sadie's skin. "Is that a threat?"

Instead of answering, she lifted a brow before turning and stomping out of the shop.

* * *

EASTERN CHECKED his phone for what had to be the twentieth goddamn time. He'd sent Sadie two messages today, and she hadn't responded to either. Why? She'd been responding to every text for the last week. What made today different?

He walked down the street, frustration brimming in his veins.

Did it have something to do with the fact he hadn't seen her in person during that time? He'd *wanted* to see her. Fuck, he'd wanted to touch her, talk to her, with every fiber of his being. He couldn't keep doing this much longer. He needed Sadie. And more than that, *Avery* needed Sadie.

But Jamie's threat toward her had made every protective instinct in him scream to life. He didn't want Sadie entangled in his mess. She deserved more than that. That's why he'd texted that they should pause things. Because he wanted to protect her.

His muscles tensed at the thought of Jamie. The woman had been blowing up his phone for days, demanding to see his daughter. To rant at him about her rights.

She didn't have any damn rights after what she'd done. He'd told her that she could see Avery when *Avery* agreed, and so far, that hadn't happened. No way was he forcing his kid to see her mother if she didn't want to. Avery had been through enough.

When the door to Sugar and Spice opened up ahead, and Sadie stepped out, his breath caught in his throat. Fuck, she was beautiful. And after a week away from her, he felt like he'd been starved of that beauty.

He forced the air to move through his lungs as he walked faster to meet her. "Hey."

She jumped and turned, pressing a hand to her chest when she saw him. "Eastern! You scared me."

He frowned and stepped closer. "Are you okay?" Was she still jumpy because of the break-in? Fuck, he'd barely checked in on her about that.

"I'm fine." She furrowed her brow. "How are you?"

Angry. Frustrated. About a million other emotions that were just as shitty. "I'm doing okay."

She stepped closer, her eyes studying his. "You don't need to pretend with me, Eastern."

"I miss you." The words slipped out completely uncensored. Not that he *wanted* to censor them.

Her eyes flared, a hint of pink tingeing her cheeks. "It's only been a week."

"Then why does it feel so much longer?"

Her chest rose as she sucked in a large breath, her gaze dipping to her feet. "Eastern..."

Something in his gut twisted because the tone of her voice told him he wouldn't like what was coming next.

"I've missed you too...but I think you were right about pausing what's going on between us until this Jamie stuff is sorted out. I don't want to make things worse."

She thought she could make things worse? For who? Not Avery. And certainly not him. That was something he'd come to realize over these last few very long days. So why would she—

He stopped, a sick feeling crawling through his veins. "Did she say something to you?"

"No. I mean...yes, she did say something. But that's not why—"

"What did she say?" He clenched his fists, trying to hold on to his anger.

"Eastern, it doesn't—"

"What did she say, Sadie?"

It took a beat, but finally Sadie lifted her gaze. "To back off. That you and Avery are hers and I'm trying to steal you both."

Rage punched through his chest. A familiar rage that he'd lived and breathed this entire last week.

"But I don't even care about that," she rushed to say. "I want to give you space so you can figure things out without having to worry about us."

"You think you and I are something I worry about?"

Her mouth opened and closed a couple of times before she lifted a shoulder. "I don't know."

This was his fault. He'd asked her to put their relationship on hold. And before that, he'd been the one who'd resisted a relationship. Apologized for touching her.

He gripped her hips, tugging her closer before lowering his voice. "Sadie, you are not a puzzle I need to piece together. You aren't a problem I need to solve. And you certainly aren't someone I want or need space from. I tried that, and it's too goddamn hard." He cupped her cheek. "Maybe that makes me a selfish bastard, but when I'm with you, I feel like I can function. I feel stronger. Like I can think more clearly."

"Eastern…" She grazed her hands down his chest. "I—"

Whatever she was about to say was cut off by the door to the liquor store opening and shouted voices ringing throughout the quiet street.

"A hundred dollars for a bottle? You having a fuckin' laugh? You're gonna send me skint, you fucking crook!"

Morris Anderson stepped out of his shop, holding Denny by his shirt collar. "I don't rip people off. I sell alcohol. You're unhappy with the price? Take your business the fuck elsewhere."

Anderson shoved Denny, who almost fell into them. Eastern quickly pushed Sadie behind him and grabbed Denny to stop him from hitting the ground.

"Hey!" Eastern barked.

Denny ignored him and lowered his paper bag to the sidewalk. "You think I'm fucking daft? I oughta teach you a lesson!"

He shoved Anderson, and Anderson went to shove him back, but Eastern stepped between them.

"Stop!"

"Oh, look, it's PC Plod," Denny growled with an eye roll while trying to wrench out of Eastern's hold. He didn't let him go, and Denny turned back to Morris. "I want my money back."

Anderson scowled at him. "Then give me the bottles back."

"You over-fucking-charged me."

"That's what the bottles cost!"

Eastern looked at Denny. "He's the store owner, so he sets the prices, Denny. You don't like it, shop elsewhere."

The man turned angry eyes on him. "Well, I can't go to the damn bar because your no-good brother banned me, and the other liquor store in town is closed." Denny shoved at Eastern, but he didn't budge an inch.

Eastern's eyes narrowed. "You drunk again, Denny?"

"Fuck off! The lot of ya." He finally managed to yank himself out of Eastern's hold before turning angry eyes to Sadie. "Careful who ya spend time with, missy. Some people ain't worth the trouble."

He grabbed his bag of liquor and stormed off while Anderson also spun around with a huff and headed back into his store.

When both were gone, Eastern turned to Sadie. "You okay?"

She nodded, concern in her eyes. "That's Denny, right? The guy you were telling me about?"

"Yeah, he's a regular at the station." He blew out a frustrated breath.

She was still watching Denny walk away when Eastern gripped her hips again. "Sadie, tell me you understand what I said."

She sucked in a breath and met his eyes. "If you want me around…I'll be around."

Thank fuck, because he couldn't go another day without her in his life. Then, because he felt starved of her, he lowered his head and kissed her.

CHAPTER 18

"*I* can't believe he said that," Elle said as she leaned over the kitchen island, eyes dreamy like Sadie had told her that Eastern had professed his love.

Sadie took out the ingredients for the apple sours. "He was pretty sweet."

"Sweet? Sadie, he told you that you make him feel like he can *function*. That you make him stronger."

Yeah, he *had* said those things. Then he'd invited her to dinner, and she'd stayed at his place the last few nights. This morning she'd woken to his lips on her neck and his hands…well, everywhere.

Her cheeks flushed as she poured bourbon into the glasses. "Even though I told him I was happy to pause things…I'm glad the break is over."

"Has he spoken to you about Jamie?"

Frustration bubbled in her. "He said she's been hounding him to see Avery, even threatening legal action."

"But Eastern doesn't want her to see Avery?"

"No, *Avery* doesn't want to see her mom, and Eastern's respecting that. And after the way Jamie acted before she deserted her daughter, I don't blame Avery for not wanting to see her."

"Me neither," Elle said quietly, turning back to the focaccia she was slicing.

They were pairing the apple sours with a board of meats, cheeses and bread. Sadie's stomach was rumbling just seeing it all come together. "Eastern has so many testimonies against her, both from Avery herself and the staff at her school, that I don't think Jamie has a leg to stand on."

"Then why do you look worried?"

Was it that obvious? She put the cap back on the bourbon and poured the apple juice. "I've known Jamie for a long time. Pretty much Avery's entire life. But I've never seen her like I did in the shop the other day. She was so angry, and that, in combination with the possibility that she's still drinking? I don't know...it makes me scared for Avery and Eastern."

"And for you."

Her eyes shot up. "I'm not scared for me."

"Sadie, she threatened you. And now that you and Eastern are back to seeing each other again..." Elle lifted a shoulder. "*I'm* worried about you."

"You don't need to worry about me. I'm fine. Better than fine. I'm back to seeing Eastern and Avery, and tomorrow, Sugar and Spice is reopening." She grabbed the triple sec.

Elle looked like she didn't believe her, but she didn't push. "Everything ready to go for that?"

"Yep. Did some prep today, and tomorrow we're a go. My grandmother is so relieved. She lives and breathes that place."

"She's lucky she had you to organize everything."

Sadie shook her head. "No, I'm the lucky one. My grandmother was all I had when my parents passed away. Even before then, when my parents worked more than they parented, she was my world. Summers here were the best time of my life."

Elle's eyes softened. "That's great."

"It must have been amazing for you to grow up in Misty Peak."

Some of the light left Elle's eyes. The woman rarely talked about her childhood or upbringing. "It was okay."

"You lived with your aunt, right?" She'd mentioned her aunt a few times but never her parents.

"Yeah, I lived with her after my dad left."

Sadie paused in slicing the lemons. "How old were you when your dad left?"

"Eight."

Avery's age. "What about your mom?"

Elle looked down at the bread like it was the most interesting thing in the room. "She left when I was five because her new boyfriend wasn't so into kids. I think my dad tried to do the single-parent thing for a while, but he just couldn't handle me on his own."

"Oh, Elle. I'm sorry."

She lifted a shoulder. "I have Aunt Jewel. I also had…"

When she paused, Sadie frowned. "You had someone else?"

"Jace, actually. Eastern's youngest brother."

"You were friends?"

"He was my best friend. Until he left for the military, that is. I swear I spent more time at his house than anywhere else."

"But you didn't stay friends?"

"He left and we…lost contact."

There was a story there, and Sadie wanted to ask a million more questions. Best friends often kept in contact when one of them moved away, so why hadn't they? And he'd had to have returned to Misty Peak occasionally during all the years he'd been away. Had they never seen each other?

So many questions rolled around in her head, but she didn't ask a single one of them. If Elle wanted to talk about it, she would.

Sadie's phone vibrated on the counter, and she looked down to see a text message.

Eastern: Sorry to interrupt your girls' evening, but I was wondering if you'd take pity on me and pick up Avery from school tomorrow while I'm at work? This might also be a ploy for me to see you tomorrow afternoon.

Her lips twitched and before she could respond, a second message popped up.

Eastern: Also, I miss you.

Wasn't he a charmer.

Sadie: Of course I can. I'll go straight from Sugar and Spice to get Avery.

Sadie: And I miss you too.

Elle sighed. "See, I want *that*."

Sadie lowered the phone and grabbed the orange bitters. "Maybe you'll get it soon."

She scoffed. "Yeah, right. My dating life is about as dead as the salmon I ate for lunch. I've tried some online dating sites, but the guys are just…"

"Not good?"

"Ha. That's an understatement. One guy actually had the balls to get angry at me for yawning during a date."

"No."

"Yes. He then put two beers in front of me to 'perk me up.' When I said I was calling it a night, he made a remark about me getting him to give up a Saturday night for such a short date."

"What an ass! I'm guessing you didn't see him again?"

"Nope. But he did text me over and over again for days, and when I didn't respond, his final message called me a rude bitch who'd ghosted him for no reason."

Sadie wrinkled her nose. "He sounds awful."

"Oh, he's just the beginning. I have a dozen very similar stories I could share, but I'll save you. I've decided dating's not for me."

Sadie gave her friend a knowing smile as she squeezed fresh lemon into the glasses. Elle was young, single, and had curves any man would die for. Not to mention an awesome personality. There was no way the woman would be single for long.

When the drinks were ready, she slid a glass across the island, then lifted her own. "Well, I'll be your date anytime you want, and if you yawn, I'll yawn with you."

"Now that's the support I need."

They clinked their glasses and Sadie sipped her apple sour, almost groaning at how good her favorite cocktail tasted. And boy, was it overdue.

* * *

SADIE GROANED as her stomach rolled. She shifted from her back to her side, grabbing her belly. Even though her eyes were closed, she knew the room was still dark. God, what was the time? Elle had only left at eleven, but for Sadie, that was a late night.

She squeezed her eyes closed, trying to fall back to sleep. Her stomach rolled a second time, and a familiar sick feeling crawled up her throat.

She was going to throw up.

Quickly, she threw the sheets off her body and turned on the bedside lamp, flinching at the sudden brightness. On her first step toward the bathroom, the path in front of her blurred, and she stumbled. She grabbed onto the bed to stop from hitting the floor.

On the third roll of her belly, she ran as quickly as her shaky legs would allow, barely making it to the bathroom before dropping in front of the toilet and throwing up everything she'd eaten and drunk that night.

Argh, she *hated* being sick. If she could choose between the flu and throwing her guts up, she'd choose the flu every time.

She wasn't sure how long she knelt in front of the toilet, eyes closed, hand on her stomach, but every time she opened her eyes, the room spun.

Jesus, what was wrong with her? She felt like she'd been hit by a bus. She couldn't be hungover. What had she had…two cocktails? Could it be food poisoning from the cheeses? Maybe she'd text Elle and find out if she was sick too.

She remained on the floor in front of the toilet for a while, and every time she thought she was okay to get up, she started heaving again, only there was nothing left in her stomach.

Her head started to ache and her stomach hurt, but she had to try to get back to bed. She couldn't spend the rest of the night here—she didn't even know what time it was.

With shaky arms, she pushed herself up from the cold tiled floor, only to stumble into the wall and have to catch herself.

Easy, Sadie, you can do this.

Her steps were slow as she made her way to the kitchen. What should have taken her a few seconds felt like half a lifetime. When she finally got there, she rummaged around the cabinets until she found the large bowl she was looking for. She also grabbed a bottle of water from the fridge. Whether she'd drink the water or not, she wasn't sure. The idea of consuming anything right now made her want to throw up all over again.

Carefully, she made her way back to the bedroom and all but fell onto the mattress. She'd barely lain down, when her stomach rolled for what had to be the twentieth time and she dry heaved into the bowl. At this point, it hurt more than anything else because she had nothing left inside her.

When she was finally done, she closed her eyes, knowing full well she'd get little to no sleep for the rest of the night.

CHAPTER 19

"What are you going to do with Sadie this afternoon?"

Avery's eyes lit up as they left the car and walked toward her school, her little hand tightening in Eastern's. "Everything!"

"Everything?"

"Yep! We'll bake and do braids in our hair and talk about boys..."

Eastern frowned. "Whoa? Back up, kid. Boys? What boys?"

Avery rolled her eyes like she was sixteen. "Dad, I can't talk to you about that stuff."

"Yes, you can. And you will. I want to know about any and every boy in your life. I'll give great advice." *Like stay the hell away from boys until you're thirty.*

"The last time I talked to you about a boy, it was when Leon Donnelly invited me to his house to play. You called Leon's mother, told her the playdate would be at *our* house with *your* supervision, and there would not, under any circumstances, be any touching."

"I don't see the problem with any of that." No, what he saw a problem with was everything *outside* of his rules. Playdates with a boy he'd never met, at a house he'd never been to? Hell no.

Her lips fell into a frown. "We never had that playdate."

Eastern squeezed her hand. "Then he scared off too easy and wasn't good enough for you."

"You always say *no one's* good enough for me."

"Damn straight."

Avery giggled. "You need to put a dollar in the swear jar."

Shit. He was already in major debt to that thing.

They were just nearing the front of the school when a car door opened across the street and a woman climbed out. He cursed under his breath at the sight of Jamie.

Goddammit. He'd told the woman to stay away until further notice.

Instinctively, he inched in front of Avery, but of course she saw her mother.

"Mom?" Avery's voice was small and uncertain.

Jamie stopped in front of them and looked down at Avery, a smile that didn't quite look genuine curving her lips. "Avery, baby, how are you?"

When Avery didn't answer, Jamie lowered to her haunches. "Can Mommy have that cuddle now?"

She held out her arms, but Avery just stepped behind Eastern, and fury pummeled his veins. "She needs to get to class, Jamie."

When Avery continued to hide behind him, annoyance flared in Jamie's eyes and her arms dropped as she rose. "I know. But I wanted to see my child."

"Now isn't the time."

"So when *will* be the time?"

He didn't want to fucking do this. Not here. Not in front of Avery.

He turned and crouched in front of his daughter. "You go get to class, okay?"

Her gaze rose to her mother, then returned to him. "Will you be okay?"

She was worried about *him*? God, he loved his kid. "Yeah, you don't need to worry about me, princess. I'm tough, remember?"

That got a small smile out of her, then she whispered, "I love you, Daddy."

"Love you too, kid." He kissed and hugged her before she ran toward the school doors.

"Wait—"

When Jamie stepped forward as if to follow, Eastern blocked her path. "Don't even think about it."

"Get out of my goddamn way!"

"If she wanted you, she would have gone to you instead of hiding behind *me*." And that fear in her eyes, fear of having to go back with her mother…fuck, it annihilated him.

"What have you said to her?"

Eastern frowned. "What are you talking about?"

"You've clearly turned her against me."

He could have laughed. "No, Jamie. You did that all on your own."

"If it wasn't you, then it was Sadie."

"Hardly. And she told me about your little visit."

Jamie lifted a brow. "So? It wasn't a secret."

"If you ever threaten her again, I'll make sure you wish you hadn't."

"Is the mighty Eastern Walker threatening *me* now?"

His back teeth ground together. "Why do you suddenly want Avery back so badly?"

She lifted a shoulder. "I miss her. And Matty wants to meet her."

If Eastern had thought he was angry before, that was nothing compared to this moment. "Matty?" Was that some fucking guy she was dating? Was she doing this for *him*?

"Yeah, Matty. We've been seeing each other for a few months.

I told him I had a daughter, and he wondered why I'm not with her. So I told him he could meet her if he wanted."

Over his dead fucking body. He inched closer and lowered his voice to a threatening growl. "Our daughter is *not* a tool for you to use to keep your boyfriend. I suggest if you don't plan to stick around and be an actual goddamn mother, then you get the hell out of Misty Peak, because it will be a cold day in hell before I let you have access to her when you don't intend to stay."

Instead of appearing angry, she just lifted a brow. "Really? Well, I hope you've lawyered up. And seeing as you won't play ball, I plan to go for full custody."

He wasn't scared, not even a little bit, because he knew there wasn't a chance in hell of that happening. "Try me."

"Don't worry. I plan to." She turned, her hair flying as she walked away.

Eastern didn't move from his spot, instead watching her as she climbed into her car and drove away, anger still beating through his veins.

When he finally felt like he could move again, he turned to storm back to his car.

"Eastern!"

The sound of Marie Alvaro's voice did nothing to help his mood. Pretending that he didn't hear, he kept moving.

"Eastern. Wait!"

He didn't stop, and when Marie grabbed his arm, she was out of breath. "Hey. Didn't you hear me calling?"

"What is it, Marie?"

Her brows flickered but she straightened. "I haven't seen those patrol cars you promised around my apartment building."

"I made sure they did a few drive-bys after you mentioned it." He started walking again, and it took two of Marie's steps for every one of his for her to keep up.

"And then they stopped? You know he's still there."

"The lurker?"

"Yes. He hangs around the building almost every night. I think it's that ex of Sadie Sandler's."

Eastern stopped and turned. "Why do you think that?"

"Because I have eyes." She touched a hand to her hip. "Look, I don't want any trouble around my daughter, so take care of it, okay? She *is* your girlfriend, after all."

Before he could get another word in, she was gone.

The next breath was more of a hiss because there were too many goddamn outliers in this town, and he was damn well over it.

* * *

SADIE MASSAGED her temple as she drove from the bakery to Avery's school. Thank God it was only a short drive, because she did not feel well today.

She'd had this headache that refused to go away all day, probably from dehydration, but the very thought of drinking water made her feel so unbelievably sick. And that wasn't even the worst part of her day. Just about everything had gone wrong at Sugar and Spice. Mixing tools had refused to work, the electronic scales wouldn't switch on, and one of the fridges had stopped working overnight, meaning that half the prep she'd done yesterday had been lost.

It had been one big, fat mess. A mess she hadn't felt up to dealing with, but she'd had no choice because there was no way she was letting her elderly grandmother deal with everything on her own.

She almost wished the nausea would come back instead of the headache. She'd texted Elle as soon as she'd woken and her friend had been in exactly the same state, confirming Sadie's thoughts that the damn cheese had given them food poisoning. Either that or the meat.

When she reached the school, she parked out front and

climbed out. The second Avery saw her, the eight-year-old sprinted forward, and the first real smile that day curved Sadie's lips.

Avery beamed. "Sadie!" She ran full tilt toward Sadie, almost sending her to the ground when she flung herself at her.

Sadie dipped her head and kissed her. "Hey, Ave. I missed you."

Avery giggled before pulling back. "I saw you yesterday morning. But I missed you too."

"Good." She took Avery's hand and headed back toward the car. "How was your day?"

"It was great!"

Over the course of the drive back to Eastern's, Avery did not stop talking. She told Sadie about her school day from start to finish, about a boy named Ethan who she had a crush on, about some new kids she played with at lunch. It wasn't until they stepped inside the house that one part of her story niggled at Sadie's mind.

"You said Miss Davies could tell you were upset this morning. Why were you upset?"

Avery nibbled her bottom lip as she lowered her bag to the floor and moved into the kitchen. "Mom was at school this morning."

Sadie's skin chilled. "Does your dad know?"

Avery nodded as she slid onto a stool at the kitchen island. "He told me to go inside, and then he spoke to her without me."

The poor kid. This was why Jamie had to leave. She was causing more trouble than good. "And seeing her made you sad?"

"It made me scared. It always makes me scared. I love living with Daddy, and I love having you back. I don't want things to go back to just her and me again."

Suddenly, everything, including her aching head, paled in comparison to this beautiful girl in front of her. She moved closer and touched Avery's arms. "Remember when I told you that Daddy was going to fight for you? I wasn't lying. He *will* fight, and he'll fight hard."

"I know. But every time I see her, I can't help but think…"

Sadie frowned. "Think what?"

"That she won't fight fair."

God, that statement was so much wiser than her eight years. "It doesn't matter whether she does or not, you're safe here with your father."

"And you."

"And me." She tugged Avery into her arms. "I love you, Avery."

"I love you too, Sadie." They stayed in the embrace for a few long minutes, and when they finally separated, Sadie tucked some of Avery's hair behind her ear. "What do you say we get your homework out of the way so we can do something fun?"

The smile returned to Avery's lips. "Like braid hair and bake cookies?"

"You read my mind."

Avery jumped off the stool and ran back to her backpack. The next couple hours were a blur of homework, baking and braiding hair. Sadie tried to forget about her headache. She even tried to sip water, but the throbbing just worsened.

When the door finally opened and Eastern stepped in, she breathed a sigh of relief. Not because she didn't love caring for Avery, but because she really needed some rest.

"Daddy!" Avery ran into her father's arms, and he threw her into the air. "I drew you a picture at school today."

"You did? Do I look good in it?"

She giggled. "You look like you. I'll show you. Hang on, I put it in my room."

She wriggled out of his arms and took off toward her bedroom. Eastern immediately set his eyes on Sadie, one side of his mouth lifting. "Hey, beautiful."

"Hey."

The smile dropped from his lips, and he quickly crossed the room. "What's wrong?"

How could he tell something was wrong with a simple *hey*? "I've just got a headache."

He pressed his hand to her forehead. "You're not hot."

"I think Elle and I food poisoned ourselves last night. The headache's probably from being sick all night."

Concern flickered over his face. "You were sick last night? Why didn't you call me?"

She shrugged. "I didn't want to worry you. You already have so much going on."

His growl was soft. "Sadie. It doesn't matter how much I have going on. If something's wrong, I want to know."

She nodded, and even that small movement hurt.

His frown deepened. "You need to lie down."

"Yeah, I'll go home and—"

"No, here."

"Eastern—"

"I need eyes on you so I know you're okay. I already feel like shit that I couldn't do that last night. Let me look after you."

His soft words eased some of her pain. How that was possible, she wasn't sure. But it *would* be nice to have someone looking after her.

Then he added, "Please?"

How could she say no to that? "Okay."

CHAPTER 20

*E*astern closed the book. Usually by this stage, Avery was asleep. But right now, her eyes were wide open and a deep frown etched her brow. "What's on your mind, princess?"

Her gaze shifted from the door to him. "I'm worried about Sadie."

He was worried about Sadie too. She'd slept through dinner, and the last he'd checked, she was still fast asleep.

"Do you think I tired her out with all the playing when we got home?" Avery asked.

"Definitely not. She loves playing with you. If anything, I'm sure that made her feel a bit better."

"Maybe you should go cuddle her. That always makes me feel better when I'm sick."

His sweet girl. He shifted a lock of hair behind her ear. "As soon as you're asleep, that's exactly what I intend to do."

"But I'm not tired." The second the words were out, she yawned.

He chuckled. "Humor me. Close your eyes and let's see what happens."

"Okay." Her eyes closed and she snuggled into his side. "Can I tell you something?"

"Anything."

"When Mom stopped caring what time I went to bed, kids at school said I was lucky. But I like this better."

The smile fell from his mouth and his hand fisted. Every so often, Avery let another little crumb of information drop about her last year with her mother, and even though he wanted to know everything, each new detail hurt like hell. Because he hadn't been here to take care of her. He hadn't even known she'd needed him so badly.

"Me too, Ave. I love you."

She sighed, and without opening her eyes, whispered, "I love you too, Daddy."

He remained beside her until her breathing evened out, then he pressed one more kiss to her head before rising from the bed. He moved quietly down the hall before stepping into his bedroom to see Sadie curled into a ball on the edge of the mattress.

Damn, she looked so small and vulnerable. He hated it. He perched on the bed and touched her forehead. Just like earlier, it wasn't hot, but still her exhaustion and headache made him worry.

"Sadie?"

Her brows drew together and her eyes tightened. "Hmm?"

"I'd like to call a doctor, just to check you out."

"No, I'm okay." Her eyes opened but they were glazed over.

He cupped her cheek. "For me, Sadie. Please."

She sighed, eyes fluttering closed again. "Okay."

Lowering his head, he pressed a kiss to her temple before rising and stepping into the living room. They only had one doctor in Misty Peak who did house calls, and although he'd never used the guy, word of mouth said that he was older and didn't put a lot of time into his patients. But he was better than no doctor at all.

He made the call and twenty minutes later, a knock came on the front door.

Eastern pulled it open. "Doctor Vincent. I'm Eastern Walker. Thanks for coming."

The man dipped his head. "The patient is your wife?"

"Partner." The word slipped out easily. "She's in here." He led the doctor into the bedroom, where it took a few minutes to rouse Sadie.

The doctor introduced himself. "Hi, I'm Doctor Vincent."

"Sadie." She pushed up into a sitting position.

"I'm going to check your blood pressure, temperature, and heart rate, then I'll ask you a few questions."

Eastern gave Sadie and the doctor some privacy by stepping out of the room. Sadie hadn't asked him to, but he wanted them to have space to do what they needed to do without his overprotective ass hovering.

Less than ten minutes passed before the doctor stepped into the hall.

Eastern frowned. "You're done already?"

"Yes, Mr. Walker. Miss Sandler is dehydrated, and she informed me that she ate some bad cheese last night, in combination with alcohol."

Eastern's frown deepened. "And you're sure that's all that's wrong?"

"She doesn't have a temperature, her blood pressure isn't overly elevated, and by the sounds of her night last night, yes, I'm certain it's mostly dehydration. Painkillers, lots of fluids, and rest is my recommendation."

Eastern should be happy, shouldn't he? So why was his gut still in a knot?

He walked the doctor out before returning to the kitchen and grabbing some aspirin and water. When he returned to the bedroom, Sadie lay on her side, eyes hooded as she watched him.

He sat on the edge of the bed and helped her take the aspirin and water.

"Why do you look so angry?" she asked quietly.

"Because he barely looked at you. Maybe we should go to the hospital or—"

"Eastern. I'm okay. My headache's actually already feeling better after some sleep. I think I just overdid it today after being so sick last night."

That *better* be all it was.

"Now, there's only one thing I need," Sadie added.

"What?" He'd give this woman the damn moon if she asked.

"You."

His brows flickered. "Sadie—"

"Come to bed. Hold me. I have a good feeling that will make me all better by morning."

The corners of his lips flickered. "Avery told me a cuddle would make you better."

"That kid's the smartest person I know."

"She'll rule the world one day." He lowered his head, touching a light kiss to her lips. "Give me five minutes."

He rose from the bed and moved around the house, checking that everything was locked up and the lights were off. When he returned to Sadie, she was asleep on her side.

Fuck, even when she slept, every part of him was drawn to her.

He stripped to his briefs before flicking off the bedroom light and sliding under the covers. The second he curled his arm around her waist and tugged her against him, she moaned...a low, deeply contented sound which slid into his chest and made every part of him that had been uneasy or unsettled instantly calm.

* * *

A STEADY THUMP beat against Sadie's ear. It was so loud, it was all she could hear. And the heat against her cheek…God, it was nice. Like the sun on chilled skin.

She nuzzled her face closer while grazing her fingers against a hard surface. Hard but also warm. Not the sun. Eastern. She didn't need to open her eyes to know it was him. His deep, earthy scent combined with the feel of his body gave him away.

Turning her head, she pressed a small kiss to his chest, right over his heart. Then another. At the same time, she trailed her hand down his body until she could feel him through his briefs.

A deep growl sounded. "Sadie. What are you doing?"

"Touching you."

His fingers wrapped around her wrist. "You shouldn't be doing that."

"Why not?"

"Because you're sick."

"Actually, I feel kind of good today."

It wasn't a lie. As far as she could tell, the headache was gone and her stomach was fine. Hell, she even felt well rested.

She lifted her head, grinning at the almost pained look on his face. "I knew I just needed you to hold me."

When he continued to look at her like a part of him wanted to run, while the rest of him didn't know *what* he wanted, she dipped her head again, pressing another kiss to his chest. He slowly released her wrist, and she continued to touch and explore him through his briefs, sweeping her hand over his hard cock. She loved every little sound he made. They were all deep and masculine and gravelly.

She began to trail the line of kisses down his chest, then his stomach. When she reached the top of his briefs, she heard the loud hiss of air between his teeth before he growled her name.

"Sadie."

Her name was a warning. A warning she happily ignored as she pulled the top of his briefs down and took out his cock. God, he was huge. And right now, he was all hers.

She wrapped her lips around his tip, only to have him growl again as his back arched off the bed. She moved her lips up and down his length as she wrapped her fingers around the base, sucking and licking. Tasting.

Every sound he made, every growl and moan, combined with those flickers of movement, made the throbbing in her lower belly intensify. She wanted more. She wanted to drive him as wild for her as she always seemed to be for him.

She ran her tongue over his tip before sucking, her palm moving up and down the base of his cock in a rhythmic motion. His growls became louder, his fingers wrapping around her upper arms and tightening.

Suddenly, those strong fingers tugged her up.

"Eastern," she gasped, but that was all she got out before her panties were torn off and the shirt tugged over her head. She was flipped onto her back, then he was between her thighs, his fingers moving over her clit.

"You destroy me, Sadie."

She sucked in a sharp breath before his lips crashed to hers.

When his fingers dipped inside her, she arched into him. "Eastern."

"So fucking wet for me."

"Now," she whispered.

Another deep, primal growl, then he pushed inside her. She opened her mouth to cry out, but his lips once again found hers, silencing her ecstasy as his tongue swept inside her mouth, tangling with hers. She groaned as he moved in long, deep thrusts.

When his mouth moved from hers, she wanted to tug him back. But those lips shifted from her cheek to her neck, his teeth grazing her skin before he sucked.

She grabbed his shoulders, digging with her fingers, sure she was breaking skin but unable to stop. It was like she was in a haze of Eastern. He was all she could feel and breathe. He was everywhere, and she was drowning in him but didn't want to come up for air.

He nibbled on her neck, his thrusts becoming deeper, harder, while all she could do was hang on. She wrapped a leg around his waist and met him thrust for thrust. Lifting her hips, taking him deeper.

When he cupped her breast, she pushed into him, a shudder running down her spine as he rolled her nipple. He did it again and again, and God, she was on fire, every inch of her.

She trailed her fingers up to his head and threaded them through the locks of his hair, where she tugged and pulled, desperately trying to anchor herself.

His mouth moved to a sensitive spot behind her ear while he pinched her nipple, and that was all it took to send her toppling over the edge. She fell, shattering below him as he kept pumping and swiping and sucking. As he continued to thrum her aching breast until finally, with his head nuzzling into her shoulder, he broke along with her.

Three more thrusts and then they were both still. For a moment, it felt like all they could do was breathe.

When he finally lifted his head, he looked at her like she was the center of his world. Like it was him and her and there was nothing that could stand between them.

Then he cursed under his breath.

She frowned at him. "What?"

"I didn't use anything."

A small smile curved her lips. "I'm on the pill."

"At least one of us was thinking."

She chuckled.

"This is probably a bit late to ask," he said, his chest moving quickly, "but are you sure you're okay?"

Despite her still-racing heart, she laughed. "Yeah, I'm okay. Guess that doctor was right, dehydration, food poisoning and alcohol are not a good mix."

Relief rolled through him. "Good. You had me worried last night."

"You don't need to worry about me."

"I'll always worry."

CHAPTER 21

Sadie put the container of cookie dough into the fridge. It had finally been fixed. Apparently, the condenser fan had broken, something that could happen as the appliance aged, and it was just really crappy timing for them.

Since the repair that morning, she'd worked nonstop, prepping items for the storefront and getting orders out.

It had been exhausting, but it was done now.

She'd told her nan a little white lie when they'd flipped the closed sign this afternoon that she was almost done with the prep for tomorrow. But if she hadn't lied, her grandmother would have insisted on staying and helping, and Sadie didn't want that. Her grandmother tried to hide the exhaustion and worry from her features, but Sadie saw it. The break-in had caused her a lot of stress, and the fact that the person had never been caught only increased that stress. Then there were all the things that had gone wrong in the shop after the reopening. And Sadie was sure Nan was worried about her too, because, well...she *always* worried about her.

She tugged her phone from her back pocket to check the time.

Holy crap, it was six o'clock!

Eastern would have finished work about half an hour ago, but he'd mentioned that he hadn't caught up with his brothers in a while. Tilly had offered to spend the evening with Avery so Sadie could get everything done at the bakery. She'd head to his house now so Tilly could go home.

She sent a quick text to Eastern.

Sadie: Sorry, only just leaving now. I'll text Tilly.

She quickly typed out a text to Tilly and had just hit send when Eastern's response came through.

Eastern: It's getting late. Everything okay at the store? I can come to you.

Sadie: Absolutely not. You deserve time with your brothers. I'm sure they've missed annoying you. Ave and I will see you when you get home.

Eastern: Drive safe. Xox

Her heart gave a little thump at his hugs and kisses. Which was silly, right? That she'd get excited about hugs and kisses at the end of a text?

But it also wasn't silly. It was exactly what she'd been craving the morning of her wedding all those weeks ago—giddiness, excitement.

After grabbing her bag and turning off all the lights, she stepped outside, only to stop and groan.

Because there, standing on the sidewalk, was Scott. God, she'd hoped he'd have gone home by now. Was he spending the entire leave he'd taken for their honeymoon here in Misty Peak?

"What are you doing here?" she asked between gritted teeth.

He pushed off the wall. "Waiting for you." He lifted a bottle of bourbon. "Bought this. Thought we could make apple sours."

If he thought remembering her favorite drink was going to sway her, he was dead wrong. "No. I have somewhere I need to be." But even if she didn't, she *would not* be having a drink with him, something he should well and truly know by now.

She walked down the street toward her car, Scott's footsteps loud behind her as he hurried to catch up. "You haven't even given me an opportunity to explain. All I want is one chance. An evening where I can tell you exactly why I did what I did."

"But that's the thing, Scott. I don't care. I don't care why you did it—the point is, you *did*. And it's in the past for me."

"It's not in the past for me."

"Unfortunately, that's not my fault or my problem."

"What happened to you?" he spluttered. "You were always my person. We could always talk things through and—"

She spun on him. "What *happened* is you cheated on me on the morning of our wedding! What happened is I realized that marrying you would have been my greatest mistake *ever*."

Pain flashed in his eyes, but she didn't feel bad about what she'd said. He didn't deserve her sympathy. He'd had no respect for the commitment he'd made to her.

Still, she softened her voice. "It's over, Scott. Go back to Atlanta. Be with your admin assistant or whoever else you decide to be with. Just…leave us in the past. We had our good moments, but they're just memories now."

"I miss you."

"*Don't*. I'm going to leave now, and I don't want you to follow me." Five more steps and she reached her car.

"Sadie, wait!"

She rolled her eyes and was about to turn and tell Scott in much more threatening words to leave her alone, maybe throw a few curses in there, when something across the street caught her attention. Or less something, as *someone*.

She frowned.

Scott grabbed her arm. "I can't just—"

"Do you see that?" She didn't take her eyes off the spot across the road.

"See what?"

Without another word, she tugged her arm from Scott's hold and started across the street. She was about halfway when she realized she was right…the thing she saw poking out from behind a car was a shoe…and attached to the shoe was a body. A very still body, lying on their side on the pavement.

Oh God.

She took off running toward it.

"Sadie! What the hell are you doing?"

She dropped beside the still form, her bag falling to the ground as she pushed the man onto his back. Her breath caught.

She knew this man. Well, not *knew* him. She recognized him.

Denny.

She felt his pulse, and her heart stopped…because there was none.

* * *

"W HAT'S PUT that scowl on your face, brother?"

Eastern lifted his beer to his lips, his knuckles white. "Everyone's annoying the shit out of me this week. Jamie. Jarrad."

A commotion from the back of the bar sounded. Fuck, even *that* was annoying him. The place was loud and rowdy tonight, particularly the group of guys in the back booth.

Kayden scowled. "I hate the guy too. Trust me, he doesn't want to find himself alone in a dark alley with me."

Cody frowned before understanding cleared his features. "He was the deputy who interviewed Tilly."

"Damn straight he was," Kayden growled. "Cuffed her when she didn't need to be cuffed. Put the damn things on too tight, bruising her wrists, and he denied her fucking water for hours."

"Has he done anything since?" Cody asked, shifting his attention back to Eastern.

"Called in sick several times and just been a general dick in the office." Tonight, he'd been the fucking comedian of the station, making chauvinistic jokes any chance he got. "Also, a few weeks ago, I overheard some deputies talking about the previous sheriff being paid off by Jarrad. They brushed it off and wouldn't tell me what they were talking about. I asked Jarrad about it tonight."

"And?" Kayden asked.

"He gave me his arrogant I'm-not-telling-you-shit expression, then told me he had no idea what I was talking about."

"Which you don't believe," Kayden said.

"Not for a second. I'll keep pushing the deputies. I've been meaning to ask Daisy too."

Cody leaned forward. "You don't have any idea what he might be doing?"

"Not yet." But he'd find out, even if it killed him. More shouting sounded from the back of the bar, making him frown. He needed a change of subject. "Has Jace officially bought the house?"

Their youngest brother, Jace, was leaving the Air Force to come home. He needed a place to stay, and their old family home, the one their father had sold to a local when he'd been alive, had just come on the market.

Kayden dipped his head. "Yep. Closing's in a couple weeks, but he doesn't think he'll make it so he's asked me to be his power of attorney to sign the paperwork. When I asked when he'd be back, he was vague about it all and wouldn't give me an exact date."

Cody chuckled. "Sounds like our brother. Never one to be tied down by a date."

"Well, something more exciting could pop up," Kayden said with a grin.

Cody whistled. "Talking about exciting, four out of the six of us will be home. Haven't had that in years."

"The odds probably won't get any better for a while," Eastern said, taking a sip of his beer. "Nylah's happy with Liam in Cradle Mountain, and Lock will probably never leave his position on his Ghost Ops team."

Kayden nodded. "Yeah, that guy's in for life. It'll be good to have Jace home though. I'm trying to get him a position working at the new skywalk, at the visitors center."

Cody's brows shot up. "Is it ready to go?"

"There've been some delays, but hopefully by the time he gets home."

Cody nodded and turned to Eastern. "And what were you saying about Jamie? She still causing you trouble?"

"She hasn't shown up again since coming to Avery's school, but her texts are nonstop." Jesus, he still got angry thinking about the school incident. "My lawyer's ready to go for when she makes a move. So far, no one's contacted him."

He wasn't sure if that was better or worse. The sooner this thing started, the sooner it would finish.

"No judge would retract your rights," Kayden said under his breath. "She fucked up. Even the school can corroborate Avery's stories. And now that she's back, she's not even trying to do better, just thinks she's entitled to Avery."

"That's Jamie though, isn't it?" He lifted the beer to his lips.

Cody's gaze shifted over Eastern's head, eyes narrowing. "Speak of the devil."

Oh, *fuck* no.

He glanced over his shoulder and, sure enough, Jamie was crossing the space between the door and the bar, gaze directly on him.

He leaned back on his stool. "What are you doing here, Jamie?"

"Getting a drink. Is that a crime?"

"It's maybe not the best choice when you're an alcoholic."

Her eyes narrowed. "I'm *not* an alcoholic. I can handle my drinks, just like my lawyer will handle getting me custody of my daughter again."

He turned to face her. "Let's say you did get custody of Avery. You *won't*, but let's pretend—what happens when your boyfriend gets tired of parenting a kid who isn't his? Or if you break up and want to get out of town again and having a child doesn't fall into those plans?"

"*When* I get custody, and *if* either of those things happen, I'll let you know my plans."

Eastern was fighting for calm when shouting sounded again from the back booth.

"Yeah, chump, chug it!"

His back teeth ground together as he glared at them. Jamie followed his gaze. "Still get easily annoyed by rowdy drunks?" she asked.

When he didn't respond, she lifted a brow, a challenge in her gaze. "They look fun. I might go say hi."

Of course she fucking would.

She slid off the stool and made her way across the bar.

"Want me to throw her *and* them out?" Cody asked the second Jamie had walked away. "I don't mind. In fact, I'll enjoy it."

Kayden shook his head. "No, let them drink and fuck up on their own. If Jamie does something wrong tonight, that's another thing to add to the list of marks against her."

Eastern was just turning back to his brothers when a text from Sadie came through. Shit, she was still at work. He quickly responded.

"That Sadie?" Cody asked, lifting another glass to dry.

"Yeah, she finished late. I offered to meet her, but she told me to stay and catch up with you guys. I don't like her being alone though, not after the break-in."

Kayden frowned. "I wouldn't like that either."

"You're in pretty deep with her, aren't you?" Cody said with a hint of a grin.

"Yeah, I am. She's unbelievable. She's in my head all the time. I can't stop thinking about her. And she loves Avery. Like, *really* loves her. Their bond is like mother and daughter."

"So don't let her go," Kayden said before he sipped his beer.

That was the plan.

Eastern was halfway through his beer when breaking glass sounded behind him. He turned to see the guys cheering and on their feet, with Jamie laughing along with them.

"For fuck's sake," Cody growled, rounding the bar.

Eastern rose to his feet and took a couple of steps toward the booth when his phone rang. He pulled it out to see it was the sheriff's office.

CHAPTER 22

Eastern climbed out of his car to see people everywhere. Paramedics. Deputies. It was fucking chaos.

But amidst the chaos, he found her. Sadie stood to the side of an ambulance, arms wrapped around her middle. From the moment he'd been told she'd found the body, all he wanted to do was get to her.

Questions had run through his head...was she okay? What state was the body in when she'd found it? Was there danger nearby?

He was so focused on her that, for a moment, he didn't see the guy beside her. Then Eastern's eyes narrowed. Scott. He had his hand on the small of Sadie's back and was standing so close his side was pressed to hers.

What the hell was he doing here?

Eastern crossed the space between them and stopped in front of Sadie. Ignoring Scott, he cupped her cheeks. "Are you okay?"

She nodded, but the nod was too quick and her eyes too wide. Not only that, but she barely looked at him.

He shifted a lock of hair behind her ear and lowered his voice so his words only reached her. "You don't have to pretend with me, Sadie."

Finally, she gave him her full attention. She'd just opened her mouth when someone called him from behind.

"Sheriff?"

He held her gaze for one more beat. "I'll be right back."

Another quick nod from her. He bit back a curse as he moved over to his deputies, Paxley and Jarrad.

"Who is it?" Eastern asked.

It was Paxley who answered. "Denny Barclay."

The name was like a punch to the gut. Denny…the town drunk. Yeah, Eastern had arrested him more times than he could count, but he'd always liked the guy.

Without a word, he walked over to the stretcher and pulled the sheet down, cursing at the sight of Denny.

What the fuck had happened? Had he drunk too much, passed out and hit his head? Had he been sick?

He pulled the sheet back up and returned to the deputies. "Any word on cause of death?"

Jarrad cleared his throat. "He had a cut on the back of his head, probably from passing out and falling down. Most likely something to do with his drinking. I'll follow up with the coroner."

"There was a bottle beside his head that was smashed, probably happened when he fell," Paxley added, voice low.

Eastern shifted his attention to the broken glass, which had been taped off.

Jarrad followed his gaze. "I've already contacted the coroner. He said he'd do a rush on the autopsy report."

"Good." Eastern shot a look over his shoulder to see Scott still standing too fucking close to Sadie. "Did Sadie call it in?"

Paxley shook her head. "Scott Chase. Said he and Sadie were walking to her car when they saw the body across the road."

A muscle ticked in Eastern's cheek. He should probably be

grateful Sadie hadn't found Denny's body alone, but he also had questions. Like why the hell Scott was with her at all.

"I'm gonna get her home." He turned back to his deputies. "You got everything handled here?"

Paxley dipped her head. "Yeah, we've got it covered. Go."

"We'll let you know if we hear from the coroner," Jarrad said.

Eastern headed back to Sadie.

"Come on, I'll drive you home."

Even though Scott's words were low, Eastern heard them just fine. "She's coming with me."

Scott scowled, a glimmer of anger in his eyes. "Don't you need to stay here and, I don't know, do your job?"

"That's not your concern." He slipped an arm around Sadie's waist and tugged her into him.

Scott stepped forward. "Hey—"

"Scott." Sadie's voice was low but firm. "Go home. To *Atlanta*. I appreciate you staying with me until everyone got here, but your life isn't in Misty Peak. This is the last time I'm going to say this —we're over."

Before Scott could respond, she turned toward Eastern and let him walk her to the car. They were halfway there when she suddenly stopped, eyes widening. "Oh God, Avery. I-I completely forgot. Tilly's probably wondering what's going on! I didn't even text her to let her know—"

"Sadie...breathe." When she just looked at him, he inched closer. "My officers called me and told me you were here. Kayden went to my house to help Tilly and let her know what was going on. Avery's being fed and bathed. She might even be in bed by now."

The air rushed from Sadie's chest. "Good. I wasn't thinking. I should have called you."

He wished she'd called him too. He'd called her the second he'd gotten off the phone with Paxley but she hadn't answered, so he'd raced here, praying she was okay.

"You were in shock." She was probably *still* in shock.

A hint of tears coated her eyes. "He was dead. I've never seen…"

"I know, honey. I'm sorry."

She sucked in a deep breath. "You knew him."

He nodded. "I did."

"Are you okay?"

"No. And I won't be until I learn his cause of death." The man had died in Eastern's jurisdiction, and he needed to know this wasn't a crime scene. That his community was safe.

She leaned into his chest, wrapping her arms around him. "I'm sorry."

"I'm sorry you found the body, honey."

* * *

SADIE CURVED her hands around her warm tea, the image of Denny's dead body still flickering in her mind even though all she wanted to do was forget.

The house was silent around her. They'd gotten home just as Avery had been getting ready for bed, and Eastern had asked Sadie—well, less asked and more told her—to rest while he read Avery her book.

Guilt laced her blood. She hadn't known Denny, but Eastern had. *She* should be the one taking care of Avery so he could rest. She should be making sure *he* was okay, but she couldn't shake this chill that had settled into her bones. And there was this sick feeling in her belly that wouldn't go away.

Denny's skin had been warm when she'd felt for a pulse. Did that mean he hadn't been dead for long? If she'd finished work a bit earlier and found him sooner, could she have gotten him help so he might have survived?

She didn't know. She probably wouldn't know until they had a cause of death.

Footsteps sounded in the hall. She looked up to see Eastern step into the living room, a concerned expression on his face as he moved toward her. He sat on the couch, immediately lifting her feet onto his lap and kneading them.

His touch...his warmth...it went so far in chasing away the cold that had crept over her skin.

"How are you doing?" he asked gently.

"I should be asking you that."

"No. This is my job as sheriff, and before becoming sheriff I was a SEAL. I've seen more dead bodies than I care to remember."

Her brows flickered. A part of her already knew that, but hearing it out loud was different. "I'm sorry."

"I knew what I was signing up for."

She watched as he rubbed her foot, the tension slipping from her limbs. "There were good parts of serving though?"

"Oh, yeah. The brotherhood was the best thing I gained. I still keep in contact with a lot of the men I served with. We also got to help people. One life saved was always worth the risks we took."

"You're amazing," she whispered, unable to hold the words in. "You know that, right?"

"No, honey. I'm just a guy trying to work his way through life one day at a time." He shifted to the ball of her foot. "You never answered my question. How are you doing?"

The image of Denny flashed back into her mind, and for a moment, she swore she could feel his skin against her fingertips. "His skin was warm."

"Doesn't mean his death could have been prevented."

How did he know she'd been thinking that?

She sipped her tea, the warm liquid slipping down her throat.

"Can I ask you something?" he asked quietly.

Why did her belly do a little twist at that question? "Sure."

"Why was Scott there?"

Ah, that was probably her fault. She should have told him

already. "He was waiting for me outside the bakery. He wanted to talk."

"About getting back together?"

"I guess so. He keeps saying he wants to discuss things."

Eastern's expression was neutral, giving her no clue what he was thinking. "Do you want that?"

Her brows shot up. Didn't he already know the answer to that? "Absolutely not."

"Because if you did want to talk to him—"

"Eastern, he cheated on me in the worst possible way. And even if he hadn't, it doesn't matter, because I'd already realized that I didn't want a life with him."

He watched her closely but remained silent.

She leaned forward. "I am so grateful for that—because now I have you and Avery. And you two are *all* I want."

One side of his mouth lifted. "Really?"

"Yeah, really."

"That's a relief. Because we want you too."

The words hit her in the chest, but not in a bad way. "You do, do you?"

"Yeah. I'm actually not sure what we'd do without you now."

"I kind of like that." Honestly, there was no kind of about it. She dropped her feet to the floor and leaned forward. Their kiss was soft and warm and comforting.

She was just slipping her hands into his hair when his phone rang.

He tugged it out and frowned. "It's Jarrad. I need to take this. I'll be back in a second."

She nodded and leaned back, nerves skittering as Eastern stepped into the hallway. Maybe she was nervous because she wanted Denny's cause of death to be something that hadn't been preventable. She needed confirmation that finding him sooner wouldn't have helped.

A couple minutes later, Eastern returned, a frown between his brows.

She straightened. "What is it?"

"Jarrad let me know that it's looking like it was a brain aneurysm. I guess that makes sense. My deputies messaged earlier and said they interviewed some people who saw him this afternoon, and he was complaining of nausea and vomiting and a stiff neck. They put it down to his drinking."

She nodded, nibbling her bottom lip. "So no crime scene."

"No crime scene."

Then why did Eastern look like he didn't quite believe it?

CHAPTER 23

*E*astern climbed out of the car and circled around to Sadie's side to help her out. They were at Cody and Harper's place for a family dinner. It was Sadie's first, and there was something about having her here, with him and Avery, that made him feel… Damn, he couldn't even describe it.

She stepped onto the sidewalk. "Should I be nervous?"

"Nervous about a dinner with my two knucklehead brothers and their partners? Absolutely not."

She laughed as she took a step toward Avery's door and helped her out. The kid was just about beaming. If anyone loved family dinners, it was her. Maybe that had something to do with her being doted on by everyone. Or maybe because there were always sweets at the end.

"Can I hold the cupcakes?" Avery asked, almost jumping in excitement. "I promise I won't eat any."

Eastern lifted the box from the back seat. "How do I know I can trust you? I'm pretty sure there were bite marks taken out of the cake at the last family dinner."

A grin curved her lips. "That was Uncle Kay's fault. He was a bad influence."

Yeah, Kayden could be a terrible influence.

"But I promise, I won't take a bite this time and I won't let *him* take a bite. You can trust me, Daddy. I wouldn't lie to you."

He frowned. "Yesterday you told me you hadn't had any sweets all day, then I found out Sadie gave you a cookie."

She laughed, the sound so sweet and airy he couldn't help but smile. "Daddy, it was a green cookie, so Sadie and I both agreed it was healthy."

His lips twitched as he gave Sadie a skeptical look.

She lifted a shoulder. "Sometimes we say these things to make ourselves feel better."

"*Please*, Daddy?"

Eastern sighed and handed the box to Avery. "Straight into the fridge."

Her eyes shone, and she nodded before running up the steps.

Sadie took his hand, the grin on her face so radiant he couldn't help but stare.

"Even if she did sneak a bite of cupcake before dinner," Sadie said, "it wouldn't be the end of the world."

He grunted before slipping his arm around her waist. "Whose side are you on?"

"Avery's. Always Avery's."

He squeezed her waist, and she laughed as the door opened and Kayden stood on the other side. He grinned down at Avery. "My favorite niece is here!"

"Uncle Kay, I'm your only niece."

"What happened to the rest of them?"

She chuckled before lifting the box. "We brought cupcakes."

"Uh, I knew there was a reason we invited you." He glanced up at Eastern and Sadie. "Hey guys, come in and get settled while Avery and I taste these cakes."

Avery shook her head. "Daddy says we're not allowed."

Kayden scoffed. "What the old man doesn't know won't hurt him."

Avery's eyes lit up, but Eastern growled. "Don't even think about it."

"Come on," Kayden whispered to Avery, lifting her in his arms.

They stepped into the living room to see Harper and Tilly behind the kitchen counter, preparing a salad and garlic bread.

Harper smiled at them. "Hey! You made it."

Eastern gave both women a hug before asking, "Is Cody around?"

"Sure is." Harper nodded toward the back door. "He's cooking the meat on the deck. Feel free to go out and do the manly thing of standing around the barbecue with a beer."

That sounded like his kind of night. He turned to Sadie. "You okay?"

"Definitely." When she leaned up to kiss him, all he wanted to do was wrap his arms around her and get lost in the kiss. But he forced himself to release her. When he turned, it was to see Kayden and Avery with their heads inside the fridge.

Oh, Jesus. He didn't even want to know. He stepped out the back door.

Cody stood over the barbecue, beer in hand. He dipped his head. "Hey, man."

"Hey."

His brother reached into the cooler and pulled out a beer for him. "Sadie and Ave inside?"

"Yeah, Sadie's talking to the women, and Avery's pretending she's not eating the icing off the cupcakes with Kayden."

Cody laughed. "That's awesome. Kayden's so different since he met Tilly. More relaxed."

"Yeah, it's great, and Avery sure loves it. He needed someone to beat the grumpy out of him."

"Well, Jace will be back soon, so if Tilly hadn't done it, he sure would have."

"It'll be good to have our little brother back with us." Eastern uncapped his beer and took a sip.

"I'm sorry about Denny," Cody said quietly, the humor leaving his eyes.

"You knew him too."

"Yeah, but I didn't have to see his dead body. Or hell, find him. Is Sadie doing okay?"

"She was in a bit of shock for a few days, but having it confirmed that it was a brain aneurysm has helped because there was nothing we could have done to prevent his death."

Cody's brows tugged together. "Yeah, just a shit situation. On a different subject, you never found out who broke into her shop?"

Eastern's fingers tightened around his beer. "No. Never found the perp. She has new, better locks on the doors, so hopefully that will help prevent anything like that from happening again."

"It's annoying that the asshole's still out there."

"Yeah, and that we don't know why they did it. They wouldn't have gotten away with much money, just the few hundred that was in the register. It's almost like they just went in there to trash the place."

When Eastern's cell rang in his pocket, he pulled it out. "Speak of the devil." He answered the call but put it on speaker. "Jace."

Air blew over the line. "Hey, big brother!"

"Cody's here too."

Cody leaned forward. "Hey, Jace."

"Ah, I get the pleasure of *two* big brothers. How lucky am I. Any nieces?"

Eastern leaned a shoulder against the wall. "She's inside, probably filling her stomach with sugar before dinner."

"Fuck, I love that kid." Jace laughed. "Just calling to let you know I'm on my way home."

Cody frowned. "Now?"

"Well, when I say I'm on my way, I mean I'm leaving tomorrow but doing a quick trip to Mexico to have some drinks with a few buddies. I might do some ATV riding through the mountains. After *that*, I'll be home."

Sounded like Jace, always the adrenaline junkie. "Need anything from us?"

"Nope, just letting you know to expect my pretty face soon."

"Good. We've missed it." Eastern wasn't even joking. Their youngest brother had always brought a lot of laughter and smiles to the family.

"You still going to work the new skywalk?" Cody asked.

"Yeah, can't wait. It's connected to the visitors center, yeah?"

"It is." Eastern headed toward the back door. "You want to speak to Ave?"

"Fuck yeah, I do."

"Language around her."

"Sorry. Fudge yes, I do."

Eastern rolled his eyes as he stepped inside, his gaze going straight to Avery, who was now wrestling Kayden in the living area. "Hey. Wanna talk to Uncle Jace?"

"Hey, Ave," Jace shouted from the phone, which was still on speaker.

Her eyes flared and she ran toward him. "Yes!"

She grabbed the phone, but before she could run away with it, he grabbed her arm. "Wait." With his thumb, he wiped off a smear of chocolate icing. "There."

"Thanks, Daddy!"

* * *

WARMTH SKITTERED through Sadie's chest at the scene in front of her. Cody and Eastern had just stepped back inside with the tray of barbecued meat. Avery was still talking to her uncle Jace on the phone, while Kayden, Tilly and Harper worked in the kitchen.

She'd offered to help—heck, she'd just about begged—but every time, she'd been told to relax because everything was just about done.

Even though Eastern and his brothers didn't have their parents around anymore, that didn't take away from their family bond. Everyone in this room *felt* like family. They felt connected and protective of one another. You could feel the love.

This…this was what she'd known was missing the morning of her wedding. This was what she'd been craving.

Eastern came to stand beside her, slipping an arm around her waist. "You doing okay, honey?"

She leaned into him. "Yeah, I love your family."

"They love you too."

She looked at him, words on her tongue. Words she'd barely admitted to herself, let alone out loud. Words she wanted to say to him, but it felt too soon.

It *was* too soon, right? To tell someone you were falling in love with them when you'd only really just started dating? But then, she couldn't control how quickly she fell for someone either.

"Oh, sugar!"

Sadie looked up to see Harper frowning. She put her hands to her hips. "We're out of mustard."

"Can we use something else?" Sadie asked.

"I could, but the salad's supposed to have a honey-mustard dressing."

"I'll run out," Tilly said, already moving around the counter.

"I'll come with you," Sadie added.

Eastern frowned. "I can go."

She shook her head. "No. Stay with your family. We won't be long. Enjoy your time with your brothers and keep Avery out of the cupcakes."

His lips twitched before he tugged her against his body. "Don't take long, or I'm coming to find you."

He probably would too. She kissed him before following Tilly out the door. A few minutes later, Sadie was in the passenger seat as Tilly drove Kayden's truck.

"Don't let me crash this thing," she said quietly. "Kayden will kill me."

"Oh yeah, a truck to most men is like a baby."

She laughed. "No, he'll kill me because *I'm* inside. I don't think he'd care much about the truck."

Something kicked in Sadie's belly. Another thing to love about this family—the men were tough, but when it came to the women they loved, they loved *hard*.

If she was falling in love with Eastern, was it possible he was falling for her too? The idea that he wasn't, that she was alone in this, made fear crawl up her throat.

"You and Eastern seem to be doing well," Tilly said, cutting through Sadie's thoughts.

"Yeah, we are. He was hesitant at first, a combination of our age difference, me being so fresh out of a relationship, and my bond with Avery. But then it was like a switch was flipped and since then, he's been a hundred percent in."

Tilly's eyes softened. "Kayden was the same. He was slow to trust in me, *and* us, but I like to think that at some point, he realized he was fighting a losing battle."

"You two are perfect together." Everyone always talked about how hard and grumpy Kayden was, but around Tilly, he was the complete opposite.

"Thank you. And you, Eastern and Avery make such a beautiful family."

A family. The three of them. It was equal parts wonderful and terrifying. Wonderful because she loved them both so much and wanted to be with them, and terrifying because they gave her something to lose.

"I heard her mother's been hanging around." Tilly's fingers visibly tightened on the wheel.

"Yeah, she said she's going to fight for Avery and keeps mentioning lawyers, but so far, Eastern hasn't heard anything. That kind of scares me."

"Why does it scare you?"

Sadie lifted a shoulder. "I guess because she was so insistent on taking action to get Avery back, but now her silence feels almost…"

"Ominous?"

"Yes. That's exactly what it feels like."

Tilly gave her a reassuring smile. "Maybe she's realized it's a fight she's not going to win. I mean, even if she hadn't done everything she's done, Avery has Eastern on her side. Hell, she's got the entire Walker family. That's not a group I'd want to mess with."

Sadie knew that. A normal, sane person wouldn't go up against Eastern and his family. But there'd been something almost wild in Jamie's eyes the last time Sadie had seen her. She could only hope the other woman had found sense and decided Avery was better off with her father.

If she really wanted to be a part of Avery's life, then she should stay in Misty Peak, wait for Avery to feel comfortable seeing her again, then slowly gain back her trust.

When they pulled into the supermarket parking lot, her phone vibrated at the same time as Tilly's. She shook her head at the text.

Eastern: Everything okay?

She looked across at Tilly. "Kayden?"

"I swear, if he wasn't so gorgeous I'd strangle him for being so overprotective."

She chuckled as she climbed out of the truck. She was about to respond when a guy walked out of the supermarket, his gaze finding hers, then Tilly's, and narrowing.

Sadie frowned. Where had she seen him before?

"I hate that guy," Tilly whispered under her breath as they crossed the lot.

"You know him?"

"Mm-hmm. He's a deputy at the station. Questioned me a few months ago after someone set me up for a crime I didn't commit. He was an asshole. I swear he gets his kicks out of making other people's lives hell."

Yeah, he did look a bit like an ass.

She was about to respond to Eastern when she remembered where she'd seen him; he was on duty the night she'd found Denny's body. But that wasn't all—he'd also been in the liquor store talking to Mr. Anderson.

The man who'd referred to him as "Dad."

It was Mr. Anderson's son.

God, she'd been such a mess the night Denny was found, she hadn't made the connection. It probably hadn't helped that the female officer had taken her statement while he'd taken Scott's.

Just before stepping into the shop, she glanced over her shoulder to find him staring straight at them...and the look on his face made unease curl through her belly.

CHAPTER 24

"*I*s this right?"

Sadie peered over Avery's shoulder. She'd picked her up from school an hour ago and brought her back to the bakery to help with cookie prep for the next day. They were working in the front of the shop at the counter while they waited for Eastern to stop by.

"Avery, that is the best-looking cookie dough I have ever seen. Have you been practicing?"

She beamed. "No. But I've been doing *a lot* of dreaming about cookies."

Sadie bit the inside of her cheek to stop the laugh. "Dreaming about cookies would definitely help. I do a bit of dreaming about cookies myself."

Avery continued to knead the dough while Sadie rolled her own dough into balls and placed them onto cookie sheets. In the morning, these would be ready to pop into the oven to bake. Her grandmother had always said chilled cookie dough was the secret to the best cookies. Well, that and plenty of sugar.

"What did you do at school today?" Sadie asked.

"Miss Davies asked us what we wanted to be when we grow up."

"Really? And what did you say?" When Avery was younger, she'd often switched between fairy and mermaid. Sometimes when she couldn't decide, it was a fairy mermaid, which honestly, didn't sound so bad to Sadie.

When the handle at the back door rattled, Sadie frowned. The door was locked, and after a few seconds the noise stopped. She was still looking in that direction when Avery answered.

"I told her I wanted to help run Sugar and Spice and be adopted by my stepmom so that you're my real mom."

Sadie's gaze shot back to Avery, her jaw dropping, heart clenching in her chest.

For a moment, she was speechless, letting the impact of those words settle deep in her chest. Then she crouched in front of Avery. "You know that I've loved you since the day I met you, right? And I don't need a piece of paper to tell me you're my daughter."

Avery's eyes shifted between Sadie's. "But what if you and Daddy break up? Or you decide to move away again?"

"That won't happen. I left for Atlanta because I thought I'd never have access to you again. It was a mistake. I should have stayed close. I won't be making the same mistake twice. And even if something *does* happen between your dad and me, he would never keep us apart. I know that with absolute certainty."

"Good. Because I don't want to lose you."

Sadie pulled her into her arms. "Me neither, baby girl."

The front door *thunked* in its frame, and they both looked up to see Scott trying to push inside, but it was locked.

Goddammit, could the man not take a hint?

She moved around the counter and put her fists on her hips. "Go away."

She had no idea if he could hear her, but he'd understand.

"Sadie…please. I came to say goodbye."

Her brows flickered and she tentatively walked forward and unlocked the door. "What did you say?"

He stepped inside. "I'm going home." He swallowed, his jaw clicking as he looked away. "I've just come to tell you that I'm done fighting for you. I screwed up, and my punishment is that I lose you. I get it. I also told my mother to stop bothering you. I would have left yesterday if I hadn't woken up sick."

She frowned. "You were sick?"

"Yeah, a damn stomach bug or something. I still feel like shit." He rubbed his temple. "Anyway…thought I should say goodbye and apologize for harassing you. For my mother's visits. Hell, even for hanging around your apartment building, hoping to get a glimpse of you."

She pulled back. "You were hanging around my apartment building?"

He scratched the back of his neck. "Yeah, I was an idiot. And trust me, I got a mouthful from that woman who used to live on our floor. She even hit me on the back of the head with her purse, told me to stay away from her daughter like I'm some kind of stalker. Which, okay, I probably looked like." He shook his head. "Anyway…I'm sorry. For everything. I didn't deserve you."

She stepped back, still not liking anything he'd done but relieved that he was leaving. "Good luck with everything, Scott."

"Yeah. Thanks."

He turned to leave but the door opened, and Jamie stepped in. One look at the other woman's bloodshot eyes and angry scowl had Sadie rushing back toward the counter and grabbing Avery.

"Hey…" Scott said to Jamie, sounding unsure. "You okay?"

Without a word, the other woman pulled her hand from behind her back and slammed him in the temple with a gun —hard.

Scott fell to the floor, eyes closed, body still.

Avery cried out, and Sadie tugged the girl behind her.

Jamie slammed the door shut before turning the gun on them. "I'm here for my daughter."

"No." Sadie didn't even pause for a breath. No way in hell.

"Sadie, I've got a gun. And you're going to hand her over right the hell now or I'll shoot you."

Fear tightened her chest, but she pushed it down. "I can't do that, Jamie. I don't know what you intend to do, but I can see you're not well. Have you been drinking?"

"That's none of your fucking business!" she shouted, causing Avery to jump. "She's *mine* and I'm taking her."

"You'll have to shoot me or take me with you then, because those are your only two options."

Avery gasped. "Sadie, no!"

"It's okay, Avery," she whispered. It wasn't, but she wasn't about to admit that to the terrified girl. Jamie had clearly been drinking, but Sadie was still hoping, *praying*, that she was in her right mind enough to remember she wasn't a killer.

Sadie's muscles twitched as she prepared to dive behind the counter.

"I can't fucking shoot you here. Someone will hear and come running," Jamie growled.

That should have made Sadie relieved. It didn't. "So take me with you. Maybe you'll get lucky enough to be rid of me somewhere along the way." Wasn't going to happen. She'd fight tooth and nail to make sure she remained with Avery.

But at the frustrated flare in Jamie's eyes, Sadie knew the woman was realizing it was the best option she had. "Fine. Back door. Now."

Sadie glanced toward the back of the shop. She obviously took too long to move, because Jamie shouted, "I said *now!*"

Sadie was careful to keep her voice gentle. "Come on, Avery."

Keeping herself positioned between Avery and the gun, Sadie stepped into the back room. She had one eye on Avery but kept looking behind her, making sure Jamie didn't get too close. Even though she didn't seem to want to shoot anyone in the store, she obviously had no problem hurting people.

Was Scott okay? He'd been bleeding, and he needed help. Would help find him in time? Eastern was stopping by—he shouldn't be far off.

She was halfway to the door when Jamie spoke.

"Stop. I'll go first. I don't trust you as far I can throw you."

Sadie tugged Avery behind her as Jamie passed them to unlock the door. Once it was open, Jamie remained where she was, holding the door in place. "Out. Try anything and I'll put you on the ground like Scott."

Sadie inched forward, keeping as much space between her and Jamie as possible as they stepped into the alley. A beat-up blue Honda sat parked by the dumpster.

The rattling of the doorknob... Jamie had tried to get in through the back.

Jamie nodded toward the car. "Get in the back."

Sadie turned to face the woman. "Jamie, you can't ask Avery to get in this car with you. You can barely stand, let alone drive."

As if proving her point, Jamie swayed before rapidly blinking. "Sadie, I'm one step away from saying to hell with it and shooting you right here and now. *Don't* push me. Get. In. The. Car."

Sadie swallowed, hating what they were about to do, but what choice did she have?

"It's okay, Sadie." Avery's small voice had her looking down. "I'll be okay."

Avery was about to climb in when Jamie's voice stopped her.

"*No.* I want *Sadie* behind the passenger seat." She looked at Sadie. "I'm not taking any chances with you behind me."

With gritted teeth, Sadie climbed in first, shifting to the far side of the backseat and helping Avery into the middle. She made sure her seat belt was firmly on before latching her own.

Jamie slid behind the wheel and started the engine. Before putting the car in drive, she massaged her temple. How much had the woman drunk? She looked about ready to pass out, and now she was going to drive her daughter somewhere?

Sadie's jaw dropped when Jamie lifted a bottle of bourbon and took a big drink. Jesus, this woman was insane!

As the car began to move, Sadie's heart pounded, and she curved an arm around Avery's shoulders, wishing she could do more to protect her. She didn't care about herself, just that she kept Avery safe.

Jamie pulled onto the main road, but her turn was wide, the tires squealing when she tried to correct herself. Her gun sat on her lap, her fingers wrapped around the grip.

Maybe they'd get lucky and someone would report Jamie for reckless driving. Sadie just had to hope that if a deputy *did* try to pull her over, she didn't do anything crazy like speed off. God, even the thought made Sadie feel sick.

Avery's chest began to heave with her rapid breaths, the smallest tremble shaking her limbs.

Sadie lowered her head and kept her voice quiet as she whispered, "It'll be okay, baby girl. You'll be okay." She didn't care that she had no right to promise Avery anything. Right now, she just needed to ease her fear.

"Stop whispering!" Jamie shouted.

Sadie looked at the other woman, anger spewing through her veins like lava. "Why are you doing this? I thought you were hiring a lawyer."

Jamie laughed but the sound was almost manic. "I tried. All the ones I could afford wouldn't represent me. Took one look at those fucking claims Eastern and the school made against me, saw he was a veteran and the town sheriff, and they turned me down."

"So this is your solution?" Sadie asked. "To get drunk and take her at gunpoint?"

That wasn't love. None of what Jamie did to her daughter was love.

"What other choice do I have?"

Was she serious? "Your choice was to do better. To make amends for past mistakes. To stay in town and be the best person you could be. To earn back everyone's trust."

Jamie's hand on the wheel visibly tightened. "Always so fucking moral, aren't you, Sadie? I used to like that about you… until I realized it made my kid love *you* more than me."

That wasn't why Avery loved her more, and Jamie knew it. "Where are you taking us?"

"I don't know. Somewhere I can get rid of you quietly and take Avery with me."

Avery's fingers wrapped around Sadie's leg, and she inched closer. Sadie placed her hand on top of Avery's and stroked her skin, hoping the gesture offered her some small semblance of calm.

Her phone vibrated in her pocket.

God, her phone! How had she forgotten about it?

Slowly, she reached into her back pocket and tugged it out, trying not to lift her hips too much so Jamie didn't notice what she was doing. Once it was out, she kept it between her thigh and the door, raising her leg slightly to keep it hidden from Jamie.

Eastern. He'd tried to call.

Quickly, she unlocked her phone and called him, switching it to silent. She waited until he answered before she spoke.

"Jamie, you can't just take me and Avery at gunpoint in a blue Honda and drive us to God knows where."

"I can do whatever the hell I want," Jamie growled.

"Stop here at the library and let us out. No one has to know."

She needed to give Eastern an idea of where they were.

"No!"

Jamie took the next right too sharply, causing Sadie to fall into the door and the phone to drop from her hold. It thudded on the floor, and Jamie's gaze twisted back at her. "What the fuck are you doing?"

Suddenly, the car swerved as Jamie pulled into a deserted parking lot behind a large building. Sadie tightened her hold on Avery.

"Give me the phone or I shoot her in the fucking leg," Jamie shouted once the car was at a complete stop.

Surely, she wouldn't shoot her own daughter. "Jamie—"

She turned the gun toward Avery, and Sadie quickly reached for the cell and handed it to her. She hung up the call and threw the cell to the floor of the back of the car.

"Good. Now get out." The gun swung to Sadie. "*Now!*"

"Only if Avery gets out with me."

"*No!*" Jamie's eyes fluttered, and she touched her head like she was in pain. "Don't fuck with me right now, Sadie. I'm right on the edge."

Sadie sucked in a long breath before unbuckling her seat belt. As she did, Jamie reached for the bourbon again to take another slug.

Sadie used her preoccupation to her advantage, leaning down and tugging Avery into a hug while discreetly unclipping her seat belt. Then she whispered into her ear, "Be brave, baby girl…and run."

Jamie was just recapping the bourbon when Avery opened her door and slipped out.

The bottle fell from Jamie's fingers. "Hey!" She jumped out of the car, but so did Sadie. Then she lunged at Jamie's legs, tackling her to the ground.

* * *

EASTERN PULLED over in front of Sugar and Spice. He was ready for this day to be over. Past ready. Jarrad had been a fucking ass all day, making snide comments about paperwork and the job load to the point Eastern didn't even want to hear his voice, let alone see his face.

He climbed out of his car, frowning when he didn't see Sadie or Avery in the window. Sadie had said they were making dough in the front room and watching out for him. They must've moved to the kitchen.

He stepped up to the door and tried the handle...unlocked. The second he stepped inside, he saw it.

A man lay on the floor, blood seeping from his head.

The *fuck?*

Eastern dropped down beside him. That's when he realized it was Scott. He checked his pulse, finding the sluggish thuds. He lifted his radio. "I need an ambulance to Sugar and Spice *now*. I have an unconscious man in his mid-twenties with a head injury."

The words had just left his mouth when Scott's eyes scrunched tight, and he groaned.

"Jesus, my head..." He reached to touch his temple before opening his eyes. "Eastern?"

"Scott. What happened?"

"I—" He glanced around the shop. "I came to say goodbye to Sadie, then..."

"Then what?" Fear churned through Eastern's gut. Fear that Sadie and Avery weren't here. He already knew they couldn't be. Because there was no way they'd leave Scott like this.

"A woman..." he finally said. "She came in just when I was about to leave. I asked if she was okay because her eyes were red, and she...she hit me. With a gun."

The fear thickened, fogging his head and turning his world from bright colors to deep, dark shades of gray.

He grabbed his phone and tried Sadie's number.

It rang once. Then a second time.

Come on, Sadie. Answer. Answer the damn phone and tell me you're both okay.

She didn't answer. The call went to voicemail. *Fuck.*

He was about to call his team at the station when her call came through. Thank God.

"Sadie?"

"Jamie, you can't just take me and Avery at gunpoint in a blue Honda and drive us to God knows where."

His blood ran cold. Jamie had Sadie and Avery.

"I can do whatever the hell I want," Jamie growled.

"Stop here at the library and let us out. No one has to know."

"No!"

There was the sound of squealing tires, then a thud before Jamie spoke again. "What the fuck are you doing?"

Avery's scream almost had his knees caving.

"Give me the phone or I shoot her in the fucking leg," Jamie shouted.

"Jamie—"

There was a gasp, then the phone went dead.

CHAPTER 25

*A*very's heart pounded loud and hard in her chest. It felt like when she woke up from a bad dream, and Daddy came into her room to tell her everything would be okay. Only Daddy wasn't here to help her this time. She didn't know where he was, but it was her job to find him.

Her feet pounded the pavement as fast as she could go and her chest hurt. But she couldn't slow down. Sadie was in trouble.

She'd swiped Sadie's phone from the floor before jumping out of the car. If she didn't call for help, her mom would hurt Sadie!

Panic and fear bubbled up her throat, but she swallowed them down. Sadie was brave, and she needed to be brave too.

When she rounded the building, she noticed a few people on the street. She wanted to run straight for them. Beg for help. But what if they *did* help—and her mom shot them? Would that be her fault?

Her bottom lip started to tremble. She bit it to keep it still.

She needed to call Daddy. He saved people every day.

Her fingers trembled as she started to type in the password on Sadie's phone. It was Avery's birthday. The day Sadie told her the code, Avery had giggled and stolen the phone a dozen times, just locking and unlocking it. Then they'd made pasta and cupcakes and fallen asleep on the couch.

She wished she could go back to that day. Back to feeling safe. To knowing *Sadie* was safe.

She tried to type in the digits to unlock the phone, but her fingers trembled so badly she kept pressing one instead of two. On the third try, tears spilled from her eyes. Tears of panic. Of guilt. Tears she couldn't stop. Sadie was counting on her, and every second that passed was another second her mother had to hurt her.

"Avery?"

Her head lifted at the soft, familiar voice.

Elle knelt in front of her, concern in her eyes. "Hey, honey, are you okay?"

She shook her head, another tear rolling down her cheek.

Elle swiped it away. "Tell me what's wrong, and I'll figure out how we can fix it."

"Mom…" A hiccup cut off her words, and her chest felt too tight to speak.

"Hey. It's okay. I'm here. Take a big breath and let the words out."

Elle stroked her back. It reminded her of the way Sadie stroked her back when she was sad. Sadie's words whispered back into her head.

Be brave, baby girl.

She straightened her spine, forcing the words out. "My mom has a gun and she forced me and Sadie into her car."

Elle's eyes widened.

"I need to call Daddy," she continued. "But I can't…my fingers won't…"

"Shh. It's okay." Elle continued to stroke her back, and it was the only thing that stopped more tears from falling. "I'm here. I'll help you call him."

She nodded, and this time when she put in the code, the

phone unlocked. She didn't need to search for her father's number, she knew it by heart. He'd made her memorize it years ago.

She typed in the numbers and pressed call. The phone barely rang before she heard her father's worried voice.

"Sadie?"

* * *

EASTERN'S FINGERS moved quickly on the keypad. He had his entire damn team of officers scouring the streets. Finding any business surveillance or street cameras that might help them locate Sadie and Avery. They'd already searched the library and surrounding streets, they weren't there, dammit.

It didn't feel like enough…any of it.

The door opened and Paxley stepped in, lips pressed into a thin line.

It was bad news. *Dammit.*

"Tell me," he growled.

"Jamie ran through a red light not far from the alley behind Sugar and Spice. The photo clearly shows her face, so we have her license plate."

"But?" He knew what was coming next, but he needed her to say it.

"But since then, there hasn't been a sighting. We still have officers on the street. It won't help though, if…"

"If they've already left town." *Christ.* He wanted to throw his damn fist into a wall.

He rose from the desk and pressed his hands to his head. He couldn't do this. He couldn't lose them. Sadie and Avery were his entire world.

He grabbed his keys.

"Eastern—"

"I'm going out to look for them, Paxley."

197

"I'll come with you."

He'd just stepped into the foyer when his phone rang. Every muscle in his body locked at the name on the screen. He answered it quickly.

"Sadie?"

Wind blew over the line. "Daddy?"

His throat closed at his daughter's voice. "I'm here, princess. Where are you?"

"Mom took me! Sadie forced her to take her too but now she's in trouble. Mom's sick and she has a gun and I think she's going to hurt Sadie!" Every word ran into the next, fear alive in her voice.

"Avery, it's okay. I'm coming. Do you know where you are?"

There was a beat of silence, then a shuffling sound before a new voice came over the line.

"Eastern, it's Elle. I found Avery on the street."

Thank God his daughter wasn't alone. "Where are you?"

"We're on Pepper Ave. I think Avery came around the municipal building. It's closed, so they might be in the parking lot behind the building. Do you want me to check—"

"*No.*" Eastern was running now. He slid into his car and Paxley dropped into the passenger seat. "I want you to take Avery away from there. Protect her. Can you do that?"

"Yes. Of course. But what about Sadie?"

"I'm only a couple minutes away. I *will* get there in time."

He had no right to promise that, but fuck, he needed it to be true.

* * *

"You *bitch*!"

Sadie ignored Jamie's screaming. She didn't think about the fear in her chest or the pounding of her heart…every part of her focused on keeping Jamie's wrists in her hold and above her head, the gun as far away from her as possible. She couldn't let go. The second she did, Jamie would shoot and she'd shoot to kill.

Sweat beaded Jamie's forehead as she threw an elbow into Sadie's cheek. Pain blasted through her skull, stunning her. Jamie took advantage, and in one fluid move, she spun them around and pressed her other arm to Sadie's throat, choking her.

Sadie tried to suck in air while never taking her hands off Jamie's wrist.

"I'm going to fucking kill you," Jamie growled.

Sadie was growing lightheaded when the arm at her throat suddenly loosened. She took advantage, shoving the woman off her and slamming her wrist to the asphalt.

The gun fell to the ground. Sadie climbed to her hands and knees and was crawling toward it when a wave of dizziness caused her arms to give way. She sucked in a large, deep breath. When her vision cleared, she lunged for the gun—but Jamie was faster, grabbing the weapon and stumbling to her feet before taking a few swaying steps back.

Sadie's world slowed as she pushed herself up, grabbing the car to steady herself.

"This is *your* fault," Jamie gasped. "All of it! If it wasn't for *you*, she might have taken me back." She blinked three times and held one arm out to her side, as if trying to keep her balance.

Despite the fear knotting her belly, Sadie shook her head. She couldn't stay silent. "No, Jamie. None of this is my fault. All I did was love your daughter, something any other mother would be grateful for. At some point, you need to accept responsibility for what you've done."

"I messed up. I *know* I messed up! But how was I supposed to get her back with you around? The *perfect* mother figure. The woman who could do no wrong."

There were so many things Sadie could say in response to that, but would she listen? Probably not.

"If you kill me," Sadie tried slowly, "she'll hate you. It will destroy any chance you might have with her in the future."

Jamie's eyes half rolled again, and she swayed even harder on her feet.

"You're not well," Sadie said quietly. "Put the gun down and we can call an ambulance."

"I'm *fine*. I don't—" She tilted drunkenly to the side.

Sadie stepped forward in case the gun dropped, but Jamie righted herself quickly, taking aim at her again.

A car suddenly swerved into the parking lot, tires squealing before it came to a stop.

Sadie's chest tightened at the sight of Eastern. He got out of the driver's seat, a deputy climbing out from the other side.

He pointed his weapon at Jamie. "Put the gun down, Jamie."

A mixture of fear and anger and frustration cut across Jamie's face. "I can't. I need her gone."

"You don't," he pushed. "Killing her will only make things worse for you. Put down the gun."

She wobbled again, her eyes doing another of those odd rolls before she blinked half a dozen times. "I just…I've made so many mistakes. I got depressed and I thought leaving would help. Then when I came back…everything was different…"

She stumbled back a step, and Sadie's throat closed—because that pistol was still pointed at her.

"Jamie," Eastern growled. "Put down the gun." The words were said slowly, as if Jamie wouldn't understand otherwise.

"I think—" Another stumble. "I think I'm done."

Her eyes rolled, and as she fell, the gun went off.

Sadie dropped to the ground, barely hearing Eastern shout her name.

CHAPTER 26

"It's a graze, Eastern."

Eastern's hands fisted as he stood beside Sadie. She sat on the hospital bed, shirt off and bandage wrapped around her middle. The doctor had just left, and *finally* it was just the two of them. "You were *shot*."

"It could have been worse."

Oh, he knew it could have been worse. So much fucking worse that he wouldn't sleep for the next month. Hell, year. "You shouldn't have been hurt at all."

She grabbed his arm and tugged him in front of her so he stood between her thighs. "Hey. Look at me."

He did. His gaze seared into her black eyes as he tried to force down the fear that simmered in his chest. She was here. Alive. *That's* what he needed to focus on.

"I'm okay," she whispered, cupping his cheek. "And so is Avery."

"I came too close to losing you both today."

"But you didn't. We're both okay."

He lowered his temple to hers, letting the warmth of her skin slip inside him and thaw some of the ice that had built from the moment he'd discovered them missing. "Thank you for protecting her."

"You don't need to thank me for that. I love her, and I will *always* protect her."

Hearing those words did something to him that nothing and no one else did. He opened his mouth, wanting—no *needing*—to tell her that he loved her. That she'd taken up a part of his heart that had forever been empty.

But before a single word could come out, the door opened and Avery burst inside.

"Sadie! You're okay!" His daughter ground to a halt in front of the bed, her bottom lip disappearing between her teeth as fresh tears glistened in her eyes. "You're hurt?"

"It's just a scratch." When Avery didn't move, Sadie held out her arms. "Can I have a hug? I think that's just what I need to help me feel better."

Avery nodded quickly, and Eastern lifted her onto the bed. Immediately, the two fell into each other's arms.

A soft knock sounded at the door. He moved over to it, expecting to find Kayden. Elle had taken Avery to his place to be with Kayden and Tilly, so he knew they had to be in the building, now that his daughter was here.

Kayden and Tilly *were* in the hall, but they stood on the far side. It was Paxley who'd knocked.

He dipped his head toward his brother before looking at his deputy. "Everything okay?"

Instead of answering his question, she nodded toward the hall, indicating she wanted to speak to him in private.

He turned to look at Sadie and Avery one more time, seeing that they were still in an embrace, before stepping out. "What is it?"

"Jamie's not doing too good. They're having trouble keeping her conscious and think she might have actually lost her eyesight."

His brows slashed together. "What are you talking about? She passed out because she was drunk, right?"

"Tests showed the presence of methanol in her blood."

What the fuck? "Methanol poisoning?"

"Yep. Doctors are doing what they can, but it's touch and go right now."

"How the hell would this have happened?"

"She was an alcoholic, right? So my thoughts are, she either made her own cheap alcohol and poisoned herself, or someone sold it to her."

Eastern ran his hand over his jaw. "We need to search her car and wherever she's been staying. Test anything you find. We also need copies of her bank statements to see where she bought her last bottle."

He just had to hope like hell she paid with a card and not cash. There were two liquor stores in Misty Peak, but there were also a number of stores in the surrounding towns…endless options. Not to mention, she might have arrived in town with her own stash. But that option was less likely, because he doubted anything she came with would have lasted that long.

Paxley nodded. "On it."

She started to turn, but Eastern grabbed her arm and lowered his voice. "And Paxley…I want a copy of Denny Barclay's coroner's report."

She frowned. "Denny Barclay?"

He inched closer. "Both Denny and Jamie were alcoholics, and these incidences have occurred in really close succession. I don't believe in coincidences."

Still frowning, she nodded. "Okay. I'll get it."

"This stays between us, okay? I don't want anyone else to know—including any other deputies at the station."

Out of all his deputies, he trusted Paxley the most. Call it gut instinct.

"You got it, Eastern. Stays between us."

He watched as she turned and moved down the hall.

Kayden walked up to him. "Hey, how are you doing?"

"Sadie got shot tonight."

His brother's brows knitted together. "But she's okay, right? You said it was a graze."

"Yeah, she's okay."

"What can we do?" Tilly asked as she came to stand beside Kayden.

"Nothing. You've done enough. Thank you for watching Avery. I'm going to take Sadie and Avery home." He needed both of them as close as possible right now.

Kayden nodded. "Of course. Call if you need anything."

What he needed was answers as to what the hell was going on with this town, and for the people he loved to be safe.

* * *

SADIE BREATHED AVERY IN. Even though the sounds of the hospital were loud around her, Avery was all she could focus on. Holding her after what they'd been through today was exactly what she needed. It finally allowed that tightness in her chest to loosen, and the pieces of her that had been torn apart this afternoon began to slot back together.

She almost wanted to cry. To never let go of this sweet child, who deserved so much more in the way of a mother.

"It's my fault."

Sadie frowned, and she pulled back to look at Avery. "What are you talking about?"

Avery sniffed. "It's my fault you got hurt. You made my mom take you to protect me."

"That doesn't make what happened to me your fault." She shifted some hair from Avery's face. "Avery, you didn't ask for your mother to do that. You didn't ask for any of this. And more than that, you didn't deserve it."

"But if you hadn't come with me—"

"I was *always* going to come with you. Always. Do you understand? There was never any other option. And that was *my* choice. I would do it again and again. Because I love you, and it is my *job* to protect you."

Her frown deepened. "So you're okay?"

"No. I'm so much better than okay, because you're safe. And that is everything."

Avery threw her arms around Sadie again. "I love you so much!"

"I love you too, baby girl."

This time, they didn't let go of each other. It almost felt like they couldn't. Not until the door opened and Eastern stepped back in. She frowned at the expression on his face. He'd looked angry all night, but right now there was something else in his eyes. Something more…dangerous.

Before she could say anything, his expression changed as he took them in. Softened. "Can I get in on that hug?"

Avery pulled away and grinned before throwing her arms around Eastern. He seemed to breathe her in just like Sadie had.

"You have no idea how good it is to hold you," he said quietly, before slipping an arm around Sadie too. "Both of you."

She leaned into them. Her family. Not by blood but in every other way. When the doctor stepped back into the room, she almost wanted to groan at the thought of letting them go.

Over the next fifteen minutes, the doctor took them through how to care for her wound before discharging Sadie. Avery fell asleep the second Eastern got them in the car.

Sadie looked over at Eastern, finally asking the question that had been on her mind since he'd stepped back into her room from the hall. "How's Jamie?"

Because this had to be about her, right? The worst-case scenario Sadie could think of was that the woman had snuck out of the hospital and now they were on a manhunt to find her. Her skin tingled in fear. God, Avery wouldn't be safe until she was found.

His brows flickered, his gaze shifting to the rearview mirror, no doubt to Avery, before returning to the road. He set a hand on her thigh. "I think it's a conversation for another time. You've been through enough for one day. You and Ave are safe. I'll tell you tomorrow. Right now, I need you to focus on healing."

"Eastern, I told you, it's just a—"

"Graze. I know. Humor me. Rest. Let me take care of everything else."

She set her hand over his and leaned her head back. She *was* safe. And so was Avery. And they were together. That was everything.

CHAPTER 27

Sadie rolled from her back to her side, a small ache from her wound making her eyes scrunch. She reached out to the other side of the bed, searching for Eastern, but all she found was cold sheets.

Her eyes popped open to see morning light slipping through the crack in the curtains, and just as she suspected, the bed beside her was empty.

Frowning, she glanced around the room.

Also empty. He wasn't there.

She was just pushing up into a sitting position when the door opened and Eastern stepped in. His gaze immediately ran over her face, then her body, even the parts of her that were covered by the sheets, obviously seeking confirmation that she was okay.

He didn't quite close the door all the way before joining her and sitting on the edge of the bed. "Hey. How are you feeling?"

"A little achy, but not too bad."

He growled low in his throat before handing her the glass of water and two small pills that were in his hands. "Pain meds."

She slipped the glass from his fingers and swallowed the pills with water, her eyes barely leaving him. "Have you been up for long?"

"Yeah, I couldn't sleep. I stayed with you for a bit, then went to watch Avery."

Her heart contracted at the pain in his voice. "She's okay?"

"Slept straight through."

"Are *you* okay?"

His brows flickered, giving him away before he answered. "I was so damn scared."

Her heart gave another tug, and she leaned into his chest, wrapping her arms around his middle. "She's okay, Eastern."

"And so are you. Thank God."

He nuzzled her hair, and she wanted to drown in all that was Eastern. In his warmth and strength. In the crisp scent that was all his.

"I love you, Sadie."

Her breath caught, and it took a moment for her to move. For the words to replay in her mind a couple of times and her head to leave his chest. "You love me?"

"I love you so much that when I couldn't reach you and Avery, it felt like the floor had been ripped from beneath me. Like my very foundation had crumbled." Tears filled her eyes as he cupped her cheek. "I love you, Sadie Sandler. You don't have to say it back right now—"

"I do," she whispered. "I love you. I recklessly fell for you a long time ago. I love so many things about you...the way you see me. The way you love and protect those around you. The way you raise your daughter. But I also love you for a million reasons I can't even begin to explain."

He swiped her cheek with her thumb, blue eyes so intense they reminded her of the ocean. "Really?"

"Yes."

His lips crashed to hers, and she felt all the things she'd been searching for since returning to Misty Peak. Love and safety and a complete abandonment of every fear and frustration. In his kiss, she found everything she'd been missing in all her years with Scott.

She ran her hands over his chest, wanting to pause this moment and get lost in it. To bind herself to the man she loved.

It was only the soft sound of footsteps down the hall that had her pausing. Sadie pulled back from Eastern, a grin on her face, as Avery bound into the room. Her smile was wide as she leapt onto the bed and threw her arms around both of them.

"Whoa, princess, careful of Sadie."

Avery's smile dimmed, and Sadie was quick to shake her head. "No. I'm completely fine. I *love* big cuddles." Then, to prove her point, she tugged Avery back into her arms so tightly that she screeched.

"How did you sleep?" Sadie asked.

"Good. I dreamed of chocolate chip pancakes with maple syrup."

Sadie laughed while Eastern gave her a skeptical frown. "Is that your way of asking for pancakes for breakfast?"

"Yes! With chocolate chips and maple syrup. You *did* say that today could be a special day of staying home and being together. Special days always involve pancakes."

Sadie nodded. "She's right, they do."

"Oh, and there was ice cream in my dream," Avery added. "Strawberry and caramel and chocolate ice cream."

Sadie's lips twitched. Who needed painkillers when you had this kid to distract you?

"Really?" Eastern asked, more skepticism in his voice now. "Anything else?"

Avery's little nose wrinkled. "Milkshakes. Definitely milkshakes."

"That's it!" Eastern grabbed Avery around the middle and tossed her onto the bed before tickling her sides and tummy.

Avery's laughter filled the room, and suddenly everything

about this moment, about this entire morning, healed any part of Sadie that still felt pain or fear from last night.

* * *

TODAY WAS everything yesterday hadn't been. The three of them stayed home from work and school and spent the day together, making pancakes, going for a walk, playing outside, and now they were making hot cocoas before they watched *Encanto*, one of Avery's favorites.

Even though they'd had a great day, Eastern could tell his daughter was exhausted. The kid would probably fall asleep before the movie was half over.

He wanted more days like this. Slow days where they just did nothing but spend time together. After yesterday, it was what they all needed.

He knew tomorrow he'd have to go back to work. Hell, even now he was waiting for the call from Paxley about Denny's autopsy report. He hadn't told Sadie about that yet. He didn't want to. He wanted to remain in this bubble of theirs for as long as possible. But she'd ask again, and when she did, he wasn't going to put her off again.

He stepped into the kitchen and moved behind Sadie to nip her neck.

She gasped. "Eastern. You're going to make me burn the cocoa."

"It'd be worth it." He trailed kisses up her neck.

"Avery will be back any second," she whispered.

She'd gone to her bedroom to change into pajamas, and yeah, she'd be back any second. "I don't care. She knows I love you."

"Does she?"

"I think everyone knew except you."

Sadie turned, her eyes boring into him. "Say it again."

"Everyone knew except you?"

She shook her head and wrapped her arms around his neck. "No. The other part."

"I love you." He'd say it a thousand times if she asked.

She stretched up, her mouth hovering a mere inch from his. "I love you too, Eastern Walker."

Their lips had just touched when her phone rang.

He growled. "Ignore it."

She chuckled before checking the screen and sighing. "I can't. It's the bakery." She clicked a key on her cell before pressing it to her ear. "Hello."

Eastern lowered his head and began to feast on her neck. Her skin was so soft, he never wanted to lift his mouth.

"Oh, okay." Sadie paused. "No, no, don't call my grandmother. I'll be down in a second."

His body locked. She was leaving?

"Okay, see you then."

He straightened, his words coming out slowly. "What's going on?"

"Marjory went home sick, and Anna only realized Marjory had the key after she'd left. They could call my grandmother, but she'll be at book club this afternoon and I don't want to bother her. I need to go down there and lock up."

"I'll come with you."

She was shaking her head before he'd finished speaking. "No. Avery's tired and we promised her a movie. Plus, she's probably already in her pajamas. I'll be back in ten minutes."

"Sadie—"

"I'm ready!" Avery ran back into the living room and dropped onto the couch. She wore her favorite pink pajama set and had a big, excited smile on her face.

"See," Sadie whispered, leaning forward and lowering her voice. "Start the movie but save me some hot cocoa."

He didn't like it. "You go inside, lock up with Anna, and leave together. Got it?"

"Well, I wasn't planning on having a solo party in the shop." She grinned as she kissed him.

After a quick goodbye to Avery, Sadie left, and Eastern joined his daughter on the couch, hot cocoas in hand.

As they searched for the movie, Avery's brow wrinkled, something she always did when she was thinking about something she wanted to say. He didn't push her, knowing the question would come when she was ready.

"Daddy?"

He smiled. "Yeah, princess?"

"Do you think Mom will be back for me?"

"No." His answer was instant, but it wasn't a lie. Even if Jamie made a full recovery, she'd be tried for kidnapping and a few other things. Jail time was certain, and after what she'd done, no judge in the country would give her custody. "You're safe with me and Sadie."

The relief in her eyes felt like a sucker punch to his gut.

He grazed her shoulder. "I'm sorry about your mom." He wasn't sorry about what happened to Jamie—that was on her—just that she wasn't the mother Avery deserved.

She shrugged. "I don't really see her as my mom, anyway."

"You don't?"

"No. Sadie's always been more of a mom to me than her. And I love that you two love each other, and we can be a family."

"I love that too." He wrapped an arm around Avery's shoulders and kissed her head. "And I love you, kid."

"I love you too, Daddy."

The movie was just starting when he glanced out the window, already counting down the minutes until Sadie got back.

CHAPTER 28

Sadie parked out front of Sugar and Spice. Her heart was so full that she couldn't wipe the smile from her face. Eastern loved her. Then, after *that* life-changing news, they'd spent the day as a family.

Images of the two of them waiting for her on the couch with hot cocoas made her heart beat just that bit faster. She was happy. So unbelievably happy that she almost didn't want to blink in case it wasn't real.

She climbed out of her car, noticing the closed sign on the door of the Misty Peak Liquor Store.

Strange. They were usually open until late. But whatever they did or didn't do was none of her business.

When she stepped inside Sugar and Spice, Anna glanced up from behind the counter. "Thank you so much for coming in. I'm so sorry to ask. We were quiet when Marjory went home, and neither of us were thinking about a key to lock up."

Anna was a newer staff member, and only the more senior staff had keys. "It's totally fine. I'm glad you called me and not my grandmother."

"She was in all morning, but she had to leave in a hurry around lunchtime. Do you know if everything's okay with her?"

Sadie cringed. Her departure was probably because she'd received the voicemail from Sadie, asking her to call. She hadn't wanted to tell her grandmother about the previous night because, of course, she'd worry…but she knew she had to.

"I spoke to her this afternoon. She's okay." She wasn't ready to share what had happened with the other employees. Thanks to town gossip, they'd find out about Avery's crazy alcoholic mother soon enough.

She scanned the clean store. "Looks like you're all done."

"Yep. We were quiet." Anna's phone rang and she glanced down at it, frowning. "Oh, it's my sitter for my daughter."

"Take it."

Anna answered the phone, her frown deepening. "Okay. Yes, I'll be home soon." She hung up and lifted her bag. "My daughter's sick. Is it okay if I—"

"Oh my gosh, yes, go. I'll lock up."

"Thanks, Sadie."

As Anna left, Sadie walked around the counter, checking that everything was as it should be. It wasn't until she reached the kitchen in the back that she noticed the bag in the trash was sealed but hadn't been taken out.

She grabbed it and opened the back door, then moved into the alley.

"You said you'd fix it!"

Sadie paused at the shouted voices. Turning her head, she noticed the screen door for the liquor store was closed, but the back door was open.

"Don't fucking shout at me, kid! If it wasn't for me, you wouldn't have *half* of what you do."

Was that Mr. Anderson? *Jesus.* He was often angry, but this sounded different.

Walking quickly, she dropped the bag of trash into the dumpster.

"I risked my *job* to pay off that fucking coroner to call it a brain aneurysm, and now someone else is in the hospital. She almost *died*! Hell, her life is *still* at risk. How am I supposed to cover up this one?"

Sadie stopped, her heart hammering against her ribs. Brain aneurysm? They were talking about Denny Barclay, right? They'd paid off the coroner? Why?

"All you had to do was take the bad shit off the shelves so no one else got hurt," the guy continued. "Was that so fucking hard?"

"This shop is full of that shit. You wanted me to just empty the shelves?" Mr. Anderson yelled.

"*Yes*! If that saved us from getting in trouble!"

Ice filled Sadie's veins, and for a moment, she couldn't move. She could barely breathe. Had they had a hand in Denny Barclay's death, then covered it up?

When the voices quieted, she forced her feet to move. She'd just wrapped her fingers around the handle to Sugar and Spice when the screen door of the liquor store opened.

"Where are you going?" Mr. Anderson boomed.

"Where do you think? To clean up your fucking mess."

Jarrad stepped into the alley—and his gaze immediately clashed with Sadie's.

Shit.

Pretend everything's fine, Sadie. Pretend you didn't just hear a confession.

She forced a small smile to her lips. A smile that took all her strength to form. Then she stepped inside the shop. Her hands trembled so badly that it took a couple tries to flip the lock.

Calm down, Sadie. Just get out of here and go to Eastern.

She repeated those words a couple times in her head before taking a deep breath and switching off the lights. In the front of the store, she grabbed her stuff and reached into her bag for her phone on the way to the door. Eastern only lived five minutes away, but even that felt too long. She needed to speak to him now, tell him exactly what she'd heard.

She was almost to the door when it opened and Jarrad stepped inside.

Fear skittered down her spine, not just at his presence but at the scowl on his face. The way he completely blocked her exit. Still, she forced her expression to remain neutral. "Hi. Sorry. We're all closed up for the day, and everything's been put away."

Good. That was good. Her voice didn't shake, and she sounded completely normal. Well, maybe not completely normal, but as normal as she was going to get.

The door closed behind him, and he shoved his hand into his pocket. "You know, sticking your nose into other people's business is rarely a good idea."

Her mouth suddenly felt dry and sticky, and it took a few tries to get words out. "I don't know what you're—"

"Don't lie to me." He pulled out his phone. "After you took it upon yourself all those other times to listen in on our business, we installed hidden cameras behind the shop."

He touched the screen and turned his cell toward her. There, on the phone, was her stopping in the alley, gaze on the liquor store door and fear in her eyes.

She took a quick step back, fingers tightening around the strap of her bag. "I heard something about emptying the shelves, that's it."

"You little liar." He moved forward, eating up too much of the space between them. "We trashed your shop, a little incentive to keep you the hell away, but you didn't take the hint, did you?"

Another step forward—and Sadie reacted on instinct, swinging her bag and hitting him hard in the side of the head. She followed that up with a kick to the balls.

Jarrad growled and hunched over, grabbing himself as she raced around him. She opened the door to run out, but Mr.

Anderson was there, and before she could fully comprehend what was happening, his fist swung toward her face, sending her world into darkness.

* * *

EASTERN GLANCED at the time on the phone, then back to the street through the window. It had been half an hour. Where was she?

He quickly typed out a text on his phone to Sadie.

Eastern: Hey! You almost home? I'm getting worried.

He stared at his phone, waiting. She always texted back right away. Hell, the three dots usually appeared the second he hit send.

There were no dots and no reply.

He looked down at Avery. "I'm just going to call Sadie."

His daughter glanced up, a frown between her brows. "Is she okay?"

"I'm sure she's fine. I'm just being my usual overprotective self."

She grinned at him. "Tell her to hurry back before she misses Luisa singing 'Surface Pressure.' It's her favorite part."

"Can't have her missing her favorite part." He pressed a kiss to Avery's head before rising and trying her number. It rang...then it rang some more. When it eventually went to voicemail, Eastern's skin felt too fucking tight. She never missed a call.

Quickly, he called his brother. Cody would be working at the bar, but Kayden may have finished at the visitors center.

Kayden answered on the first ring. "Hey, Eastern, everything okay?"

"Any chance you're free to come over and watch Avery for me?"

"Now? Sure. Tilly and I are just heading home. We can be there in five. Everything okay?"

"I'm not sure. Sadie went to Sugar and Spice to lock up, but she's been gone too long and isn't responding to texts or answering my calls."

There was a short pause. "But Jamie's still in the hospital, right?"

"Yeah, I just…I need to check on her."

"Got it. Four minutes."

Eastern had just hung up when his phone rang, Paxley's name showing up on his screen. "Paxley. You find anything?"

"Actually, I did. We found a bottle of bourbon and a receipt from the Misty Peak Liquor Store in her car. She'd purchased them yesterday morning. We've had the last drops of bourbon in the bottle tested, and it's positive for methanol."

Fire burned in Eastern's veins. "So Anderson's been selling homemade alcohol to up his profits." And Jarrad was probably in on it. That had to be what the conversation he'd overheard at the station was about. Jarrad had been paying off the previous sheriff to keep him quiet, and some of the deputies knew about it.

Shit. Once this was over, he'd have to clean house at the station and get rid of all the dirty officers.

"Looks that way," Paxley said. "I looked into Morris Anderson. He lives on a huge property. When he purchased it, the place already had a pole barn. It would be the perfect place to set up a home distillery. All he'd need to do is add some ventilation."

Eastern cursed. "You get a warrant for his property?"

"Yes, his property and his shop."

"Good. Go to his property. I'll go to his shop." He just had to hope like hell this was completely separate from the reason why he couldn't get in touch with Sadie.

He hung up and moved back into the living room to crouch in front of Avery. "Hey, princess, I'm just going to go out for a second."

Her brow scrunched. "Sadie isn't okay, is she?"

Damn, his daughter was too perceptive.

He tucked a lock of hair behind her ear. "I'm going to make sure she is."

Avery seemed to think about that for a moment before nodding. "Good. Bring her home, Daddy."

One more kiss to his daughter's head and he rose to his feet. He'd just put on his shoes and strapped on his holster when a knock came at the door.

Tilly gave him a small smile when he opened the door, while Kayden's features remained unreadable.

"Thanks for coming." Eastern tilted his head toward the living room. "She's in there."

Tilly nodded and headed inside.

Kayden remained where he was. "I'm going with you."

Eastern shook his head. "This is official sheriff's business."

"No. This is you checking if your girlfriend is okay. I'm coming."

He didn't have time to argue with his brother. He cast one more look into the living room to see Tilly beside Avery, arm around her shoulders, before stepping outside. He sped the entire way to the bakery, making it there a hell of a lot faster than he should have.

The first thing he saw was her car. When he pulled up behind it, he noticed the door to Sugar and Spice was closed and the lights were off. Not only that, but the liquor store also had its closed sign on.

A mixture of fear and uncertainty stabbed at his chest, but he pushed it down and climbed out of the car. Kayden was silent behind him as they moved to the door of Sugar and Spice. Eastern tried the handle.

Locked.

Kayden tugged off his jacket. "Here."

Eastern took it and wrapped it around his fist, then he punched through the glass. The sound of smashing glass barely registered as he reached inside and flipped the lock.

Again, there was no immediate sign of Sadie. No voices. No sound of movement. Nothing but eerie silence.

He ran into the kitchen. The back door was closed and locked and the room was dark.

"Eastern."

He sprinted back into the shop to see Kayden holding Sadie's phone.

"It was under a chair."

Dread twisted his gut and he searched the floor. That's when he saw tiny specks of red by the door. He lowered to his haunches.

Blood. It was definitely blood.

The ringing of his phone barely penetrated the haze of panic filling his lungs. It was only when Kayden pulled the cell from his pocket and handed it to him that he answered Paxley's call.

"Paxley."

Wind blew over the line. "It's here, in his barn. Anderson has an entire distillery operation going on."

"He took Sadie." The words rushed from Eastern's lips.

"*What?*"

"I don't know the details. But someone took her, and my gut says it was him. I want an APB out on him and Jarrad."

"Jarrad?"

"Yes. He's involved in this operation with his father. Do it. We have to find them, and we have to find them fast."

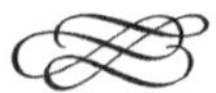

CHAPTER 29

Sadie groaned as she rolled onto her back. God, her head was killing her. Why? Was she hungover? Had she injured herself?

She tried to touch her temple with her right hand, only to stop. Something around her wrists, binding them together.

A chill swept over her skin because it almost felt like…rope?

Suddenly, her last memories came back to her. Overhearing the conversation in the alley from the liquor store. Jarrad coming into the store and attacking her, then his father…

Jesus, Mr. Anderson had *hit* her.

Her eyes flashed open, but there was only darkness. She couldn't see a thing. Not only that, but there was the dull sound of an engine beneath her.

They'd put her in the trunk of a car.

Her breaths became choppy, a sick feeling swirling in her belly. She'd never been a claustrophobic person, but here, tied up and stuck in this small space, the fear almost choked her.

Closing her eyes, she forced her body to relax. For the air to move slowly in and out of her lungs. Panicking wouldn't help. What she needed was a weapon. Yes—a weapon.

Blindly and with bound hands, she felt around the trunk, her fingers running over paper and empty boxes. She reached over her head and to her sides. Nothing. Nothing but trash.

She was about to give up, the panic once again crawling through her veins, seizing her, when her hand brushed over something hard and cold. It wasn't until her fingers examined it more closely that she realized what it was…a lug wrench.

This. This can be used as a weapon. It was heavy, and if she swung it hard enough, she could do some serious damage.

As the car continued to move, she held the wrench in both hands, focusing on remaining calm until she had to act. It wasn't until the car stopped that her pulse spiked again.

It's fine, Sadie. You can do this.

She counted in her head as a way to distract herself, all the while keeping her muscles tense and waiting for the trunk to open.

The sound of a car door opening and closing sounded. A second later, the trunk opened—and she swung.

The person cursed loudly when the wrench made contact, and immediately she swung a second time. But strong fingers wrapped around the wrench before ripping it out of her hands. Then she was violently pulled from the trunk and thrown to the ground.

She didn't have time to avoid the kick to her ribs. Pain flared through her abdomen. Then a second kick, and if possible, this one hurt worse. It felt like fire searing through her.

"Jarrad. *Enough.* Throw her over your shoulder and let's go."

"She hit me in the face with a fucking wrench, Dad!"

Sadie moaned and curled into a ball, grabbing at her ribs, the air wheezing in and out of her chest.

"First she beats you at her shop, now she gets you in the face. You can't defend yourself against a pathetic *woman?*" There was humor in Mr. Anderson's voice. "Stop being a pansy and throw her over your goddamn shoulder."

Jarrad grunted before reaching down. The second her stomach hit his shoulder, she cried out. Holy shit…the pain was like nothing else. It felt like a knife to her abdomen.

"Shut up, or I'll kick you until you pass out," Jarrad growled.

He started walking, and every step was as torturous as the last, agony punching through her ribs. Something was broken, she could feel it.

"You sure there won't be anyone in these mountains?" Mr. Anderson asked.

"I'm sure. The skywalk finished a couple weeks ago, but it isn't open yet. The visitors center is closed, but even if it wasn't, it's in the other direction. Trust me, the area's deserted. No one will be here, and when I tell you no one will find her body in the section of the mountains we're going to, I'm not fucking joking."

Her heart rattled. Jesus. They planned to kill her and leave her in these mountains. She tried to move, but the second she even twitched, pain blasted from her ribs.

"Wait—did you see that?" Mr. Anderson asked, abruptly stopping.

Jarrad stopped as well, and the jarring motion made her groan in pain. "What?" he asked.

"I swear I saw something on the skywalk."

Jarrad scoffed. "Don't be ridiculous. I told you, there's no one here. The sun's setting. Everyone's long gone for the day. You really think I'd bring us out here if I wasn't certain it was deserted?"

A grumble sounded from Mr. Anderson. "Fine. Let's go. What are we doing about that girl in the hospital?"

"I went to the hospital and tried to look at the chart, but Walker had stationed Angie at the door and she wouldn't allow me in the damn room. Bitch. If we're lucky, they'll look at her history of being an alcoholic and put her condition down to drinking too much."

Alcoholic…were they talking about Jamie? Did this have

something to do with the reason Eastern had been acting strange after talking to his deputy yesterday at the hospital?

"And if not?"

"I don't fucking know, do I, Dad? I guess we find the doctor who diagnoses her and pay them off before Eastern the Boy Scout finds out. It's exactly why I told you to trash the rest of the shit—so this didn't happen!"

"Don't act all high and mighty with me. You've been just as much a part of this little operation as I have. And you certainly haven't complained about the profits."

So these guys were making their own alcohol, and *badly*, by the sounds of it. Making people sick, *killing* people, then covering their tracks.

Assholes.

Jarrad shuffled her higher on his shoulder, and she cried out. At this point, her entire rib cage hurt so much she was almost numb to the pain.

Something on Jarrad's hip flashed in the fading light, catching her attention. She frowned, forcing herself to focus through the pain. Was that...the butt of a gun? No, it couldn't be. He wouldn't be so stupid as to leave a gun within reaching distance. Unless he thought she was too injured to reach for it?

And yeah, it *would* be hard to get to the weapon. But she had to try. They planned to kill her and leave her somewhere no one would find her. They'd actually admitted it.

She didn't move immediately, instead taking a deep breath of courage and preparing her ribs for the pain...because there *would* be pain.

Three seconds. She counted them down in her head.

Three...two...one...

She lunged.

"What the fuck?"

Ignoring Jarrad's growled words, she wrapped her fingers around the grip of the gun, yanked it out and fired at Jarrad's leg.

He cried out, dropping her to the ground. Pain flared from her ribs, racing down every limb of her body, but she ignored it, lifting the gun and pointing it at Mr. Anderson. He was already pulling his own weapon from its holster.

Sadie fired first—and her breath stopped when blood bloomed across his shirt.

Oh God…she'd shot him! She'd shot *two* people. She'd never shot another person in her life!

Mr. Anderson dropped to the ground, grabbing at his chest.

She spun to face Jarrad, but he'd already snatched up the fallen gun from Mr. Anderson and was limping behind a tree.

She didn't think. She just jumped to her feet and ran.

* * *

JACE WALKER LEANED over the railing of the skywalk, the cool evening air brushing over his skin.

Home. He was finally home. A part of him still didn't quite understand why he'd left his career as a Tactical Controller. He'd loved his job. Fuck, he'd lived and breathed it. The second he'd graduated high school, he hadn't been able to leave Misty Peak fast enough, to get out of here and make something of himself.

Yet…here he was, back in the town where he'd grown up, for reasons he didn't quite understand. Because he was done chasing adventure? Because somewhere along the way, he'd started craving something else? Something slower?

Even though he was here, he didn't know if he knew how to *be* here. He'd been chasing anything that got his blood pumping for so long, he wasn't sure he knew how to stand still.

He reached beneath his shirt and traced the tattooed ink on his skin.

You're too loved to lose.

He read that message every day. In her handwriting. With her voice in his head.

A small whisper inside him said that maybe *she* was the reason he was back. Because it had been too long since he'd heard that voice for real...the gentle tone that had always kept him calm.

He dropped his hand and looked out over his mountains again. When he was a kid, he couldn't wait to get out, but now, being back, he had to admit that all he felt was...relaxed. At the way the air whistled through the trees. The sway of the branches. It was peaceful. Calm. Two things he needed.

He closed his eyes, breathing in that fresh air.

He was just opening them again when movement from below caught his attention. He frowned at the distant sight of two men and...shit...was that a woman dangling over the taller guy's shoulder?

The older man looked up suddenly, and Jace shifted around the bend in the skywalk so that he was shielded by a tree. He pulled out his phone. His brother was the town sheriff. Surely he'd want to know about this.

The phone rang. Then it rang some more. When it went to voicemail, Jace hung up but tried again. This time, Eastern answered.

"Jace, now's not a good time."

"I think you'll want to hear this. I'm at the skywalk, and I just saw two men moving through the woods, one of them with a woman over his shoulder."

There was a pause before Eastern asked, "What do they look like?"

"One older guy, maybe mid-fifties. It's the younger man who has the woman. I only saw the back of her though. She has long black hair, I think?"

"Sadie." His brother sounded winded, as if he was running.

Jace frowned. Eastern had briefly mentioned the woman he was seeing. Wasn't that her name? "Sadie? She's missing?"

"Yeah. Where in the skywalk are you?"

Jace opened his mouth, but anything he was going to say was

cut off by the sound of a gunshot. And judging by Eastern's sharp intake of breath, he heard it too. Then a second gunshot sounded.

Jace raced down the skywalk to get back to the forest floor.

"I'm sending you a pin of my location. I'm going after them, brother."

CHAPTER 30

*A*ir soared in and out of Sadie's chest and pain radiated from her ribs, but she didn't stop or slow. She couldn't. She wasn't sure how long she'd been running, seconds or minutes. Time had blurred together, the fear and adrenaline fogging her head.

Sharp branches scratched her cheeks and arms, the gun heavy in her hand.

A gun. She was holding a *gun*. One that she'd used to shoot both Jarrad and Mr. Anderson.

Nausea rolled in her belly at the memory of the blood on Mr. Anderson. The way it had spread so quickly across his shirt and soaked through his fingers.

She pushed it down. If she hadn't shot him, he would have shot *her*. And now Jarrad would be coming after her. He had a weapon too, and he wouldn't hesitate to shoot to kill. All she could do was hope and pray that the bullet she'd put in the back of his leg slowed him down enough that she could get away.

But God, was she even running in the right direction? She didn't know these mountains well enough, and even if she did, fear was messing with her head.

She rounded a tree, only for her foot to catch a root and send her to the ground. With bound hands, she wasn't able to catch herself while also holding the gun. Pain exploded through her ribs, halting her breath and making her groan in agony. She rolled to her side, holding her middle, begging the pain to subside.

When footsteps sounded in the woods, she ground her back teeth together and forced herself to her knees.

Oh God, where was the gun? It was getting so dark, she could barely see a thing. And the cover of the trees was doing nothing to help her.

She ran her fingers through the dirt, desperately searching.

Come on, come on, where are you?

"Get the fuck out here, Sandler!"

She flinched at Jarrad's shout. It was distant, but not so far off that she couldn't make out his words.

"You fucking *shot* me and probably killed my father. You're gonna pay!"

Her fingers brushed over cold metal.

Yes.

Quickly, she grabbed the gun and crawled behind a tree. She tried to force her breathing to calm. Force the short, jagged breaths to deepen. It wasn't easy when the pain in her ribs was like a living, breathing creature, squeezing her from the inside.

She wrapped her fingers so tightly around the gun that her knuckles ached.

When the silence around her stretched, her belly began to cramp and an icy chill swept over her skin. At least when Jarrad had been yelling at her, she'd known approximately where he was. How far. How much time she had to prepare. When he was quiet, he could be anywhere.

Her heart began to pound so hard that every beat felt like a punch to her ribs.

Then she heard it—the small snap of a stick right beside her.

She swung the gun around, but before she could fire, it was whipped out of her hand in a move so skilled and efficient, she barely felt the weapon being removed from her hold.

Then she was lifted and spun…and suddenly there was a body behind her, a hand pressed to her mouth.

She grunted at the ache to her ribs but still tried to fight. To kick and hit and do what she could to get away—until a voice sounded in her ear.

"You're safe."

She stilled. That wasn't the voice of Jarrad or Mr. Anderson.

"I'm Jace Walker."

Her eyes widened. *Jace Walker?* As in—

"I believe you're dating my brother Eastern. Not sure why you'd pick that knucklehead, but here we are. I called him. He won't be long."

Eastern's brother was here…and he was *joking* with her. Was she dreaming? Maybe she'd passed out somewhere along the way.

But if she wasn't, if this was real, then Eastern knew where she was. Not only that, but he was coming for her. And until he got here, his brother was keeping her safe. A brother who was former special forces, just like Eastern.

"I'm gonna take my hand off your mouth, but I need you to remain quiet. Okay?" His deep, gravelly voice sounded so much like Eastern's.

She nodded quickly.

He removed his hand slowly, like he was scared she was still going to scream or make a noise.

"You're hurt," he said quietly. It wasn't a question.

"My ribs…I think some are broken."

A small growl sounded from him.

She turned her head, just making out the blue of his eyes in the little remaining light. Eyes that looked eerily similar to Eastern's. But that was where the similarities stopped. While Eastern had dark hair, Jace had light. He also had lines around his eyes… laugh lines?

Despite their situation, he grinned at her. "Hey there, gorgeous. Don't worry, I may look all sex and charm, but I know how to handle myself in a dangerous situation."

She blinked. How could he be so calm at a time like this? "I shot two people."

Some of the humor left his eyes. "I hope you shot to kill."

"Maybe one of them. I don't know."

He seemed to take that in for a moment. "If I've learned anything in my life so far, it's that sometimes people don't deserve the air they breathe. You may have just done a lot of people a favor."

A noise crackled from not too far away, like the crunch of leaves under feet.

Jace put a finger to his lips before lifting the gun. The weapon looked at home in his hand, as if he'd fired it a hundred times before.

"You really gonna make me search for you all goddamn night, Sandler?" Jarrad shouted. "You're just delaying the inevitable. You. Will. *Die*."

Jace tensed. "Fuck, I hate this asshole. I'm kind of looking forward to getting rid of him. Stay down for me, darlin'."

He shifted to stand, but then another noise sounded, this one from farther away. She just made out the grin on Jace's face before he whispered, "I believe we have company."

Her heart leapt in her chest. Eastern? Was he here?

"I'll be back. Just gonna let my brother know where we are."

Before she could ask him how he planned to do that, Jace moved, running so fast he was a blur in the darkness, darting from one tree to another.

He didn't even try to be quiet…but maybe that was the point.

Then Jace fired.

* * *

EASTERN MOVED QUICKLY through the mountains. He'd called in other officers, but they weren't here yet. For the moment, it was him and Kayden and, when they found him, Jace. Thank God Kayden had insisted on coming, because even though he knew these mountains, had grown up in them, Kayden led the local SAR team.

They moved quickly and quietly toward the location Jace had sent. Every muscle in his body was tight, every fear in his mind alive and spiraling.

Were they too late? Had those gunshots he'd heard over the line been aimed at Sadie? Jace had hung up to go find her, and so far there'd been no update. He just had to hope that his worst nightmare hadn't eventuated and she was alive, somewhere in these mountains.

He leapt over a stump and rounded a tree, only to grind to a halt at the sight in front of him.

Morris Anderson, on the ground, blood soaking his chest.

Kayden reached down and felt for a pulse. "He's alive, but only just."

Was that the bullet he'd heard on the phone? *Fuck*, Eastern was praying that was the case. He surveyed the trail, seeing a small splatter of blood on the ground just a couple yards from Anderson. Was it Jarrad's or Sadie's?

Following the trail of blood with his gaze, he noticed it led south. He took off, hearing his brother's footsteps behind him. He was by no means quiet. If he had to choose between quiet and speed, he'd choose the latter.

His feet pounded the ground, Glock heavy in his hold. He'd done a hundred missions during his time as a SEAL, all much more dangerous, but this was different. This was personal.

If Jarrad had harmed a single hair on Sadie's head, Eastern would kill him. Tear the asshole apart with his bare hands.

The trail of blood had already disappeared when a gunshot sounded. It was like a blow to Eastern's abdomen, and for a moment it felt as if the air had been ripped from his chest. But thanks to the shot, he corrected his course slightly and forced his legs to move faster. His arms to pump harder.

He heard Kayden branch off. Not a surprise. He'd go after Jarrad from a different direction with the aim of boxing him in.

When the deputy finally came into view, Eastern stopped, Glock raised and pointed at the son of a bitch's back. "Drop the gun, Jarrad, and put your hands up."

The muscles in Jarrad's back visibly tensed, but he didn't move, his gun still aimed at a tree in front of him.

Kayden stepped into the clearing from a point diagonal to Eastern. "Drop the gun, asshole...*now*."

Still, Jarrad continued to stand there.

Jace stepped around the tree in Jarrad's sights, pistol raised. "You're surrounded, man. Drop your weapon."

Several seconds passed, all drenched in a heavy silence, as everyone waited to see what he would do.

Suddenly, Jarrad growled and spun toward Eastern.

Before Jarrad could fire, three gunshots exploded through the air—one from Eastern, and one from each of his brothers, every one a kill shot.

Jarrad dropped, blood seeping from his chest, back and head.

Then Sadie appeared from behind a tree, and she was all he could focus on. All he could see. He took off toward her and wrapped her in his arms.

She groaned, and he immediately pulled back.

He scanned her body. "You're hurt."

"Ribs," she gasped. "But I'm okay."

He looked down and noticed the rope around her hands. *Motherfuckers.*

He grabbed a small knife from his holster and sliced the rope off before gently tugging her back into his hold. "Never again, Sadie. I can't let you out of my sight ever again."

He knew the absurdity of that statement. At some point, he'd have to. But right now, all he could do was hold her, and thank whoever was looking out for her tonight that she was alive.

CHAPTER 31

Eastern kept his arm wrapped around Sadie's waist as the paramedic cleaned and covered the cut on her forehead.

Fury filled him, but he pushed it down. She didn't need his anger right now. This week had been hell for her after two attacks...*two*. He needed to be calm for her, even though calm was the last thing he felt.

When the paramedic was finally finished, the guy tugged off his gloves. "All done, Miss Sandler. The graze on the head is cleaned up, and I think you have one, possibly two fractured ribs, so I'd recommend you go to the hospital and get an X-ray."

"Can it wait until tomorrow?" she asked. "I'm so tired."

Eastern inched that bit closer. She was coming down from the adrenaline high, which would no doubt make her exhausted.

The paramedic paused. "As long as you're breathing okay, pushing the X-ray to tomorrow should be okay."

When the paramedic walked away, Paxley headed over. The deputy had been waiting for a chance to speak to Sadie. He couldn't interview her himself because it was a conflict of interest.

He lowered his head to Sadie's ear. "Are you okay to speak to some officers tonight? If not, I can get them to wait until tomorrow."

She shook her head. "It's fine. I'll get it over with while we're here so I don't have to do it tomorrow."

So damn strong.

Paxley stopped in front of them. She looked at Eastern, and he gave her a small nod before she faced Sadie. "Miss Sandler, I'm Deputy Paxley. Can you talk to me about what happened tonight?"

Sadie nodded. "I went to Sugar and Spice to close up the shop. I told the other worker, Anna, to go home, but before I left, I took out the trash." She frowned. "I heard Mr. Anderson and Jarrad arguing from inside the liquor store. The screen door was closed, but the back door was open. They were talking about a problem Mr. Anderson was supposed to fix but hadn't. Jarrad said he'd told his dad to take the *bad shit* off the shelves."

She paused, and Eastern gave a gentle rub to her shoulder before she continued.

"Jarrad said he'd paid off the coroner to label a death as a brain aneurysm. I assumed he was talking about Denny."

Eastern shared a glance with Paxley. So the coroner had falsified a report and a death certificate for money. Looks like his job had just gotten busier.

"He also said something about another person being in the hospital and what had happened to her could be linked back to them," she finished.

"Jamie," Eastern and Paxley said at the same time.

"What happened next?" Paxley asked.

"I ran back into the store, but when I tried to leave, Jarrad came in. I fought him off but by that time, Mr. Anderson had arrived, and he hit me. I woke up in the trunk of a car, and when the car stopped and the trunk opened, I again tried to fight, smashed Jarrad in the face with a lug wrench, but Jarrad threw me to the ground and kicked me twice, and that's when I hurt my ribs."

Anger rolled through Eastern's veins like fire. If the son of a bitch wasn't already dead, he'd kill him a second time.

Sadie sighed. "We were up here, and they were talking about where they were going to leave my body. I was on Jarrad's shoulder when I grabbed the gun from his holster and shot him. I also shot Mr. Anderson. Did he...is he dead?"

Eastern's jaw clenched. "He's alive." Not that he'd be upset if the guy died.

The air rushed from her lungs. "I didn't kill anyone."

"You didn't kill anyone, honey," he confirmed.

"I ran and hid, and Jace found me just before you came," she finished.

Eastern's gaze shifted to his youngest brother, who stood talking to other officers. He was so fucking grateful to him. He had no idea what Jace had been doing in the forest tonight, especially when no one had even known he was back in town yet, but he didn't care. If he hadn't been here, things might have ended very differently.

"Thank you, Miss Sandler." Paxley glanced at him and pulled out her phone. "Here are photos of the barn on Morris's land."

Eastern took the cell from her fingers, the muscles in his forearms tightening at the images. There were large distillery machines and bottles and containers everywhere. How long had they been doing this? Their setup looked well established—and huge. So big that they couldn't have just been selling at their shop. Did they distribute to other liquor stores in the state?

That was a question for another day. "Thanks for all your work on this, Pax. I need to get Sadie home now."

She nodded, and just as she walked away, paramedics came off the trail pushing a stretcher with a body bag on it.

Jarrad. His father had already been taken to the hospital while the paramedic looked over Sadie.

Carefully, he lifted Sadie into his arms and carried her to the car. When she was comfortable in the front seat, he stood to find Kayden and Jace behind him, both with grim expressions on their faces.

"She okay?" Kayden asked.

"She will be. A cut on her forehead and we'll get her ribs x-rayed tomorrow."

Jace crossed his arms over his chest. "What happened to our safe little town? There were never any murders or kidnappings when I lived here."

"No shit," Kayden said under his breath. "There's been too much going on lately."

"Well, lucky I'm here to get everything back on track." Jace grinned.

Of course their baby brother *would* joke at a time like this. "What were you doing out there?"

"Checking out my new workplace." His gaze moved over the dark landscape, and by the look on his brother's face, Eastern was certain there was more to it than that. Jace liked to come off as the carefree one, but he was deeper than he let people realize.

"Thank you," Eastern said firmly. "Both of you."

Jace dipped his head, and Kayden clenched his shoulder. "Get her home, Eastern."

* * *

Sadie lay on her side, eyes open, watching Eastern as he slept. She'd slept for an hour or so, but now she was wide awake, everything that had happened tonight...hell, the last couple nights...playing over in her mind like a bad movie she couldn't get out of her head.

She'd shot people tonight. Almost been shot herself. And yesterday, she and Avery had been kidnapped.

Yep, she probably wasn't going to get any more sleep tonight.

Quietly, she rolled to her other side, gritting her teeth to stop the groan from the pain of her ribs. She'd heard fractured ribs hurt, but she'd never thought they would hurt *this* much. Not that she knew for certain they were fractured, but with the amount of pain she was in, even after taking medication, they had to be, didn't they?

She carefully climbed out of bed, relieved when she didn't wake Eastern. The poor guy must be so exhausted. There'd been lines under his eyes all night, and the stress…God, there'd been so much lately.

She padded into the kitchen and grabbed some more pain medication and water. As she swallowed the pills, her gaze moved over the shadows in the backyard. It was strange how these huge life events could happen and leave you feeling completely changed, while everything around you remained the same. And she would be forever changed, but she also felt immensely grateful to be living in a town with people she loved. Who worked so hard to protect her.

For a few minutes, she just watched the leaves in the trees flutter in the slight wind. The moonlight as it cast a dim glow over the grass.

She placed the glass into the sink and walked down the hall to Avery's doorway.

Warmth skittered through her chest at the sight of the girl asleep in her bed. She lay on her belly with the sheet and blanket kicked off, her little cheek pressed into the pillow. Some of the pain and tension eased from Sadie's body. There was something about looking at a child you loved that almost felt healing.

Without making a sound, Sadie crept forward and pulled the blankets over Avery's small body. But she didn't straighten right away, instead lowering her head and pressing a gentle kiss to her cheek before whispering, "I love you, baby girl."

Avery moaned, snuggling deeper into the bed before mumbling, "Love you too, Sadie."

A small smile curved Sadie's lips, the first one all night. How she'd heard and replied without waking, Sadie had no idea, but she wasn't questioning it.

Sadie rose and moved to the door, but instead of going back to the bedroom, she just leaned her shoulder against the door-frame and watched the slow rise and fall of Avery's back.

When gentle hands slipped around her waist, she gasped.

"Why are you up?" Eastern asked, mouth going to the side of her neck, where he kissed her.

She relaxed back into him. "I couldn't sleep and just found myself here. She's so beautiful."

He set his chin on her head. "She is. Just like you."

"I love her so much. Sometimes I just ache for her to be mine."

"She *is* yours." The answer from Eastern came so quickly and firmly, she turned to look at him.

"She feels like she's mine."

He slipped a lock of hair from her cheek behind her ear. "Family isn't always blood. It's the people who love us the hardest. And she loves you, Sadie. She loves you so much."

Tears filled her eyes. "I'm so lucky to have you both."

"No. *We're* the lucky ones."

He lowered his head and kissed her, his lips caressing hers and making every tight muscle in her body loosen.

He lowered his head to her ear and whispered, "Come to bed with me."

She nodded, and he lifted her into his arms so that her cheek was right over his heart, and she listened to that heart beat as he carried her back to bed.

CHAPTER 32

Sadie leaned back in her seat, a smile playing at her lips. It was Monday evening, and they were having a family barbeque at Eastern's house with his brothers, their partners and Avery. Well, technically her house too, because a few days ago, they'd officially moved all her things from her apartment to here. Well, Eastern had. With her fractured ribs, she was pretty much useless.

She stroked Avery's hair as the eight-year-old sat on her lap eating chips. A week had passed since everything had happened with Mr. Anderson, Jarrad and Jamie. Jamie was still in the hospital, and from what Sadie had heard, it would be a long road to recovery. Mr. Anderson was also still hospitalized, but he'd get out sooner and be taken straight to a cell.

Sadie was recovering from fractured ribs, but she felt grateful that was *all* she was recovering from. Things could have been so much worse.

Her gaze lifted to the four men standing around the barbecue. She hadn't seen much of Jace in the last week, but she would forever be in debt to him for what he'd done for her that night. If he hadn't been in those mountains and called Eastern when he'd seen her… God, she didn't even want to think about that.

Her hand tightened on Avery's hip, and she shifted her attention back to Harper and Tilly, who were talking about the visitors center.

One thing Sadie was absolutely certain of was how grateful she was to be back in Misty Peak and part of this family. It was crazy that just a few months ago, she'd been living a completely different life.

"Sadie, we've been doing all the talking," Harper said, cutting into her thoughts. "How are you doing?"

"I'm good, actually. I've taken some time off work and so has Eastern, and we've just been spending time as a family." She pressed a kiss to Avery's head.

"Your ribs healing okay?" Tilly asked.

"Well, Eastern's barely let me move, so rest has been kind of mandatory. Hell, he's been carrying me around the house like I'm incapable of getting around myself." Not that she minded being pressed against Eastern's chest. "Plus, I've been on a strict pain medication schedule."

Harper, Tilly and Elle had also been paying her regular visits, always with food and treats and coffee. There was also her grandmother, who sometimes visited multiple times a day, and again always with food. She was surrounded by a community she hadn't expected when she'd come back to town, but man, was she grateful for it.

"Good," Harper said with a smile. "And what about your grandmother? I know she wasn't doing too good after she found out about everything that happened."

"She's still worried. Every time I mention coming back to work, she refuses to let me."

Tilly's eyes softened. "Not a surprise. Twice you were attacked in that store."

"Yeah, I know. And I wish I didn't even have to tell her. I'll ease my way back into work eventually." She tickled Avery's side. "We went in yesterday though, didn't we?"

Avery giggled. "Yeah, and Sadie got me a double chocolate chip cookie."

Tilly's eyes widened. "Double chocolate chip?"

Avery nodded. "Yep, and we bought more for tonight, but Daddy says I have to wait until after dinner to have one."

"What a party pooper," Harper said with a grin.

Sadie looked over to Eastern again, her heart doing a little skitter in her chest. His head was thrown back and he was laughing at something Jace said. It appeared Jace was definitely the joker of the group. Not a huge surprise. That job usually fell on the little brother, didn't it?

When Eastern's gaze found hers, his smile softened and he winked. Even now, her pulse went into overdrive at every small gesture from him.

"Bet he's glad you came back," Tilly said softly.

She looked at the other woman. "*I'm* glad I came back. It's kind of crazy, but the morning I was supposed to marry Scott, I just *knew* I should be somewhere else. It almost felt like I had this other life waiting for me. I didn't understand it at the time...now I do."

Tilly squeezed her shoulder. "You were meant to be here."

"It definitely feels that way."

Avery looked up at her. "Sadie, I'm cold."

"I'll get your jacket from inside." She kissed Avery's head and was about to shift the girl off her lap, when Avery gave her that cheeky grin of hers.

"Actually, I think a hot cocoa might warm me up."

Sadie's lips twitched. The sneaky kid. She lowered her mouth to Avery's ear. "Just don't tell your dad." Because hot cocoa probably fell into the same category as cookies, right?

"Thank you, Sadie. I love you."

She'd never tire of hearing that. "I love you too, baby girl."

They both stood. Avery took her seat as Sadie moved into the kitchen, all the while knowing just how incredibly lucky she was.

* * *

EASTERN SIPPED his beer as he watched Cody work the grill. Jace was telling them some long-winded story about a teammate who'd passed out after a night of drinking and woken up with no clothes and all of his shit stolen. Eastern was sure some of the story was being embellished, but then, that was Jace, always ready to make people laugh.

His attention shifted to Sadie. She sat across the yard with the women, Avery on her lap. He'd woken every night during the last week, having to remind himself that the two people he loved most were alive and safe. That they were right there with him.

Sadie's ribs would take a while to heal, and he'd been making sure she took the time to rest and barely lift a finger. When her gaze found his, he smiled and winked at her. Pink tinged her cheeks. Damn, she was beautiful.

"Looks like you found a good one while I was away," Jace said, pulling Eastern's attention back to his brothers.

"We've all found good women," Eastern said, lifting his beer to his lips. It wasn't a lie—Sadie, Harper and Tilly were the best women he'd met.

Kayden nodded. "Damn straight. Sadie doing okay after everything?"

"Yeah, she's strong. Stronger than me, anyway. But I can't get past how close I came to losing her." His fingers tightened around the neck of the bottle.

Cody gripped his shoulder. "But you didn't. She's here. Alive. Safe."

"Yeah. That's what I need to keep reminding myself."

Jace frowned. "So the asshole you found in the mountains, Morris, is he…"

"Alive. But the second he's out of the hospital, he's going to be dragged into prison for the rest of his life." He didn't stand a chance of avoiding his fate.

Charles and Lenard had also been arrested for taking bribes to keep their mouths shut about Jarrad's little operation. They'd pled innocence and were awaiting trial, but they both knew what was coming.

The coroner had also been arrested.

"What about Jamie?" Kayden asked.

Eastern frowned. "She's still not doing too well. Her eyesight in particular isn't great. They're not sure if it will ever go back to what it was. I did go visit her a few days ago, and she was pretty quiet. Just told me again that she'd made a lot of mistakes."

"She did," Kayden agreed. "Avery deserves more. I'm glad she has Sadie."

Eastern nodded. "Me too. She also has you guys and Harper and Tilly."

Jace cleared his throat. "And now that I'm back, I can take my rightful place as favorite uncle."

Cody shoved his shoulder. "Get off it. I'm the favorite and we all know it. That kid loves my bar pretzels."

Kayden frowned. "Hey! I'm the uncle who takes her for cookies at Sugar and Spice. She tells me I'm the favorite every time."

Eastern chuckled as he shook his head. "She loves all of you. We *all* do."

Kayden looked at Jace. "So, now that you're back, you and Elle gonna be as close as you used to be?"

There was a flicker of emotion on Jace's face. It came and went so quickly, Eastern couldn't quite name it.

"I actually haven't seen her yet. I need to visit her at the café."

Once upon a time, the two had been inseparable. "When was the last time you saw her?"

"Dad's funeral. We didn't get much of a chance to talk though. I pretty much came and went."

Eastern remembered. They'd each handled the passing of their father very differently. Kayden had been angry. Cody and Eastern were the stoic funeral organizers. Nylah was emotional. Lock had been nearly silent, while Jace had arrived then left so quickly, barely *anyone* had talked to him.

"The friend she worked with, Macy…she was killed not too long ago, right?" Jace asked, brows tugged together.

Eastern's features hardened, but it was Kayden who answered. "Yeah. Stabbed to death in the mountains. Thank God the case got solved and the murderer was identified, but it doesn't bring her back."

Jace's frown deepened. "Elle doing okay since?"

"She seems to be," Kayden said. "But I think she's good at keeping her feelings to herself."

Jace nodded. "She was always like that."

"You all moved into Mom and Dad's old place?" Eastern asked.

Jace nodded. "Sure am. It's like I'm sixteen again, only stronger and better looking."

Cody scoffed. "You wish."

Across the yard, Sadie and Avery rose from the seat, and while Avery sat back down, Sadie made her way into the house.

Eastern set his beer beside the grill. "I'm just gonna head inside." He turned back to look at Jace. "It's good to have you home, brother."

"It's good to be home."

Eastern crossed the yard and stepped into the house through the back door, finding Sadie looking through the back window. She turned and smiled at him. "Hey."

He crossed the small space between them and gently slipped his arms around her waist before kissing her temple. "How are your ribs?"

"They're fine. I took my pain medication, and I barely feel a thing."

"Good. What are you doing in here?"

"I'm not allowed to tell you."

He looked at the milk heating on the stove and the cocoa and sugar beside it. "You're making hot cocoa for Avery."

"What are you, a detective?"

"No, just the sheriff of this small town." He nuzzled her neck. "You're too good to her."

"No such thing."

She sighed and looked out the window again. "We're really lucky, aren't we? To have all these people who care about us."

"Yeah, honey. We are. But I'm the luckiest because I have you and Avery."

She turned in his arms and looked up, emotion thick in her dark eyes. "Everything just kind of feels perfect tonight."

He cupped her cheek. "Good. You deserve perfect."

"I love you, Eastern Walker."

He lowered his head and hovered his mouth over hers. "I love you so much, I *ache* for you." Then he kissed her.

CHAPTER 33

"So basically, you'll be ensuring people are staying safe, taking any tourists who'd like a guide onto the skywalk, and for the real daredevils, setting up and running rappelling sessions."

Jace nodded as he wrapped his fingers around the railing of the skywalk. It was pretty fucking magnificent up here and pretty cool that rappelling was going to be offered. The rappelling would take place in the center of the skywalk, where a big tree connected to the walk. "I can't wait. You've done a good job of setting this up."

Tilly lifted a shoulder. "Linda did the groundwork. I just came in at the end to grab all the glory."

Kayden scoffed. "I don't think so. You've done a lot to make sure this was finished when it should be." He kissed her temple.

Jace grinned. "Shit, you guys are too cute."

He moved back toward the end of the skywalk. In the coming week, he'd get trained on the rappelling side of things, but he doubted they'd get a whole lot of interest in that. What people really wanted was to see these mountains from high up. And yeah, he was looking forward to spending his days up here too.

"Don't think I've ever been called cute before, but I'll take it," Kayden said.

Jace threw a glance over his shoulder. "Only when you're with her. On your own, you're like a poor man's Henry Cavill."

His brother shoved his shoulder, and he bit back the grin.

They made their way back to the visitors center, which was only a few minutes' walk. On the way, Tilly and Kayden spoke about the most recent changes to the center and the influx of tourists over the last few months.

He liked Tilly. And he could see why his brother liked her. She was friendly and had a good sense of humor. Plus, she was smart. You could see the intelligence in her eyes. When he'd first heard the two were dating, he'd been surprised, given who her father was and what he'd done to *their* father. Kayden had always taken that the hardest. But they'd obviously worked through their differences.

When they reached the visitors center, they walked through the foyer into her office.

Tilly sat at her desk. "I'll just print the job offer for you to read through and sign."

While Kayden perched on the desk, Jace's gaze moved to the door. "Is Elle in today?"

Tilly didn't look at him as she responded. "She sure is. Made my day with a double-shot latte this morning."

Suddenly, his feet twitched to go and see her. He hadn't made contact with her since he'd been back. It was so fucking strange to be in this town, the place where so many of his moments had been spent with her growing up, yet *not* be with her now.

"Go," Kayden said, clearly seeing the need in his eyes. "The forms will be here when you get back."

He dipped his head and left the room. For some damn reason, nerves began to tighten his stomach as he stepped onto the back deck. Which was fucking ridiculous. He never got nervous. He could literally walk in front of a crowd of a million people and crack a joke without a single stutter.

He stepped into the café—only for his feet to grind to a stop. Because there she stood, behind the counter. She was side-on as she worked the coffee machine, her blond hair pulled up into a ponytail, with small wisps of hair falling over her cheeks.

Something slammed into his gut. Some sort of emotion he couldn't name, though it felt familiar.

Fuck, she was beautiful. She'd always been gorgeous, but after not seeing her for so long, it felt like he'd been starved of that beauty.

She turned toward the customer across the counter, and when she pushed the coffee forward, her lips spread into a smile that was so radiant, the air was knocked from his lungs.

Shit, he felt like he'd been sucker punched.

He was still standing there, probably looking like a complete fucking idiot just staring at her, when her gaze shifted and, finally, she spotted him.

Suddenly, every moment they'd ever shared together flashed through his mind, thrusting him back fifteen years. To a simpler time, when they'd been kids...and he'd made the mistake of thinking he'd always have her.

But nothing ever lasted forever, did it? Not really.

For a moment, her eyes flared, surprise whipping through their depths. Then it was like a shield came up, and her expression blanked.

He moved forward, forcing a huge-ass grin to his face. "Hey, Tink. Miss me?" Using the nickname he'd given her all those years ago also shot him into the past.

"You're back." Her voice almost sounded breathless.

"I am. Tilly and Kayden were just taking me through a few things for the skywalk. Thought I'd come over and say hi."

Her brows flickered. "So...you're working here soon."

"Sure am. Ready to see me every day?"

Something that looked eerily like pain flashed in her eyes. But then she blinked.

Frowning, he inched forward. "Hey. I probably should have said this long before now, but I'm sorry we lost contact. I'm hoping we can find our friendship again." It wasn't a lie. His friendship with Elle had gotten him through some of the worst times in his life as a kid.

Her lips parted, like she was surprised by his words. "Maybe. But you'll probably be too busy settling back into town, and I'm always pretty busy here."

"We were never too busy for each other before."

She swallowed, her voice quieting. "That was a long time ago."

Then why did it feel like just yesterday? He lowered his own voice. "You going to make me fight for this friendship, Tink?"

"No, I...you..." She cleared her throat. "Let me get you a welcome-back-to-Misty-Peak drink."

"How about our usual?"

The first flicker of humor crossed her face. "Our usual was a mocha with about five teaspoons of sugar."

"Serve me up."

"I am *not* serving you that."

"Come on, Tink, for old times' sake."

She cocked her head. "Jace, we drank that when we were fifteen. By any adult's standard, it's disgusting."

"How do you know? Have you had it recently?"

"I don't need to drink an over-sweetened mocha to know that it doesn't taste good."

One side of his mouth lifted. "Do you treat all your customers like this?"

"If a customer asks for a particularly disgusting drink, then yes, I warn them."

"Consider me warned."

She stared him down like she was waiting for him to change his order. Wasn't going to happen, he was in too deep now. Plus, when he said he was going to do something, he did it. And right now, he was committed to drinking his over-sweetened mocha just to prove to her that he could.

She crossed her arms. "Fine. But if I make this, I expect you to drink it. *All* of it."

"I'd drink sewage water mixed with dish detergent if *you* made it for me."

She rolled her eyes before turning, her ponytail flicking behind her, and even that simple action reminded him far too much of his sixteen-year-old best friend who'd never hesitated to put him in his place.

As she made the drink, he gentled his voice. "I'm sorry about Macy."

The muscles in her back visibly tensed. The two had been friends even before they worked together. "Thanks."

"Are you okay?"

"Of course."

He wasn't sure if he believed her, but he nodded anyway. "Good."

He spent the entire time she made the drink studying her. Memorizing the little flickers of movement. The way she glanced over her shoulder every few seconds as if checking if he was still there.

When the drink was ready, she heaped teaspoons of sugar into the cup, gave it a stir, then pushed it across the counter and crossed her arms. "There you go." There was a challenge in her voice.

Luckily for him, he loved a good challenge.

He lifted the drink and sipped, the sweet liquid curdling in his gut. Fuck, it tasted worse than he remembered. But it also didn't, because it brought back so many memories.

"So?" Elle asked.

"Delicious."

She rolled her eyes a second time. "Liar."

"I'd never lie to you." He held the cup out to her. "Here, try it."

"No."

His lips twitched. "Come on, Tink. I dare you."

There it was, the spark in her eyes. Because she'd always been just as competitive as him.

She wrapped her fingers around the cup and lifted it to her lips. When she sipped the warm liquid, shock lit her expressive eyes. Because everything that drink had brought back for him, she felt it too…she didn't need to say it out loud for him to know. The long afternoons together. The weekends on the deck of his house.

She handed it back. "Disgusting."

He grinned. "I'm really looking forward to seeing more of you, Tink."

Her chest rose and fell on a deep breath. "It's good to see you again."

It wasn't good. It was a million little things, a million emotions, but *good* didn't even begin to cover it.

He gave her one last smile before stepping out of the café, and that's when he realized that for the first time in a long time, he finally felt like he could breathe again…because of her.

Order book four in the series, RECKLESS FAITH, featuring Jace and Elle, NOW!

ALSO BY NYSSA KATHRYN

PROJECT ARMA SERIES

Uncovering Project Arma

Luca

Eden

Asher

Mason

Wyatt

Bodie

Oliver

Kye

BLUE HALO SERIES

Logan

Jason

Blake

Flynn

Aidan

Tyler

Callum

Liam

MERCY RING

Jackson

Declan

Cole

Ryker

BEAUTIFUL PIECES

Erik's Salvation

Erik's Redemption

Erik's Refuge

SHORT CHRISTMAS STORY

Hidden Shadows

RECKLESS SERIES

(series ongoing)

Reckless Hope

Reckless Trust

Reckless Fall

Reckless Faith

Reckless Love

JOIN my newsletter and be the first to find out about sales and new releases! CLICK HERE

ABOUT THE AUTHOR

Nyssa Kathryn is a romantic suspense author. She lives in South Australia with her daughter and hubby and takes every chance she can to be plotting and writing. Always an avid reader of romance novels, she considers alpha males and happily-ever-afters to be her jam.

Don't forget to follow Nyssa and never miss another release.

Facebook | Instagram | Amazon | Goodreads

www.ingramcontent.com/pod-product-compliance
Lightning Source LLC
Chambersburg PA
CBHW061541210726
48287CB00006B/2040